DUKE REDEEMED

BRIMSTONE LORDS MC TWO

SARAH ZOLTON ARTHUR

At last
I met the one I dreamed for all along
When life had gone and done me wrong
My reward for stayin' strong

At last
When you needed me, I came through
In your darkest hour
Fate brought me home to you

I found a partner when none would take
A family to call my own
We held on when they thought we'd break
My flights of fancy, flown

I'm alive, not just livin' thanks to you
The past remains the past
For all you've done I'll shout to the heavens
That you're with me at last

-At Last

First Print Edition: December 2017

Irving House Press

P.O. Box 5738

Saginaw, MI. 48603

1

DR. BRENNAN/ CAITLIN

The curvaceous woman moans loudly, arms wrapped around his neck and back. She rubs her indecently clad skin over most of his body, kissing on his chest and neck as they stand outside his club room while I pass them on my way to Elise's. He has his hand on the knob pulling the door shut.

Their presence in the hall perfumes the air with alcohol, sex and really bad decisions.

No shirt, he's wearing only a leather vest exposing all his expanse of beautifully ripped chest dusted in dark hair and covered in tattoos. His arms. His chest. I'd bet any amount of money, his back too. All covered in tattoos.

Beyond the dusting of hair on his chest, he hasn't bothered to button up his jeans. I swallow down the lump in my throat, embarrassed that I'm unable to tear my eyes away. Even more embarrassed that I stop moving altogether, to openly gawk at the man. But when I say he's beautiful, I mean, *He. Is. Beautiful.* In that gruff, gritty, could kick your ass without breaking a sweat kind of way.

My eyes follow the line of coarse hair trailing down from

his navel, a runway pointing to the root of what promises to be a long, thick good time. When I move my gaze back up, I find him glaring at me through heated eyes. Not the good heat, the lip licking, '*I want you*' way which would work for me, as I clearly want him.

No, he looks on me with a something else kind of heat.

My lips part, and I feel myself beginning to sweat under his intensity. I clear my throat knowing I have to gain back control of the situation. I ask, "Is Elise inside?" Pointing to her door two doors down.

He says nothing, just stares at me like I'm the dim kid in class.

Control, Caitlin. Get back the upper hand, I silently motivate myself. In order to do that, I train a condescending smile across my face, and raise one brow. Then I ask again, slowly and drawn out, "Is Elise in her room?"

His face turns harder than it looked only seconds before, I'm sure not understanding the audacity of someone, especially a woman, speaking to him in such a manner. "Watch it," he grumbles.

"Come on, Duke." The woman hanging all over him, whines in a breathy, '*just had great sex but I'm ready for more*' kind of voice. And that's my cue to get the heck out of here.

"Never mind." I wave him and his attention away. "I'm sure she is. Have a nice day." Then I turn my attention from the man and force myself to walk like I'm not trying to escape which is especially hard pulling a plastic cart on wheels behind me. The cart keeps catching on my heels, causing me to wince each time because having a heavy cart attack my heels hurts.

I only give a light knock on Elise's door. If the baby is sleeping, I don't want to bother him yet. As I wait for her to answer, my back to him, the back of my neck burns from his stare. I feel it. He's there, watching me.

And even if I didn't feel him watching, I'd know it the way Elise pulls open the door and steps into the doorway. She glances at me briefly, but only briefly because her eyes dart over my shoulder and stick. A sort of half-smile smirk dusts across her face before she moves back out of the way.

"Hey Elise, how are you?" I ask as I move into her room.

Today I'm at the Brimstone Lords compound for Elise's six-week checkup, post baby Gunner's delivery. Her husband is out on a run. That's what the men call them, even though I know he and two other MC brothers are out searching for Livvy Baxter. They're lucky, as in lucky to be alive, as she and Elise were unfortunate players in that crazy, murderous Houdini's psychotic show. Bad business, that was. I got the details first hand, but even if I hadn't, their stories were the top news stories all over the country.

"Good. Thanks for coming down," she says in what I can only describe as a forced cheer. I've been coming around here for close to a year now, and Elise Hollister is usually quite open with me.

I pause before replying, waiting to give her the opportunity to come clean on whatever has her troubled. She stays silent. On a sigh, I shake my head once and pick back up. "Not a problem. I know the drill. Any cramping? Started your period yet?"

"No cramping, and yes, period here and gone."

While I look for a place to set down my purse, she hops up on the bed. Then I walk to her bathroom to wash my hands. "Good. That's good. So, how's our boy been?" I call through the door left open, though not loud enough to startle the baby.

"Busy. Can't wait for him to get home." She giggles. At least that seems genuine.

"I meant the *baby* boy."

"Beau can be quite the baby."

Now we both giggle quietly as I can see the little bundle of joy wrapped up and sleeping soundly in a bassinet.

"*Ugh.*" I blow out an exasperated breath. "That's all men."

"Don't I know it. I live in a biker compound."

"I'm going to check you first and then I'll check Gun. Let him sleep a little longer."

I turn around to the plastic bin on wheels that has all my equipment inside, unlatch the locks and flip the lid open. What I need is right on top.

Once I've pulled the portable stirrups out, I order Elise to strip down for me while I secure them to the side of the bed with clamps, then gesture for her to lay down. This is one of those naked appointments, as she calls them.

Her feet up in the stirrups, legs spread, bottom to the edge of the bed, the appointment is as comfortable as I can make it. Her body visibly tenses, as everyone's does, when I don my gloves and lube her up. She shudders at the speculum. No one likes a cold, metal cylinder shoved up inside their lady bits. But as most of my female patients are, she's a trooper.

She's healed nicely and the insides look good.

After Elise is dressed, I hand her off a script for birth control as well as an already filled case. The woman needs to start them ASAP. When her biker husband gets home, after already having had to go six weeks without getting any, I know where his head—both his heads—will be at.

But neither Elise, Boss nor I want her preggers with baby number two just yet. And from what Elise has shared, her man isn't the best with condom usage.

"Any big plans tonight?" Elise asks while slipping her yoga pants back on, an innocent question, but it jars just the same.

Much to her chagrin, I have to wake the baby to check him out, too. He squirms and coos. Not the case at his last checkup where I neglected to blow on the stethoscope to warm the metal. Gunner wailed. A meltdown of epic-newborn proportions.

Boss looked ready to rip my head clean from my body. And it wasn't because I made his son cry. It was because I made his son cry after we'd finally, *finally* gotten him to *stop crying*.

Two weeks straight of colicky baby crying, the new parents were about ready to crack. We'd nixed the breast milk, but had to figure out a formula which wouldn't cause gas.

With too many choices, on about formula number five, we hit. So enter me and my stethoscope mishap. Despite a miserable boy, I miss the newborn stage.

Gunner is a happy baby now. Incredible what a change in diet did for his constitution. They're doing a great job with him. Thus far he checks out completely healthy.

We leave her bedroom. She and a wide awake, wriggly Gun walk me through the common area, where the glutton for punishment that I am, looks for Duke again. The MCs president. I've known him as long as I've been coming here. As Elise's doctor, at first. But being a family practitioner, I started caring for a few of the brothers as well.

But not Duke. He's strong and charismatic. Personally, I think he's so tough, he scares the illnesses away. And for some reason, he can't stand the sight of me. He legitimately bristles whenever I come around. Then we end up snapping at each other or are reduced to speaking in sarcasms, like in the hallway earlier.

A damn shame because when he has those tattoos on display, and he's in full MC President mode, exuding all that power and badass-ness, even though he's normally not my type, *lord help me*... I'd put hand to forehead and swoon if I didn't think Elise would want to know why. I'm not in the mind to give up that ditty of information about myself just yet, if ever.

She continues out into the paved courtyard with me, and we stop at the trunk of my Jeep Grand Cherokee. I flip the hatch door and begin to heft boxes inside. My Cherokee color is Cayenne, and it's sexy as hell. I let Jade pick it, she liked that it matches our hair. When we moved to the mountains, I upgraded from our little sedan. I didn't think a sedan would be safe on slick winter mountain roads.

"*Caitlin*," Elise says to grab my attention. *Oops*. "Any big plans tonight?" she asks again, I assume, because she asks it with a bit of emphasis. I've been in Thornbriar for months and still haven't managed to form any real friendships. Acquaintances, sure. Yet every night when I'm done doctoring, my butt is at home on my sofa watching television with my four-year-old. Most people don't even know I have a daughter.

She's at daycare during my office hours. I usually stop by the grocery store before I pick her up to avoid the inevitable "I want... I want... I want" in a preschooler's whine. I love the girl but that gets annoying.

My little Jade, anyone who has seen her eyes knows why I gave her that name. It's our extremely Irish heritage. She's the spitting image of her mama. Both my parents were born over there. Jade had been born when I was living there taking care of my grandmother before she passed. Though, my little girl happens to be much more popular. She's going to her first friend sleepover tonight. So no, no plans. A Friday night and I'll be where I usually am.

"Nope," I answer Elise. "My ass will be sitting on the couch watching the History Channel."

"Why don't you come hang? Trish is coming over with Sneak. Maryanne will be here too because Tommy is working and won't be home 'til late. We're having a girl's night in."

She pauses, then, "And I think Duke'll be there, too. I mean, as an FYI." Although her words sound benign, spoken in a casual tone, she keeps peering over my shoulder, out toward the gate and main road.

"Do I need to bring anything?" I ask, peering over my shoulder as well. When I turn back to look at her, she's wearing a troubled face, I guess, which wipes any thoughts of '*Duke being there*' out of my mind.

Though, she clears it quickly enough. From troubled to blank. "Just your cute face and an appetite for junk food and gossip," she jokes. "The prospects have already done the shopping. There'll be alcohol for those of us who can drink and fake-ohol for those who can't. And we're making our own pizzas."

"Wow... um... sure. If you think it'll be alright with the guys."

"Please, you'd be doing them a favor, not having to keep me company." She shifts Gun in her arms. "Most of them would prefer to be off getting laid."

She just had to tell me that, right? Now I have images of sexy bikers getting laid, or rather one sexy biker, in particular, getting laid, sifting through my head. "Right. Then what time should I be back?"

"Seven is when the other girls are showing. Is that too late?"

"Sounds perfect to me." I finish packing up my car and move to say goodbye to Elise and Gun when she grabs my elbow softly to stop me from leaving. "What's up?" I ask.

"Nothing... uh... be careful, okay?"

That's an odd sendoff, adding to her odd behavior out here. I take advantage and ask, "Be careful of what?"

"It's really probably nothing."

"Let's assume it's something, what would that something be?"

Elise moves in closer and drops her voice. "When you come here do you, uh, do you ever get the feeling of being watched?"

What? "No. Not that I've paid attention. Have you?" It's been less than a year since she'd been kidnapped by Houdini and buried alive. The choice came down to saving Elise or catching Houdini. Boss saved Elise. That means that psychopath is still out there somewhere.

"Well yeah. When I leave the compound and sometimes when I stand out here for too long. It's just leftover anxiety, I'm sure."

"Have you told Boss?" I ask.

"*No,*" she says way too quickly, almost a whispered shout, startling the baby. "He'd freak. He'd come back. He'd tell the other brothers."

"Yes, but Elise." I pause. My turn to lay a hand on her arm. "You were kidnapped. He needs to know."

"Beau is off trying to find Liv. I want my friend found. And more than that, I want him home. We've spent so much time apart. I want my family back together. Under one roof. It's selfish, I know. But if he comes home now, he'll only have to leave again. Plus, I never leave the compound without a guard, so I'm cool, you know?" She tries to sound unaffected, but I can see through her façade.

I open my mouth to tell her what I think of that idea when she cuts me off. "Please don't say anything."

Do I agree to that when I don't agree? But she's my friend, I think. Or at least starting to be my friend. I can't betray her trust, even if for a good reason. Letting out a slow breath, I decide on how to answer. "Okay, for now. But you need to tell him. If not for you, think of Gun."

This answer seems to appease her, she smiles a genuine smile, even if it doesn't reach her eyes. Then she nods and steps back. I take that as my cue to climb inside my car and actually leave.

A prospect stands out front by the fence, he pushes open the gate for me and shoots off a two-fingered salute as I pass through. This new crop of prospects is something to behold. If I were a few years younger and didn't have a child, I'd work him like a stripper pole, not that I've ever worked a stripper pole. But I'd heard the saying numerous times from Elise and her friend Maryanne Doyle, and it seems apropos here. His small name patch, the one on the front of his vest stitched just above his heart, says Jesse. Though, I believe his mother did him a disservice with that name. She should have called him *Eye Candy*.

They must like him. Gate duty is pretty important, especially in their world. From the way Elise explained it, all prospects start off doing the shit jobs that no one wants. Unclogging toilets, cleaning up vomit after a party, cleaning up after the party. Making a four a.m. food run when a member has a sweet tooth. They like you, trust your loyalty to the club and the brothers, they'll move you up to the gates. From gates, it's protection. You prove your grit, then you get patched in. There's no timeframe.

You might be cleaning puke for two years; you might only be on the gate for a month.

The whole dynamic is pretty fascinating.

Jesse looks like he'd show a girl a good time. Too bad there's only one man I'd honestly consider going biker for. And I have to remind myself that he can't stand the sight of me. God, that gritty voice gets me every time. Not blood, but liquefied want courses through my veins. Pumping through my erratically beating heart. No other way to describe it.

Plus, and this is important, it has been *so long* since a man has done that to me. Not since Aiden, Jade's daddy, left Jade sad and me broken hearted for a new life and a new woman he'd been talking to online in Australia.

What kind of man leaves his toddler daughter to move to another continent?

But we survived.

I hope Mr. Sexy Biker won't be there tonight. Seems since I first took Elise on as a patient, I close my eyes and dammit if it isn't him, those lines, probably from his years of smoking, surrounding a pair of gray, bordering on silver, eyes that stare back at me.

Apparently, I'm more obvious about my attraction to him than I mean to be. Usually Elise drops little tidbits of information about him when I'm at the compound and he's around, trying to pique my interest. "He's only like, thirty-eight years old. That's a lot of good years left to uh, do whatever one might do with a man like Duke." Or "He likes his pieces, but Duke hasn't been in a relationship since his wife died. He's very loyal."

I actually never thought she'd try to coordinate a meetup where Duke and alcohol were involved. I mean what else could that FYI of hers mean?

A shiver runs the length of my spine just from thinking about thinking about him.

"Mama!" Jade rushes to me, slamming her tiny body against my legs and wraps her arms tightly around my knees, which me being five foot nine and all legs, is where she reaches.

Scary how the mind can wander so much that a person can lose consciousness to the world around them. I don't remember driving here. I don't remember getting out of the car. I don't remember walking through the parking lot or inside the building. None of it.

My girl and her preschool were my destination, but holy

cow, I need to be more careful. *And* to stop lusting after someone I'd never stand a chance with. I'm no biker babe.

Shaking my head, I chuckle at that thought. Me, as a biker babe? The idea is even too ludicrous for my imagination.

Get your act together, girl.

After disengaging Jade from my legs, I take her hand and we walk back to get her bag and sign her out.

"Miss Jenny, I'm going to a sweepover at my fwiend Macy's house. It's her birfday."

"So you've said," Miss Jenny answers, chipper as always.

"I'm sure about a million times today." I joke.

Miss Jenny rolls her eyes but then shakes her head yes, laughing as she does.

We gather Jade's bag, lunch pail and jacket, sign her out and say goodnight to the staff. Then my little bundle of energy beats me to the car where I've unlocked the doors from my key fob.

She's already sitting in her car seat in the back, waiting for me to buckle her in, by the time I reach her.

"I'm not 'posta eat dinner wiff you. Macy's mom is makin' us birfday burgurs before the cake." My princess kicks her dangling legs excitedly.

"Well then, let's get home and get your bag together so you can have those birthday burgers. Okay?"

We ended up packing half her room into her overnight bag, but she was so excited to be going to an actual sleepover, she didn't want to forget anything.

Now I've got sweat-drenched hands gripping the steering wheel tighter than the situation warrants. It's just girls' night in at the clubhouse. A chance for me to make some friends.

After dropping off Jade, I swung back by my house to gussy myself up in that using makeup to make me look naturally flawless way. I don't want any of those bikers to think

I'm there for anything more than to hang with the girls. But I don't want to look like Medusa either. It's a fine line.

Jesse is no longer on the gate when I pull up. Another prospect lets me through. I might not know all of them, but they all know me from my time taking care of Elise.

I walk in wearing a white fitted babydoll Tee under my black lamb's leather jacket, black skinny jeans and ballet flats. My hair is down, all the buoyant curls springing in a sort of tamed hysteria. They've never seen me with my hair down. I kind of feel like Sandy from the end of Grease. At the *first* double-take from the first biker, I pause long enough to look over my shoulder and coo, "Tell me about it, *stud.*" Then I keep walking as if I'd never stopped, to begin with.

2

DUKE

Jesus Christ. When I got back from my ride, my club was overrun with pussy not available for fucking, and they're still fuckin' here.

Boss's old lady and her girls' night in. All of 'em except for Trish, sucking back tequila like they just invented the recipe and are trying to get it right.

'Course, drunken pizza making was pretty entertaining. Rounds of mozzarella stuck to the ceiling until the prospects scrape it down.

Sneak has his cell out snapping off pictures to send to Boss. The women have been dancing on the bar singing Taylor Swift songs for the last half-hour. Taylor Swift *in my club*.

And shit, Dr. Brennen up there shaking her ass. That woman has moves. What I wouldn't give to bury my dick deep inside that undoubtedly sweet pussy. Bet the carpet matches the drapes. She seems too good to wax. That's fine. Shit's better than fine. I prefer some stubble. Trimmed, but I like the scrape of coarse hair against my cheeks when I feast.

Then there's her fucking hair. Seeing all those curls

cascading down her back. No bun. My fingers itch to run through those glossy, soft strands. *No, dammit.* I'm not even attracted to redheads. Give me a sexy burnished chestnut any day. Dawna had thick burnished chestnut hair, when she wasn't on the chemo.

I need to calm my dick down. I need to get laid. Vicky-Lee, my regular piece is great with her mouth, but I need something more than she gave me this morning. Besides, she ain't here because I stupidly agreed to keep 'em out tonight. What the fuck was I thinking?

Sneak uses his two fingers to whistle at his woman using Tommy Doyle's wife as a pole for a pole dance, even though she ain't drunk. Once Gun was conceived, Trish put Sneak on a mission to put a baby in her belly, too. So now she's knocked up, just starting to show.

When I turn away from the PG stripper show, the good doctor is down on her knees, writhing over the counter like she's riding an imaginary dick.

Then the strangest thing happens. Her phone rings, and right in the middle of a gyration, she answers it.

"Hello?" She sounds off, concerned. Since it's a one-sided conversation, I don't know who's talking to her or what they've said, but she shouts, "I'm coming. *Oh god…* I'm coming. Keep her head and neck immobilized."

The doctor pushes off the bar top and slips. She'd have face planted if I hadn't caught her.

"Get off me," she says instead of thank you. "I've got to go." And I notice her pulling keys from her pocket.

Fuck that. She can barely walk, I ain't letting her drive. "You ain't driving."

"I have to go. I have to go *now*." She wrenches from my arms. But I ain't drunk and catch hold of her belt loop to stop her.

Split second decision. "You need to go, I'll take you," I tell her. And I know the second the words leave my mouth shit's about to get real between us. Because Dr. Brennan is the kind of woman you get real about, and you do it quick.

Her eyes go wide and for a moment, I think she's gonna fight me. But nah. She turns to me and I can see the fear and pain on her face. What the hell was that phone call about?

"We have to go now," she says, giving in. Though I have to keep my arm around her to keep her upright.

Once we're out the door, I steer her away from my bike toward my old pickup sitting outside my doublewide. She looks confused since clearly bikers ride bikes, but hops in without a word. God knows I've seen that kind of fear in a person's eyes too many times to count, so before she even has the seatbelt clicked, I've already backed out of my spot and am headed for the gate.

Thornbriar being so tiny, it takes us only six minutes to reach… well it's a house in one of the nicer sections 'a town. The doctor jumps from my truck before I park and runs up to the door. There's a woman waiting for her with the door open.

The woman, not noticing me or not caring, starts to shut the door, but I wedge my hand between it and the frame before she could shut me out.

"Ambulance is on the way," the woman tells Dr. Brennen.

"Thank you," she answers, dropping down next to a little girl laying at the base of a set of carpeted stairs, running her hand over the child to check her out. The kid already has a neck brace on.

"We used the brace from when Jack broke his collarbone and wasn't supposed to move his neck." The woman, whose home we're in, says as she absently runs her hand up and down the back of a boy standing next to her. He must be Jack. "We were careful."

When the doctor nods, I assume the woman means getting the brace on.

"*Mama...*" the little girl cries to the doctor.

Mama? You gotta be kidding me.

That's the calm before the shitstorm. Not two seconds after, red flashers from the ambulance light up the nighttime sky, and paramedics flood in with a stretcher. They try to do their job while a still quasi-buzzed doctor barks orders. I've heard doctors don't make good patients, so I can only assume how bad they can be when their kid is involved. Making it doubly bad when a buzzed doctor's kid is involved.

And I know they've reached their limit on patience with her when they don't invite her to ride to the hospital along with 'em, stating not enough room in the back. She looks panicked.

"Come on." I grab her hand, and we move back out to my truck, following closely behind the ambulance.

The shitstorm gets worse when they wheel the little girl into emergency. On duty doctors take custody of the child and start to assess. Then tell Dr. Brennen they're taking her back for some scans.

I thought parents were allowed back to those things with little kids, but they won't allow Dr. Brennen back, and let me just say, that woman has a mean streak and a vocabulary to make the saltiest sailors blush.

When the door swings shut behind the doctors and her little girl, that's when I watch Dr. Brennen's shoulders fall and she burst into tears. Shit, I hate when women cry. So I really hate seeing *this* woman cry.

"Come on, now. None 'a that." It's the only way I know to console her. That, and wrapping my arms around her. And I'm not sure if she forgot who's holding her, but once in my arms, she buries her face in my shirt, continuing to shed those tears. And fuck if she don't wrap her arms around me, too. Holding me, letting me hold her.

She's tall for a woman, but I still stand a head and neck over her. Which puts the top of her head at the perfect height to drop comforting kisses on if I get bold enough. Her scent, she smells like vanilla. Like a bakery, and it drives me nuts. I have to fight to keep from getting hard, since this ain't the place or time for it. Like ain't it enough she's a classy broad, class and those luscious curves in all the right places, but she has to smell like a fucking bakery? I'm a saint for corralling my dick the way I have.

When her crying slows and she pushes back from my chest, I don't let her go. Despite her initial protest, she stays in my arms for the entire twenty minutes it takes for the on-duty doctor to return with scan results. And I still don't let her go then, twisting her around, but with my arm slung around her waist so we stay connected.

"Sprained, not broken." He assures her. "We're moving her to a room now. Follow me."

Since it ain't my place no matter how good she feels in my arms, I finally get my head outta my ass and loosen my hold so she can follow, only to have her grab a hold of my T-shirt to drag me along behind her. I'm shocked. But I guess even doctors need moral support sometimes.

They're fitting the kid with a neck and upper chest brace when we walk into the room. The girl is out, which no one seems worried about, so I assume it's medically induced.

"She needed sedation to be scanned. Just as a precaution to keep her immobile, but she'll have to stay overnight for observation because of the concussion."

When the on-duty doc notices Brennen still crying he tries to comfort her, shifting the chart in his hands so he can rest one on her shoulder. "Come on, we got lucky," he says. It's probably an innocent gesture. Part 'a good bedside manner or some shit. Hell, she ain't even mine, yet I don't like this guy touching her because he's more the type a class act like Dr. Brennan should be with. "You know as well as I do how much worse it could have been."

Then he pats the arm he had his hand resting on, and turns to walk out.

I stay standing like an idiot because I ain't sure what else to do here. Finally I decide to give the woman privacy and turn to give her just that when she stops me, this time, with her words. "You can call me Caitlin, you know."

"*Pardon?*" I ask, rubbing the back of my neck.

"My name. You always call me Doc or Dr. Brennan. But you can call me by my first name, Caitlin."

"Okay, Caitlin. How you holding up?"

"I know you don't like me, so it was good of you to help the way you did. *Thank you.*"

Well shit. She thinks I don't like her.

"You gonna be okay?" I point to the door so she knows my intention to leave. Apparently, that was the wrong thing to ask as she breaks out in a fresh round of tears. Looks like I ain't leaving anytime soon.

Instead, I pick up the hospital version of a club chair, this one a pastel pink vinyl, to move it closer to the bed. Then I sit and grab a still tearing Caitlin by the waist to pull her down onto my lap.

"She'll be fine," she whispers, then hiccups. And I think she's trying to convince herself more so than me.

What am I doing? I ain't had a woman on my lap who I wasn't fucking or getting ready to fuck since Dawna left this world. But every breath she breathes against my neck, where she's tucked her forehead, makes me forget a little more why I don't do this shit. You fuck, you don't get hurt. Period.

Son of a bitch, if I don't fall asleep in that chair with Dr. —*er* Caitlin—on my lap. We sleep the whole night. I know because when I wake up, the room is flooded with natural light, I got a kink in my neck and my dick is harder than granite because of her ass rubbing on it while she was passed out, but damn if she ain't pretty when she wakes up. Fucking gorgeous. Pale, peaches and cream skin, only less peaches and a hell of a lot more cream to her complexion than even most redheads.

She stretches and turns her head to look at my face, then startles as if she forgot whose lap she cuddled against last night. *Fuck, I just used the word cuddled.* This woman's gonna fucking turn me into Boss if I ain't careful. My VP is more whipped by his woman's pussy than just about any brother I've met. Elise is sweet, smart and feisty when she needs to be, not to mention fucking hot. *Still...* I shake my head to erase the image of Boss's old lady, because I got old lady material on my lap.

The funny part, Caitlin don't move. Her cheeks stained a gorgeous pink. She lowers her eyes and smiles coyly. "You stayed," she says softly, almost surprised.

"I could hardly leave with you sitting on my lap." The morning makes my voice sound grittier than usual. Most women would flinch from the tone. Not Doc. No, not *Caitlin.*

"Thank you." Before I know what's happening, her face descends and her plump, heart-shaped lips press a gentle kiss to the corner of mine.

Her touch, her kiss should freak me the hell out. I ain't kissed another woman since Dawna. I fuck, I eat my fill. What I don't do, what I never fucking do, is kiss. It hurts too much when it ends. When you want more, but can't have more. My skin starts to feel tight. Not because of the kiss, but because of how badly I want more.

In a sudden bout of self-preservation, I grip her upper arms to push her off my lap. "Gotta piss," I tell her.

Caitlin continues to smile, though less coyly, more assessing, then presses a second kiss, this time squarely on my lips. It's longer, though just as gentle. Then she stands. "You need a smoke, too. Although as a doctor, I should advise you to quit."

How the fuck does she get me?

But as she stands from my lap, I know without a doubt that she does. She pats my chest, and turning her attention back to the little girl mumbles, "Outdoor smoker's lounges... only in Kentucky." Then she blows a strand of hair that had fallen in front of her eye out of her face.

Cute. Sexy. Sweet. Smart. Caring. *Dammit!* What I need to do is walk away right now. Bypass the *Kentucky* smoker's lounge outside and head for my truck. Head for the compound. There's gotta be a piece still around this morning. Maybe a hot mama that's down to fuck. What I don't need is to stay anywhere near Dr. Brennan.

I nod, then get the fuck out of there. Only I don't make the break for the parking lot. I press the down button on the elevator that'll take me to the smoker's lounge. A courtyard out behind the hospital.

There are two older guys, a chick, and a kid who doesn't look older than sixteen already in the courtyard sucking down smoke when I enter. They all look beaten down, but the kid won't look anywhere but his shoes. I watch him closely. When he finishes his first smoke, he pulls a soft pack of Reds from his jeans' pocket and tips the package for another but it's empty. The kid growls loudly, crushing the pack in his hand and whipping it to the ground.

When I catch his eyes, they're glistening, and I get it. That's real heartache right there. I'd recognize the signs anywhere. He's about a second and a half away from losing it. So I do the only thing I can and reach inside the pocket of my cut to pull a hard pack of Reds. Without words, because with that level of pain, he don't need some stranger's words,

I hand him off a couple of cigarettes, then light one of my own.

Quietly, we all sit on benches or lean against the exterior brick wall while the courtyard fills with a gray haze around our heads. When I'm finished, I snuff out the nub against the ugly beige, plastic ashtray and toss it inside with the other butts, and turn to go back inside. Again, like a fool, I walk to the elevator and push the button for the fifth floor. The stainless steel doors slide open, and I climb aboard.

Caitlin's sitting on the side edge of the bed, running her knuckles down the side of the little girl's cheek when I knock on the doorframe to announce my arrival. The girl is awake, though appears groggy. And for the first time, I'm able to get a good look at her. She's the spitting image of her mother. Showing the kind 'a beauty I know when she's older, poor Caitlin's gonna have her work cut out for her keeping those horny boys at bay. The woman's gonna need a man around to pick up the slack. Someone who can put the fear 'a God into any pubescent fucktard who thinks of putting his dick anywhere close to that little angel.

Shit. I should leave. I'm the kind of man who can put the fear 'a God into a pubescent fucktard. The last thing I need is to be considering becoming that man. *Get the fuck outta here, Duke.* But I don't take my own advice, no matter how good that advice is. And that's because Caitlin smiles at me. Her bright eyes saying she's glad I've come back. That twinge of glorious pain, the kind of pain a man usually wants to feel hits my heart. I recognize that kind of pain, too. Though I ain't felt it since that first day on the beach with Dawna.

Prettiest thing I ever saw, at least up 'til now. She was a few years younger than me and she'd missed so much school, her mama decided to homeschool.

She'd been in remission the first time we met. Thick, burnished chestnut hair swayed as she sashayed, swaying those hips which for sure caught my attention next. And the kicker, she didn't even realize she was doing it, getting me harder the longer I watched.

Dawna was sixteen to my Twenty. Some of my buddies knew who she was and told me not to bother with the home-schooled freak.

I, however, thought more with my dick and my dick told me any girl who looked that good in a bikini, it had to get to know intimately.

When I plunked my cocky, dumb-ass body down on the bank next to her and her sister, it was done because I was done for. That gorgeous, petite woman became my world.

"Hey, Duke." Caitlin actually leaves her little girl's side to come to me, meet me halfway inside the room. I blink back the thoughts of Dawna. Can't be thinking about her when I got Caitlin here with me, especially not when she wraps those thin, shapely arms up around my neck, resting her cheek against my collarbone.

My arms, I bring around her waist to hold her back. She feels good here. I hate that she feels so good here.

"Who's dat, Mama?" The little girl's scratchy voice pulls my attention away from the gorgeous woman who I should be smart enough to walk away from, but clearly, I ain't. A full night of her sleeping on my lap, no sex involved, tells me I ain't smart enough for that.

Doc drops her hold from around my neck and shifts around to face her daughter. She glides one of her hands down to lock with mine and drags me over to the bed. "This is my friend, Duke."

"He the one who wides motocycwols?" the girl asks. She has her hand raised to her mouth like she's whispering her question so I don't hear, though she says it full volume. And what the fuck does it mean? Did Caitlin tell the little angel about me specifically, maybe because I brought her here? Or had she talked about the club in general?

"Yes," Caitlin tells her. "He's the one who rides motorcycles. But he brought his truck to take us home in."

That her way of telling me she wants me to stay until the girl gets released? Why do I like the thought of that so well?

Both Caitlin and her daughter look to me as if waiting for me to introduce myself. I say the first thing that comes to my head. "Hey, Peaches."

Caitlin chuckles, probably because her daughter scrunches up her nose at the endearment. "My name is Jade," she says. "Nowt *peaches*."

"Yeah, but you got peaches and cream skin like your mama. So it's either that or creamy." I tease.

Jade giggles her high-pitched little girl giggle. "I wike peaches."

And the way she giggles, fuck, I'd hardly know she'd been injured last night. Let alone how bad it could have been.

Then Caitlin, one hand still locked with mine, grabs a hold of one of Jade's, and looks between us. "The nurse came in for a vitals check and said the on-duty doctor should be around with the discharge papers in about a half hour, which means we'll be here for another couple of hours, at least."

"Giving away doctor's secrets?" I ask with an eyebrow raised. Fuck, am I *flirting*? What the hell is wrong with me? I don't flirt. Ever.

When she levels that smile of hers on me again, *shit*. I know I'm in trouble. I *was* flirting and Caitlin *likes me* flirting.

I sit down on the club chair next to Caitlin, who's resumed her spot on the bed next to Peaches, and for the next two hours, I get to know the little angel.

Before they're finished with the discharge, I swing back by the clubhouse to grab Peaches' booster seat from the back of Doc's car, and give the order for one of the prospects to drive it to her house once I call. After that, I swing by the pharmacy and grab a buzzer. It's loud, really fucking annoyingly loud. So when Caitlin is off somewhere in the rest of the house, if Peaches needs her mama, Caitlin will hear her.

Finished with my errands, I drive back to the hospital to pick up Peaches and Doc and to drop 'em back home for a little bit 'a girl time. Though not before I tell 'em about the prospect bringing the car and handing off the buzzer to Jade, explaining what it's for. Even with Peaches on her hip, Caitlin bends the top half of her body into the cab and draws my face to hers for a quick lip touch.

"Thank you," she says. "For everything." We kissed three times now, and all three 'a those times she initiated. I have a mind to initiate the fourth, but don't get the chance when she gently shuts the door and walks inside her house. Her little girl waving at me as they go.

I wait until Jesse pulls the Jeep into Doc's driveway. He runs the keys up to the porch, knocks on the door, and when Caitlin answers, she smiles at him, they share a laugh then she shuts the door and he runs to climb into my truck.

"She's something," he says while clicking his seatbelt in place. "Good choice, Prez."

Now prospects think I'm hot for doctor? I can't deal with that and straight up ignore him altogether. A short grunt is the only response he gets.

The punk laughs at me.

With so much on my mind, we drive back to the compound in total silence, I don't even bother with the radio. Not a prospect, but Blaze is on the gate and opens it to let us in when we arrive. Blaze is a patched-in brother now. Something don't feel right. Then Jesse taps my shoulder and points for me to look over to the right where a large group of brothers, including my two lieutenants still in town, stand in a huddle.

"What the fuck is going on?" I bellow. Truck parked, I stalk towards my brothers.

They're standing around a long, thin, white box with a red satin bow affixed to the lid. The kind the flower shop in town uses for long-stemmed roses. I know because I used to buy Dawna roses once a week right up to the week she died. She loved 'em.

Sneak looks up at me and breaks the huddle apart so I can get to it. "Tommy's on his way," he tells me.

Jesus.

"What now?" I ask. Sneak, because he's the one wearing the gloves, bends down to pull the top off the box. It's long-stemmed roses alright. Dead, withered, black long-stemmed roses. The note laying on top says 'Congratulation on your little *angel.*' The 'angel' is underlined. If that ain't a threat, I don't know what one is. And it's signed, H.

"It gets worse," Carver, my other lieutenant, says.

Worse? How could it get worse?

Sneak bends down to pick up a photo from the bottom of the box, stem end. Carver is right, shit got worse. Again, with Sneak's wearing the gloves, I let him show me instead of taking it from his hand, so as not to leave my fingerprints. It's of Elise and baby Gun taken here on the compound, probably through one 'a those telephoto lenses. *The bastard has eyes on Elise and Gun.* The photo was just taken yesterday. Elise has Gun, and she's standing next to Caitlin's Jeep, talking to her.

"Who dropped this off?" I ask, trying like hell but failing to keep the bite from my voice.

Bobby-Wayne, one of the newer prospects, speaks up. "It was a Hildegarde Flowers driver." Hildegarde Flowers. Yep, that's the flower shop in town, alright. "He drove up to the gate, said he had a delivery for Elise Hollister and handed me a clipboard with a paper to sign for the delivery. So I did. But I got nosey and opened the box."

Well thank our lucky-fucking-stars the kid got nosey.

I run my hands over my face and grumble. "Anyone call Boss?"

"Not yet. We still need him with Chaos and Blood. And you know, he hears this, he's on his way home." Carver. He's right. We need Boss to stick with Chaos and Blood. Liv. Damn that woman. She should've kept her ass here with her man and her brother who love her and would die to keep her safe. Damn all women.

This is the last shit I need to be dealing with. I sigh, then order, "Double Elise's guard. She don't leave the compound without at least two 'a you, got me?" When the men mutter their agreement, I turn to the three I want specifically on her. "Blaze, Blue and Hero," I yell loud enough for Blaze on the gate to hear. "You all got Elise duty." Then quieter I ask, "Anyone tell Elise?"

Rounds of "Nah" or "No way" or "Fuck no" travel around the group.

"Good. *Don't*. She don't need to worry about this. We already got one stupid woman on the run." Caitlin Brennan came along at the wrong time. Houdini going after Elise again, and I can't stop thinking about how bad I want to fuck the good doc. Maybe I just need to fuck her and get it over with. Nah, I need to let her alone and never look back. "Let me know when Tommy gets here. I'm going in for a drink."

3

CAITLIN

"Duke? What are you doing here?" I ask the sexy biker at my front door.

He holds up bags of groceries in each hand for me to see. "You need to eat." Then he pushes his way through the door, moving me aside with his large frame, in the process.

His boots clomp against the hardwood flooring as he makes his way to the kitchen. Like he's been in my house a hundred times, though today is his first visit.

I blink at an empty doorway, unsure of what is happening at the moment. Then once I get my wits about me, turn to follow him. When I reach the kitchen, he's pulling items from the plastic bags. Some he leaves on the counter and others, he opens cupboards to look for places to put the boxed or canned goods.

"I have a pantry." I point to the door next to the utility room. "All my cans and boxes go there."

With a full armload, he walks to the pantry. It occurs to me he won't be able to open the door, and so I jog to reach the handle before he drops boxes all over the floor.

The thing about Duke, when he looks at me, it's as if he's

accessing the innermost recesses of my mind and heart. Even for the briefest look, which he gives me now. It's as unnerving as it is exhilarating. What does he see when he looks at me?

How do I measure up with the women in his past—and why do I care about the women in his past? They're none of my business.

Though he is here, isn't he?

No one is forcing him to be. But what does he want? Why *is* he here?

Duke shuts the pantry and slips out of his cut, that's what Elise told me the vest he wears with the big patch indicating he's a member of the Brimstone Lords is called. He slips it off his shoulders to drape over the back of one of my high-backed, wooden kitchen chairs. Then he walks to the sink to wash his hands.

Turning back to me, he grunts out, "Pan."

Again, it takes my brain a second to kickstart, but I go to the pots and pans cupboard under the counter next to the oven and pull a cast iron skillet with a lid out for him.

"Might as well pull a pot, too. Big one," he says.

I watch in bewilderment as the man works at the counter, this time ripping open a box of cornbread mix.

While he's busy I move to the dishwasher to pull the measuring cups from the clean dishes and grab him the carton of eggs from the fridge.

Duke pours the oil into the measuring cup and cracks one of the eggs into the oil, whisking them together with a fork, then he pours the mixture into the skillet. The man works comfortably in my kitchen. I can't wrap my head around this personality one-eighty he's spinning. For almost a year I've seen him grumble, grunt and bark orders at his MC brothers. I've seen him accept touches from the women who hang about the clubhouse and even the starts to some pretty bawdy activities with them.

He uses my electric can opener to open a can of cream corn and dumps it into the skillet before giving the whole thing a mix. Though he hadn't preheated the oven. I help with that because it gives me something else to focus on, even for a moment.

Sure I'd thought he was sexy before. Commanding and always charismatic in the way he holds himself and takes charge of any given situation, at least any given situation I'd been around to witness. I guess that's why he's their president.

What am I supposed to do with this new information? That he can be sweet and kind, and now domestic? I'd wanted to sleep with him before. But the man he's showed me yesterday, and now today, that's not the kind of man you simply sleep with. That's the kind of man you lose your heart to. The kind you give of yourself completely. He's a paradox of the greatest order. Who would have thought?

While we wait for the red light on the oven to turn off he opens a package of ground beef and dumps it in the pot. It hits me, the cans on the counter, the meat in the pan, he's making chili for us. Chili. I love chili.

My stupid heart fills with warmth for the enormous biker filling my kitchen.

Emotion clogs my throat, but I swallow it back without calling attention to it. "Can I get you a beer?"

On a nod, he uses a spatula to mix the beef. "Two," he says.

He opens the oven to place the cornbread inside while I pull three beers and put the eggs away.

Duke twists the cap off the first Guinness. He takes a long drink, then twists the cap off the second Irish stout and pours it into the pot with the meat. It fizzes, perfuming the whole kitchen with a deliciously meaty-yeasty smell. Duke and chili, it's a heady combination.

Mid-dinner preparation, he pauses to flick on the old radio secured beneath the top cupboard next to the refrigerator, where Ann Wilson from Heart belts out some amazing high notes about a magic man. I'd never understood the lyrics before. That is, I'd understood the meanings behind them, just not the emotion. Now, in the kitchen with my very own magic man, I understand completely. That's after only a few kisses shared between us.

My belly pangs, and not from want of food. To distract myself from these understandable, yet wanton thoughts, I start to open the cans.

It doesn't work when he puts his hand up. "Stop. *Sit,*" he orders. Duke Ellis, Brimstone Lords President, is cooking *me* dinner. I don't think any man has ever made me dinner before. Even through the late-night study sessions when a boyfriend should. Or when I started as an intern with crazy intern hours. Jade's father never lifted a finger to help me.

God, I remember a few arguments when he'd yelled at me because I'd chosen to catch up on sleep rather than get dinner on the table for him once he got home from work. He, I'd found out *after* we began living together, had very '*traditional*' expectations for gender roles, unfortunately.

Well, Duke's wish is my command, at least right now. I hoist my bottom up onto the countertop, my bare feet dangle over the side.

The burly man grabs my foot to run his fingers over my glitter-pink polish. It's just a touch on my foot but constitutes more intimacy than I've had in years.

I laugh uncomfortably. "Jade likes pedicures. Typically, we do it when we're home. Friday or Saturday nights."

"You always use glitter?" His laugh is not uncomfortable but teasing—in a good way.

"No. Not always glitter but Jade always picks."

"So you don't go out, then? At all?" he asks.

I shake my head. "That night at the clubhouse was my first night out since Jade was a baby. There's just not enough time in the day. And I have to trust people to care for her. Look how that turned out. I sent her to her first sleepover, she ended up in emergency."

Before I'm ready for him to stop touching me, because honestly, the contrast of his smooth skin and rough, calloused fingers— I suck in a sharp breath and shudder. If it wouldn't be so obvious as to why I fanned myself, I'd fan myself. His feather-soft caresses simultaneously calm me and shoot white-hot tingles up my leg.

The man is a serious tease whether he knows it or not. Yet in the tradition set down by the centuries of serious teases before him, he ends the foot fondling to stir the chili simmering on the stove.

I don't even freak out that he'd neglected to rewash his hands before picking up the cooking utensil. A freak-out might deter him from making a move like that again, and I'd greatly enjoy for him to make a move like that again.

Besides, it's *my* foot. I know my showering habits, so I figure I'll be fine this one time.

"Right, no going out with your girls. Does that go for dating, too?" He asks, pulling me back from the mental shut-down which *he* caused. It's a good thing he's cooking and not assisting me with a patient.

"*Dating?*"

"Yeah, you know—where a man picks you up and takes you out to dinner, or where the fuck ever." He picks up the can of tomatoes and one of the cans of beans to dump into the pot.

"A man? I don't think I remember what one looks like."

His eyes grow huge, choking on the drink of beer he'd just lifted to his mouth.

Abruptly, I take in how what I've said might be construed and attempt to backpedal. "I mean a man on a date. Not saying you aren't a man. You're actually quite manly, um... strong... confident... handsome."

The word vomit keeps spewing from my mouth while Duke throws his head back and laughs loudly. Still deep. Still gritty. Still unbelievably sexy. The sound reverberates throughout the kitchen.

Oh god, had I told him he was handsome?

I bring my bottle up to my lips. What I need to do is shut up now. But I've once again given him the upper hand, which means I have to act fast to get it back and cock an eyebrow his direction. "*Tisk, tisk, tisk,* if that was your way of getting me to divulge what I think of you. Men like you needn't fish, Mr. Ellis," I say, then take a long drink. Hoping to all get out, that it sounds more confident than I feel saying it.

At least my voice didn't tremble.

Duke turns from the stove to push my hand, and thus my bottle, away from my mouth. I guess I sounded confident, because then he kisses me.

No, no. Not just a kiss. His beautiful, slow, sensual assault on my lips far surpasses any ordinary kiss. Dominant and powerful yet allowing me the time to respond.

He smells of cigarette smoke and tastes of Guinness and tobacco, and when his tongue parts my lips, I open fully to receive all he's willing to give. The full Duke Ellis experience. His touch, his feel, his taste overpowers my senses, making me dizzy. As he presses harder, I feel it. The moment my bones liquefy, and I become pliant in his arms. All that liquid pooling in my lady bits between my thighs.

I can't even move my arms to hold him back, having lost all body control when I became liquid.

Slowly, he begins to lay me down, my back against the counter. He hooks one of my legs around his hip and begins to stroke me over my shorts, but right there. Right where I need him to touch me. Every nerve ending in my body ignites with burns and tingles. Torturously decadent burns and tingles. *Oh god, so good. So good.*

Of course, right as he pushes up my T-shirt going in for the kill by tugging on the cups of my bra, right as he has me ready to jump out of my skin from the continuous stroking and now nipple rub, the timer for the cornbread goes off. I am fortunately shocked back to my senses.

This isn't me.

I don't do one-night stands. Especially not in my house. In the middle of the day. Between cornbread and chili preparation. And not with a scary biker who has shown his sweet side in recent days but didn't like me until my daughter went to the hospital, and has probably had more women in the past month than I've had men in my entire life.

Considering all this, I push him off. "Cornbread," I say lamely.

He laughs. Shaking his head, he touches my nose as if teasing a small child, then turns to grab the potholders I have hanging from a magnetized hook on the refrigerator. Pulling the sizzling hot skillet from the oven, he then places the golden-brown goodness on one of the back burners to cool while I right myself.

For the next twenty minutes, he prepares chili. Dicing condiments like raw onion and avocado. He opens a package of shredded sharp cheddar cheese and a bag of corn chips. He does all this while ignoring the fact that with a kiss, the man knocked my world off kilter.

How could I go back to my life before he touched me when my body is still fizzing from his touch? And that's without coming. The man is dangerous. I assumed old age would be the death of me. Who would have thought life as I'd known it would end with a kiss? From Duke Ellis, of all people.

He doesn't announce it, but I know the chili is done when he opens the cupboard to take a couple of bowls out. So while he ladles up a heaping mass of beans, meat, and tomato sauciness for each of us, I jump from the counter and walk to the fridge where I grab us each another cold brew, twisting off the caps. I toss them in the trashcan next to the pantry and hand his off. I lean my hip against the edge of the counter and watch him sprinkle cheese and onions on top of one of the bowls. "That's for you, right?"

"You don't like onions?" he asks.

"Oh, no. I like onions, just not that many. I don't want hair on my chest." I joke.

His eyes drop from the bowl to my chest, almost glazing over as he stares, then he clears his throat. "I see your point. Any objections to cheese?" he teases back.

"Nope. I love cheese. Avocado can find a place in almost any meal and corn chips—" Instead of continuing, I give him a look to convey *'enough said.'* Because who doesn't love corn chips? "Would you like to watch a movie while we eat?" I use my chin to gesture to the living room.

"Yeah, Doc. That sounds good." Not waiting for me to lead the way, he picks up his bowl with one hand and his beer in the other, and walks back toward my big, fluffy, denim-covered sofa. A sofa sectional is perfect for snuggling with little girls or hot bikers. Cleans easy in case of spills. As I watch his retreating back, I realize how much I like him in my space.

His gate screams confidence. Strong, power in every step. The way his muscles move, it's like he's stalking—almost cat-like—even though it's only to my sofa. He can't help it.

When I join him, he's standing next to the coffee table, not sitting.

"Something wrong?" I ask.

"You got coasters or some shit you want me to use?"

The man smokes, swears too much, and heads a motorcycle club. But asks if I use coasters? Another sweet act from the man who continues to surprise me.

When I don't answer, he clears his throat. "Women usually want coasters so as not to ruin the coffee table with water spots."

I look down at the painted white, chipped, has-seen-better-days coffee table made from salvaged wood Jade and I had "rescued" according to her, from a beach in Ireland before we'd left. She'd loved it so much that I paid the hefty sum to have it shipped back here to the U.S. To my parents' house, where we stayed when we first moved back.

"No," I finally respond. "No coasters here. Jade and I live comfortable. A home should be a safe place, an escape from the world outside. You want to put your feet up on the coffee table to get comfortable, I won't complain. The only thing I ask is boots off first, because germs close to food." I scrunch my nose.

"Fuck, you ain't who I thought you were." It's a strange response. Not said hurtfully, more like, dare I say, reverently.

4

CAITLIN

To get the movie watching underway, I set my drink and bowl down on the tabletop, sit my butt down on a cushion, scoop up the remote, and pause to listen for Jade. When I don't hear any buzzer or little girl noises, I assume she's still resting. With a quick glance over to Duke to urge him to get situated, I press the pay-per-view button and begin to scroll.

"What do you feel like watching?" I ask.

Duke's response is to sit down right next to me so our thighs press together, and he plucks the remote from my hand to take over scrolling duty.

I turn to stare at his audacity.

That's when he decides to explain, "There's pussy domain and there's dick domain. When a dick is around, remotes fall squarely into dick domain." He explains without looking at me but continuing to peruse the movie options.

Dick domain? I bite back the laugh. It's been Jade and me on our own for so long, even before her dad left us, looking back on the situation with a less love addled mind. I forgot how possessive men can be about the television. And yes, it's my house, but the man cooked me dinner. I don't have the heart to argue it out today.

He stops on some action-packed, espionage shoot 'em up. The kind full of explosions and too many bullets shot from a clip, magically without needing to be reloaded.

Duke toes off his boots, hoists one foot up and rests it on the table, then crosses the other overtop. I hand him his bowl then his drink, which he tucks between the sofa arm and his body. And in a move I don't expect, he pulls me, chili bowl and cornbread in hand, so I'm half on top of him. We're leaned so close together that I have no choice but to fold my legs and tuck them under me, pushing my toes under the cushion next to me to get more comfortable, if that's possible. Because as I've found, Duke Ellis, Brimstone Lord President, happens to be damn comfortable.

It's awkward at first, the way he pushes my head to rest on his shoulder. An awkward way to eat. But I don't move from the spot until it's time to set my bowl down. Then he tugs me right back into my previously held position.

In a particularly gruesome death scene full of blood and guts, I gasp and tuck my face into Duke's T-shirt, burrowing deeper into his side. He chuckles at my reaction, the sound vibrating his broad chest while the solidness of him beneath me makes me feel safe and warm, if not slightly put-off.

"What are you laughing at?" I demand, though my words hold no heat.

"You deal with blood and guts on a daily basis, and a crappy movie grosses you out?"

Incredulously, I roll my eyes. "I see the aftermath of explosions and gun fights. I'm not there while they happen, just help after they do."

He stops laughing then. "My uncle, the man practically raised me after my pops got sent down—*prison*—he was the president of the club. My uncle. And the club's dirty money took care of us kids." Duke doesn't go on, staring back at the television. But he can't start a story like that and not finish, so I lay my hand against his chest, giving it a slight bit of pressure in a way, to tell him it's safe to go on.

On a nod, he continues. "It's nothing. Just—my mother couldn't object to us hanging around the club because my uncle wanted us there *and* she accepted weekly deposits into her bank account. He didn't have any sons. When my older brother Rex turned eighteen, he patched in. Started his prospect period when he turned sixteen and got his license. Same with me. For two years, I did every disgusting job my uncle and brother and all the men could think of."

"Okay?"

"You wanted to be a doctor, I'll bet your whole life."

Slowly, I nod.

"I never had dreams like that. I just always knew I'd follow my family into the club. That was, until I met Dawna. Then I knew I'd follow the family into the club and marry Dawna. Every decision I made was for one, the other, or both."

"And now?" I ask, swallowing hard. For some reason nervous about his answer.

"Now, for the first time in my life, I want something just for me."

I don't know how to respond, so I lean up, close my eyes and press my mouth to his. I mean it to be quick. But in true Duke fashion, the fashion I've found since spending time with the man both when he liked me and didn't, he folds his body over mine to take over the kiss like he takes over everything.

Taking over the kiss, for Duke, means nipping, licking and pressing deep and long. The glide of his lips, wet, silky smooth decadence, like the finest Belgian chocolate. And as everyone who has been to Europe knows, Belgians make the finest chocolate.

Drinking in all that's Duke, I feel intoxicated. Aside from his mind-blowing lip prowess, I think he just told me that he wants me. Me. Though the question is for how long? Does he only want sex? Or does he *want me*, want me?

I'm a mother. If he only wants sex, I suppose I could do that, but he can't show up here. He can't spend time around my daughter, get her attached and then scrape us both off like her father did. I can't let that happen again. We'll need boundaries.

"Duke." I finally pluck up the courage to say, breathy yet firm. Or as firm as I can make it being this tuned on. His mouth stills, though his lips stay pressed gently to my neck, and the pulse point, pulsing erratically where his lips point.

I gather my thoughts by closing my eyes, then open them and push back so I can look him in *his* stunningly gray, almost silver eyes. "If you want sex from me, I've never been anyone's uh—*side piece*—before." And I clear my throat for something to do because of how intensely he's staring. "But well, you know I like you, and can probably do that. I just can't have you at my house. I'm a single mom. I can't have Jade get attached—"

"Shut it, Doc," he says right before he kisses me again. Hard, openmouthed and *passionate*. And as he continues to kiss me, Duke grabs the hem of my shirt and whips it up over my head with no preamble, leaving me in only my pale, lacy blue bra.

He only gives slight acknowledgment with a quick smile before he moves his hand to unfasten the back clasp. Then he tugs the straps until my bare breasts stand exposed, my nipples at attention. My breasts aren't huge. They aren't mosquito bites either. Mostly pert—I'd had a baby, after all—and proportional for my size.

The perusal he gives them is so much different than that of my bra.

"What?" I ask, wanting to cover up, yet not making the move to do so.

"I'm not gonna fuck you today. Though Doc, I gotta taste you. Been dying to taste you and that peaches and cream skin for so fucking long."

"*Taste me?*" I'm hesitant. Partially from being out of breath from his kisses, and partially unsure of what parts he wants to taste. Oh, but I find out.

Duke reverently plumps my breasts together before sucking on one of my nipples, deep and hard. The nip he gives it surprises me, and I jolt. He releases it, and blows delicately over the heated red mark he's left, swipes his thumb over the whole areola, and then switches to give the other attention. It. Feels. Good.

I thought the burning tingle before, on the counter, was good—and it was. But this, if he keeps it up, I could orgasm. From nipple stimulation. Over two years since a man's mouth has touched me, and that man is Duke, and his mouth feels *that good*. My breaths come in pants. Shallow. "Oh god, *Duke*." I sigh.

"Think you're ready for me." He grumbles then, "Gonna fucking taste you."

Before I can register what's happening, he releases my nipple with a pop not bothering to soothe the sting of that nip, because his hands suddenly become busy when he rips my elastic-waist shorts down my thighs, along with my panties. Then he kisses my lips hard one more time and removes my shorts and panties the rest of the way, tossing them to the floor.

He flips me so I'm no longer angled partly on the bottom cushion, but so my back presses firmly against the back cushion of the sofa, drops to his knees in front of me and spreads my thighs, holding me wide open with his hands at my knees.

"Carpet matches the drapes..." he murmurs. "Trimmed not waxed... thank fuck..." And then he, no other word for it, digs in. I've never had a man go at me with such relished, reckless abandon as Duke. The feeling so intense, so overwhelming, my thighs strain to snap together, to give me some relief from his tongue assault, though Duke is strong and keeps my legs splayed wide.

"I... oh god, *Duke*." A tinny feeling fills my head, my breaths no longer come in pants as I gulp to try and fill my lungs with any air at all. There's a loud ringing in my ears, and I close my eyes, pressing them tightly together. So tightly that black spots pop behind my eyelids. His tongue assault is relentless. He drops his hand from one of my knees to fling my leg over his shoulder, then takes his free hand, trails two fingers along the slick wetness he's created, and plunges those two fingers inside me to compliment his cunilingual ministrations.

Even without enough air in my lungs, I gasp at the intrusion. He crooks his fingers forward, hitting a spot no man has ever hit before. My entire body seizes up, and it happens. I *explode*. He growls, feasting through my climax. Continuing to pump his fingers. Continuing to draw out my orgasm.

I shake uncontrollably when he finishes. Maybe from the shock, since my body has never experienced such an extreme orgasm before, or maybe... maybe because it's Duke who gave it to me. Can I even allow that thought to take root?

Then surprising me further, Duke stares at me a beat before he hollers, "*Fuck*." And then pushes up from his spot kneeling on the floor, which means my rubber band legs flop from his shoulders awkwardly.

I pull my knees together, my skin suddenly flushing a self-conscious bright red, redder than my hair, as he sits to slide his boots back on. Focusing on whatever he's decided to focus on so he doesn't have to look at me, Duke stands and walks into the kitchen.

I hear the scrape of him grabbing his keys from the counter and the swish of moving his cut from the chair, then he walks back through my living room and out the front door without even saying goodbye. Leaving me naked and confused on my sofa.

What just happened?

He said he wasn't going to fuck me. Only wanted to taste. I thought that meant he wanted more with me. Well, his actions tell me where I stand with Duke. Men like Duke Ellis don't want to start things with a single mother. It hurts. Though, in my experience, that's all I can expect from a man. Hurt. They suck down all the fun parts of life and then leave you without any inclination that this had been the plan.

I'm an educated woman, yet there I go, falling for it again. The problem is, I don't know what about me drives them away. I'm not clingy or whiny. I even told Duke I'd sleep with him without any attachments. Though, no attachments doesn't mean no goodbye. No, *'hey thanks for a good-time, we should do it again'*, or even a pat on the knee in passing to let me know all's well. Aiden asked me out. Aiden told me he wanted me to move in with him, and when I told him I was pregnant, acted over the moon. But it was all a lie. The truth of the matter is, I repel men.

The tears, unfortunately, begin to pool in the corners of my eyes.

How can one woman be so unlovable?

Reaching down, I pluck my shorts and panties from the floor where Duke had tossed them, and shimmy them back into place. Then pull my Tee over my head, not bothering with the bra. It's not like I'm leaving the house with Jade on bed rest for the next couple of days. As if sensing that I'm thinking of her, Jade's buzzer goes off.

"Coming," I shout to her, jogging up the stairs to her room, entering with a fake plastered-on smile. "Hey Princess Jade."

"Peaches, Mama."

I wince but shake it off. "That's not my nickname for you. I call you Princess Jade. You know that."

"But *I wike Peaches*." She wobbles her bottom lip after drawing out the word peaches, meant to really put a point on that little girl whine of hers. She's a pro.

But I'm a mom and thus immune to lip wobbles and little girl whines. Though, my baby girl *is* injured, so I refuse to argue with her over this. I pinch the bridge of my nose, then sigh and change the subject. "What did you need?" I move closer to place my hand on her forehead and stroke her hair.

"I'm hungwy."

"You want some chili?" I ask.

"You made chiwi?"

Not wanting to deal with the aftereffects of Duke having been here and Jade not getting to see him, and since she wouldn't be seeing him again, I lie. "Yes."

"Okay Mama, can I have chocwet miwk?"

"Sure, baby."

Then I turn to run back downstairs.

I ladle her a small bowl of Duke's delicious chili, butter a slice of cornbread, and mix up a glass of chocolate milk. Everything is placed on a serving tray that has small legs at each of the corners to form a table, which I'd pulled from the cupboard above the refrigerator. We typically use them for eating breakfast in bed, or eating dinner in front of the television.

Back upstairs, inside her room, I set the tray down on her desk to prop several pillows behind Jade's back and neck to give her more of a seated upright position. Then I set the tray on her lap and hand her the remotes to her pink princess flat screen and the one to play DVDs.

Before I leave, I load the DVD player with her favorite princess movie, move to kiss her forehead, and walk to my room to shower.

Duke's sweet, sensual touch lingers on my body. I have to get it off. Erase him from my memory. I loved hanging with the women at the clubhouse, but they belong to the Lords. I belong to no one, and since the clubhouse belongs to *him*, well, I'll have to stay away. At least Elise got a clean bill of health. If she needs me once her husband returns, I'll see her at her house.

The water scalds my '*peaches and cream*' skin to bright strawberry. Not that it makes a difference, he's not just *on* my skin. In a couple of days he'd gotten *under* it. I turn the water off and step onto the fluffy, powder blue bathmat, letting the water drip down my back and legs. Eventually, I pull an even fluffier powder blue towel from the bar next to the bathtub, bend so my hair hangs flipped forward in front of me, and wrap the towel around my head like a pretty, pastel turban.

I slip on my favorite lavender, terrycloth robe, tie it securely around my waist, and walk back to Jade's room to check on her. She happily sings along with the blonde princess on the screen, so I don't bother her. But move back downstairs to find a plastic container to store Duke's leftover chili in.

When I find one big enough to fit it all, he'd made a large pot, I take a smaller container for Jade and me to have tomorrow. The rest I scrape into the larger container and stow it in the freezer. After, I find a zipper bag for the rest of the cornbread, wash up all the dinner dishes, make sure the doors are locked, then I sit on the sofa avoiding the spots where Duke played with me, and turn on the History Channel. A WWII documentary. Cannon fire blazes across the television. Loud *booms* erupt through the speakers.

What would normally hold my rapt attention, barely registers. I watch blankly, numbly. I'd feel bad about moving Jade and I again, because she's popular here among the preschool set. She has a best friend, is going to slumber parties and everything. But maybe, even though Thornbriar needs a doctor, maybe they don't need Caitlin Brennan as a doctor.

Eventually I nod off. Until I hear a crash from upstairs that startles me awake. I jump from the sofa, remembering that I'd neglected to take Jade's tray, and figuring she'd fallen asleep. The tray must have crashed to the floor.

In Jade style, she remains sound asleep. Luckily she ate every drop of her chili, so even with the bowl tipped upside-down on her carpet, there's none to stain. Sippy cup of chocolate milk drained, too. Careful to keep quiet, I collect the dishes and walk back downstairs to wash hers out.

And because the shit of the night refuses to end, when my hands are wet and sudsy, my phone rings. I wipe them on my robe and run to answer it. There's no need to look at the number because the location tells me everything I need to know. It's an out of country number. Sydney, Australia flashes across the screen. I huff out a breath big enough to blow the hair dangling in front of my eye out of the way.

Aiden-Freaking-Murphy.

Um, *no*. He abandoned us for a woman in Australia. I don't even care if he's dead and calling from the underworld. For three months I was stuck in Ireland by myself, closing down my grandmother's estate, not that she had much of one left. My grandma liked to, as she'd said so many times over the years, "suck the marrow from the bones of life."

I had a two-year-old who kept asking where her daddy was. Yet there was me, sitting by the phone hoping, praying that the jerk-face would call to tell me he'd made a terrible mistake.

So many tears shed over him, I couldn't keep count. And then when he finally called, he didn't want me, he didn't even ask about *his daughter*. Oh no, Aiden wanted the freaking antique locket he'd given me on the night he asked me to move in with him. It was his grandmother's locket. A locket he'd found out was, "worth a mint."

What? Did he want to re-gift his gift of love? Or maybe he intended to sell it off to take his woman on a tropical vacation.

Either way, I wouldn't send it. It was a gift. Though, Aiden was so right, it *was* worth a mint. And any chance of reconciliation vanished with that phone call, after which, when I told him I wouldn't give back the locket, he cleared out Jade's saving's account that we'd started for her when she was born.

Yeah, guess what looser? I keep staring at the words Sydney, Australia. Now I *can't* send it. Because when I *sold it*, the mint the gold exchange paid me funded Jade and my move back to America.

He calls now every five or six months. I've never answered, not once. In honor of my grandmother, I took a sabbatical from work so Jade and I could travel the country a little before we had to commit to a location. But once I settled in Thornbriar and opened my practice, it wasn't hard for him to find my number and for the calls to start up again. You can find almost anyone through the internet.

The ringing finally stops. Hopefully this time he'll get it. I won't answer his call. I'll never answer his call.

5

CAITLIN

It's been five days since Duke showed at my home, cooked me dinner and gave me the single best orgasm of my life. I took the week off to see to Jade's recovery, referring my patients to Dr. Brighton, the only *other* general practitioner in town. Older than dirt and thinks women have no place in medicine. Hell, he thinks women have no place out of the kitchen, which is rough for my female patients he has to see, but my daughter comes first.

She'll always come first.

Her bruising has been healing nicely. Come Monday, I'll have to go back to work. But for today, after I got my girl bathed and dressed, we loaded in the car to head to Nashville. I've been thinking Nashville might be a nice place to move. So we're having a girls' day to check it out. Just the two of us, since we don't have anybody else.

We're about fifteen minutes outside of Thornbriar when some jerk, probably texting and driving, passes us but veers back over too soon, cutting me off. I swerve hard to the right to avoid a front end to tailend collision, but he sideswipes my car, forcing us off the road.

I lose control, pulling hard left on the steering wheel in an effort to straighten us out, at the same time I slam on the break. We end up skidding on the gravel. The rear of the Jeep clips the rock and bounces off, swinging us around until we head-butt the mountain. My front airbags deploy, as do the side-curtain airbags. I turn to check on my daughter, scared in her car seat.

A hit and run. Exactly what I don't need today, or ever.

The seatbelt has Jade's little body pressed taut and erect against the seatback. She wears a stunned face, and her bottom lip trembles, but otherwise she appears to be fine. "What happened?"

"Someone hit us, Princess Jade. How are you? Does anything hurt, baby?"

"No Mama," she answers right away, though it's with a thickness to her voice.

"Are you scared?"

Slowly, she nods, continuing to hold back the tears by trembling her little lip.

While reaching into my purse on the floor of the passenger side—it had been thrown from the seat—for my cell phone, I try to reassure her. "Okay, you're okay Jadie. I'm going to call for help."

About ten minutes after my call, a police cruiser rolls to a stop behind us, all six plus feet of sculpted Sgt. Tommy Doyle exits the vehicle. I know him from around town, but also, he's Elise's husband's best friend. I got to hang out with his wife Maryanne that girls' night in. She's a paralegal at Brown, Morris and Lazinski, in Bartleton, one town over. Funny, beautiful, a delight to be around.

Tommy approaches our car, and I roll down my window. "Sgt. Doyle." I greet him.

His gaze cuts from my car to my eyes. "Girl please. You

partied with my wife. She likes you, which means I like you. Which means to you, I'm Tommy. Not Sgt. Doyle."

A laugh bubbles up, a laugh because he's so downhome, so personable, that I can't help it. "Okay."

"So what the hell happened?"

It takes me ten more minutes to explain everything that went down, since I have to pause in several places for him to write down the account on a tablet, while asking poignant questions along the way. When finished taking my statement, he calls the tow for us.

Tommy waits with us until the tow shows. Ellis Auto & Towing written in bold, red lettering across the side of the truck with the phone number printed below. *Crap.* Ellis Towing? Duke's company.

One of the brothers, a man called Sly, exits the vehicle where he saunters up to us, greeting Tommy before taking in my car and giving a low, slow, over dramatized whistle. Sly's long, dishwater hair he keeps pulled back in a ponytail, hangs down his back. And his cut is visible from beneath his coveralls because he neglected to button them all the way up, probably on purpose to show his affiliation with the Lords.

He's very handsome, too. A full beard. Deep blue eyes. Chiseled jaw and high, straight cheekbones. And no wedding ring, which means he undoubtedly has a whole slew of females hanging around at any given time, for any level of companionship.

"Hey Dr. Brennan, this doesn't look too bad. Still, how ya doing?"

Shoot. He's nice, too.

"Uh, we're fine. Thank you for asking."

"We?" he asks, then peers inside the backseat. "*Shit.* You got a baby in the back."

"I'm not a baby." Jade protests loudly. "I'm in pweschoowl."

"Sorry, little miss." He smiles a beautiful sly smile, and I get it, the nickname. "Forgive me." He finishes then turns to Tommy. "Can you take them? I don't have room for the booster in my truck."

"No problem," Tommy answers.

I'd probably be able to drive my Jeep back, even if it limped down the highway, if it weren't for the airbags having deployed. It hurts my heart to see half the hood of my car smushed like an accordion, and the bumper partially hanging off, but I'm thankful the safety cage did its job and kept us from feeling the brunt of the crash.

Tommy kneels into the backseat to unhook Jade, then grabs her and her booster. This section of highway is carved through the center of a mountain. High, jagged, barren rock faces to both sides of us. I suppose we got off lucky. Some sections have mountain to one side, but then only a railing, then drop off to the other.

Sly helps me from the vehicle, holding my hand while he leads me to a safer spot along the shoulder. He drops it when Tommy passes my daughter off to me, though he does it lingeringly so I'm forced to shift Jade's bottom into one hand until he finally releases the last finger.

It's unbelievably loud with the cars whipping past us, and there's a choking stench of exhaust hanging over our heads. Jade holds tight like a baby spider monkey clings to its mother, so much that my pale yellow 'Trust me, I'm a doctor' T-shirt rides up the back exposing a large expanse of skin. I attempt to pull it down as we walk our way over to the police cruiser, to no avail.

Before we move to leave, I set my girl on the hood of Tommy's car to perform a quick onceover. Eye check for dilation. Sound of her breathing. Any new bruising or pains. Everything checks out. The crash wasn't that bad, more scary than anything.

Not a moment later, Sly leans inside my car to turn it on and set the gear to neutral in order to hook it up to the flatbed. "I got this," he says to Tommy. "See you back at the shop."

Back of the cruiser, Tommy drops Jade's booster in the center and hooks her in, then holds open the passenger front door for me.

I slide in and buckle my seatbelt, watching as he rounds the hood of the car to fold himself behind the steering wheel. Starting the engine, he checks his mirror then pulls a u-ie. As he straitens out of the U-turn, he flips off the flashers. Day ruined, we head back toward Thornbriar.

"You don't have to take us to the shop."

Tommy raises an eyebrow at me. "Oh no? Do you need me to take you to the hospital?"

I shake my head. "I think we're good on that front."

"Right, then don't want your car fixed?"

"Well yes, sure I do. But you can drop us at home. They can call me with the estimate. Maybe I'll just get a new car."

Blinker on, he merges with the off-ramp. "You got something against Ellis Auto & Towing? Don't think I didn't see your face when the truck pulled up."

"No. It's not *my* problem. For some reason, Duke doesn't much like me. And Ellis's is his company. So it would be better if *I* wasn't around."

In that moment Tommy's look goes from questioning to beautifully mischievous. "Is that so?" he asks. "No, I think I better take you to the shop. If nothing else, Boss would want me to take you there since his wife's your friend. To make sure you're okay, and all. Elise would freak out if he didn't."

On a huff, I cross my arms over my chest, wincing slightly from the movement. I probably have a bruise from where the seatbelt pulled taut. Rather be bruised than dead. Although we didn't hit hard, an accident is an accident, which means it could have ended badly. "Really, I should just go—"

Up until now, Tommy had been friendly and a downhome good 'ole boy. That friendly, easy-goingness evaporated with the blink of an eye. "I said I'm taking you to the shop. So I'm taking you to the shop."

Since I don't know what to make of the finality of his words, his tone, I decide for the moment not to argue my point any further. Though I don't engage him in anymore friendly banter, either. Why should he care so much if I see Duke or not?

The cab of his cruiser becomes an awkward place to be. Until, oblivious to all of it, Jade begins to sing her favorite song. Her little girl voice almost hits all the notes to *You Are My Sunshine*. And I begin to sing along with her, turning to look at her face as I do. Surprisingly, Tommy Doyle begins to sing with us, too. He catches Jade's eye in the rearview mirror, and they smile at one another.

Without thinking, I blurt the first thing that comes to mind. "You and Maryanne should have a kid."

His eyes cut to me, then back to the road. "When she wants it, we will. 'Til then, I'm enjoying time, just me and my wife."

Our conversation ends when Tommy clicks on his blinker once again, slowing to a snail's pace, and turns into the lot of Ellis Auto & Towing. Standing out front of Ellis Auto & Towing, wiping his hands on a greasy rag, is none other than *the* Ellis of Ellis Auto & Towing, himself. Icing on the cake, the scowl forming across his face as we lock eyes.

Sgt. Tommy Doyle fixes his gaze on Duke, back on me, and chuckles while turning into a spot then cuts the engine.

In the time I take stalling to get out of the cruiser, Tommy has Jade in one arm, her head resting on his shoulder, while carrying her booster in his other hand.

Duke approaches. *"Peaches,"* he says to Jade. Not even a hello for me. But then he reaches his hands out to her, and because for some reason she's taken with him, Jade reaches back, twining her tiny arms around his neck.

"You hurt anywhere?" He asks and sounds *concerned.*

"No," she answers, moving her head to lean, not on Duke's shoulder as she had Tommy's. But because of the sheer size of him, Jade places her head against his chest and snuggles to get comfortable. He's so sweet to her. I don't know what he says because he whispers in her ear, but her little head bobs up and down in agreement to whatever he's said.

Nerves that I'd managed to keep in check during our ordeal finally catch up. I feel hot, my cheeks and the back of my neck. A nauseous feeling forms in the pit of my stomach. Water, I need to splash water on my face. "Is—uh—" I clear my throat. All male eyes dart to me. "Is there a restroom I can use?"

"Yeah, use the office one. It's cleaner. In the lobby, through the door behind the desk. First door you come to," The biker president offers.

"Thank you."

After following Duke's directions, I find myself standing at the sink, cold water running. The cold coming off the stream hangs in the air around the basin and feels good. I breathe it in for a few seconds then pull several sheets of brown paper towel from the metal dispenser and run them under the faucet to get them soaking wet. I place most of the drenched towels against the back of my neck. The others of the stack I use to cool off my face. And I keep repeating the actions until the nausea subsides completely.

Not nearly ready to face Duke Ellis, but knowing I really have no choice since he'd been the one holding my daughter before my anxiety-fueled retreat, I throw the paper towels in the trash and straighten my shirt and hair back to respectability, then return to the group outside.

A pleasant surprise, Sly is standing between Duke and Tommy, the three men faced toward me in a wide-legged, manspreading, semi-huddle. They appear to have been talking about me. The evidence of that being when the conversation abruptly stops upon my arrival. Sly looks me up and down. There's a glint in his eyes joining the wicked grin on his lips when he finally pats Duke on the shoulder and starts for me.

Duke's arm, the one not holding Jade, shoots out to halt him to the spot.

Tommy's hands go to his hips with his head bent down. It's apparent by the way he bites his top lip, he's trying and on the verge of failing not to laugh.

Several more of the men have come out of the bays, partly I'd guess to get a better look at the damage inflicted on my pretty Jeep from the accident. The other part to watch the byplay. Though, I can't think about that.

Seeing it up on the flatbed, it hits me that we're going to have to find a ride to the next town, bigger than Thornbriar by a town and a half, to rent a car now.

"Hey pretty lady," Sly calls out, drawing my attention away from my poor broken ride. "You got your color back."

"My color?" I ask.

"Yeah, you were looking a little gray when I got to the scene."

I hadn't realized. Tommy asked me if *I thought* we needed to go to the hospital, but he never said, *'Hey Doc, you look sick.'*

"Well, that tends to happen when you're the hit in a hit and run. I'm better now, though. Thanks for your concern."

"Where were you heading?" he asks.

"Jade and I were going to do a girls day in Nashville." I

swear I see every man in the forecourt cringe when I mention Nashville. What's wrong with Nashville?

"By yourself?" Bizarrely comes his next question.

"Yes. Jade and I have traveled quite extensively by ourselves." What? Because I'm a woman I can't follow highway signs or a GPS? "And I want, no strike that, after today, I *need* a really good coffee. A Frappuccino." To accentuate my need, I throw my hands out in front of me, then pull them back to hook my thumbs in my belt loops when the men laugh at me. I'm not being funny.

"If you can give me about a half an hour, I'd be happy to take you." Sly then surprisingly, generously offers.

As if the universe wants to remind me how much I don't understand men, or at the very least, a certain black-haired, goateed, tattooed man, Duke breaks from the group, still carrying Jade, to walk over to me.

"Won't be necessary, brother," he says to Sly as he slides *his arm* between my arm and torso to hook around *my waist*, pulling me snug against his side.

Some of the brothers smile, some stare down at their feet, shaking their heads. Sly simply answers, "Gotcha."

But I'm confused. Too confused to let it go. "Hey Prez, what's going on here?"

Instead of answering me, he hollers over to the brother called Crass, a new transfer from the Illinois chapter of the Lords. He came into the picture around the same time I did. The man Boss and Elise named their son Gunner after, I'd heard all about how he'd almost lost his life protecting Elise when she was being actively hunted by that biker, murderer and genuinely bad guy from a rival club, Houdini.

I didn't have to imagine, because I lived their surprise along with them, when he turned out to be Boss's *thought to be dead* cousin, Logan Hollister a.k.a. the reason Livvy took off. Since he tried to kill Liv, too. And the nutcase is still out there somewhere, roaming free and able to strike again. He might even still be hanging around Thornbriar, if Elise's feeling of being watched holds merit.

Yes, so Duke calls out to Crass, "You call me with the estimate, yeah?" Though it's formed as a question, it's an order.

"Sure thing, Prez. You got it." Crass calls back from the backend of the flatbed where he examines my poor, banged-up Cherokee.

Why call Duke and not me? It's *my* Jeep. Curious and slightly aggrieved, I try to get him to talk to me. "Hey Prez..." Nothing. "Duke..." He continues to ignore me. Which means it's time to try something new. "Chief?"

Finally a reaction. "Chief?" he asks.

"As in Commander in Chief. You know, because you're the president." That garners a laugh from the big guy.

"Come on," he whispers in my ear before he moves his lips to press a sweet kiss to the side of my jaw. Now he has me really confused. The man holds my daughter. His arm around my waist. And he kissed me in front of his brothers.

Men.

6

DUKE

"Alright, Doc. Let's get you some coffee." I give her arm a little squeeze to get her moving. She wants to argue, can see it written all over her gorgeous face.

Though she don't argue. She opens her mouth then closes it. Opens then closes it. Opens then closes it before giving up. "There's no good coffee in town," she finally settles on.

"Thought we were headed for Nashville?"

"Um…" Her heart-shaped lips press together.

Is it bad how much I get off stumping her?

"Tommy," I call out. "We need Peaches' booster in the back of my truck. Gotta get my girls something cold to drink."

Her feet stop abruptly as she turns her head to glare at me. "*Your girls?*"

Tommy, the son of a bitch, just about busts a gut laughing, but he does it while walking the booster over to my truck. I can see why he'd find it funny and give him that play. Hell, if I wasn't sitting in the middle of it, if it was one of the other brothers, I'd find the whole thing fucking hilarious.

"Duke—*Chief*, when um... when did we become your girls?" she whispers.

I set a drowsy Jade into the backseat and secure the seatbelt around her. I don't bother to answer until her door is shut, and Tommy's left us for his cruiser, out of earshot. Only then do I lay it out for the good doctor.

"You crawl into any man's lap at the hospital when your girl's sick, and sleep there all night? Let 'em give your girl a nickname?" I ask, pulling a cigarette from the pack I keep in my front vest pocket and light it. Won't be smoking while we drive, so I take the opportunity while I got it. Plus, it gives me something to do with my damn hands.

"No," she answers.

"You let just any man come over and cook dinner for you and your girl? Watch movies?"

"*No*." She repeats herself, stronger this time.

"You kiss any man the way you kissed me?"

She throws silent attitude at me by folding her arms under her tits, but refuses to answer.

So that's when I go in for the death blow. "You let *any man* eat you out 'til you come so hard he could drown from your juices?"

That got her. Those stunning jade green eyes of hers go wide. "I did not come that hard." She protests.

Yeah, she protests, but those wide eyes got heat behind 'em, and I stare, almost mesmerized by her chest raising and lowering from the shallow breaths she struggles to take. Caitlin knows what we shared that day, how wild she went that day. And from the hungry look she tries to hide, I know she remembers I'm the one who made her wild.

"Doc, *you did*. And that's what makes you *my girls*."

"But you left. No goodbye. You just left."

Why did I even bother to hope she'd let that slide, at least for now? I know I owe her an answer, an honest answer.

"Listen honey, after what we did, what you gave me, had a lot to think about."

"You didn't bother to say hi to me when I showed up here today. You didn't say word one until Sly showed interest. Then you decide to piss in my corner?"

"No, told you. Had a lot to think about. Sly sniffing around made me realize if I don't claim what's mine, someone else might try. And I can't have that because I'll kill any fucker who sniffs around you."

"Come on, Chief, be reasonable. You can't—"

"You let me in, Doc." I tell her something she already damn well knows, take a long drag on my cigarette and blow the smoke away from her and the car. "You gave me the green light, which means we're a go. Both know we been dancing around this shit for close to a year. You could've been a bitch when Jade got hurt, pushed me away. You didn't. So yeah, I can and I will." Then to drive my point home, I motion between her and Jade in the backseat. "*My. Girls.*"

She swallows hard as her features soften. Those green gemstones focus solely on my tired eyes. "I have to admit," she says, breaking out that damn sweet, shy disposition, which does all kinds 'a shit to my insides, cheeks blushing strawberry. "I like thinking of us as your girls. We haven't been anyone's girls in so long."

"You gonna keep staring at me or you gonna kiss your man?" Because I really need to feel those soft lips against mine. *Now.*

She swallows hard a second time. "I'm going to kiss my man." Then she presses into me, up on her tiptoes, because I'm so much taller. She tilts her head and covers her mouth over mine. Lips to lips. "You taste of tobacco and mint," she says, still pressed against me.

A taste I give her more of when I take over the kiss, first throwing the butt on the ground so I can wrap my arms around her neck, then shove my tongue in her mouth. My fingers, I twine through the hair at her nape. And… fuck me, she moans. Right there in the parking lot of Ellis Auto & Towing. I slide my hand from around her neck down to her sumptuous, rounded ass and press our bodies flush, grinding my pelvis against hers. It's torture, but I couldn't stop if I wanted to.

"Ho-*ly* shit," someone grumbles loudly. "I should've got there first." Then I know it's Sly who opened his yap, and laugh at my good fortune because yeah, he should've gone for it. He'd be dead because I would've gutted him. But at least he'd have died knowing how Doc smells up close and the taste of her lips. The feel of her body pressed in all the right places as she kisses with everything in her.

She moves back only slightly from me and turns her head. "Caitlin," she calls out for no apparent reason.

"What?" He calls back.

"Caitlin. You guys can call me Caitlin. That's my name."

Right. Got it.

"Alright Doc, *now* let's get you some coffee." It's selfish, but I want her all to myself. The brothers can get comfortable calling her Caitlin later.

"No good places in town," she teases.

"Thought we were headed for Nashville?" I play along.

"Oh yeah, that's right," she says then presses another kiss against my mouth. "I could kiss you all day." At first I think she's being cute, but then, seeing the way she sucks in her bottom lip, biting down, I realize it was an accidental admission. One she really meant. Sly could've tried to get in there, but she's mine all the way. Those words just proved it.

"Caitlin," I growl. "Get in the truck." Because goddamn I want to taste her again, but I want to do it in a way we won't be interrupted by one of my brothers.

She hurries around the hood of my pickup to slide into the front seat, and automatically buckles herself in.

I move with my head held high, shoulders back, not on top of the world—I *own* the fucking world—and fold in behind the steering wheel, crank the engine, then back out of the parking spot.

After straightening out the frontend, I take her hand and move it to rest on my thigh, dangerously close to my dick. Part of me hopes she'll take the initiative to move a little closer. Since she don't, I press my hand over hers to keep it in place.

And we drive.

"You and Peaches eat barbeque?" I break the silence after a good twenty minutes of reliving that kiss and her sweet words over and over in my head. Feeling her hand in mine. The hum of the wheels rolling against the blacktop sound in the background.

Instead of giving me an answer, she stares out her window and mumbles, almost a whisper, so I can't fully understand her words. Then it clicks as I listen to the last of her thoughts. "...I'm his girl. I'm Duke Ellis's girl."

I kind of snicker under my breath and give her hand another squeeze, not expecting that reaction. "Yeah, honey. You are."

That's when she turns her head to look my way and blinks her eyes twice, as if to clear her mind. Or maybe realizing I'm in the cab with her, or hell, that she spoke out loud. "I... um... don't really know what that entails. Does this mean we're exclusive? Or um, am I expected to give up other men but I'm supposed to look the other way when you've got a taste for one of the pieces?"

Fair enough question. Well, the first one, anyhow. I was married to Dawna for fucking years and never looked twice at a piece. Right up 'til the end. Even after she decided to stop the chemo that had made her so weak, it had been months since we'd been able to make love. Because with Dawna, it was always making love. She didn't see the fun side of sex. The stress relief. The hot make up. She only wanted the intimacy. And because she was sick so much of our time together, I gave in and didn't argue because I didn't want to make her sicker.

That's how I'm about to answer when she goes on. "Maybe we should work out the logistics of this relationship before we get too far in it."

Doc ain't sick, so I ain't tiptoeing around her when I get pissed, and that last question of hers pissed me off. "I think you know the answer to that," I tell her, thinking that'll be the end of it. But no.

"Okay," she says. "Logistics take two. Is this an exclusive thing between us or—" Doc cuts herself off to look out the window again, watching the mountains whip past us. Then she finishes in a jumble of words, "orareyoustillseeingotherwomen?"

"Come again?" I ask.

"You heard me." She fixates her glare on a small, nondescript green bug holding on for dear life to her side mirror, so not to look at me, and adds, "*Never mind.*"

"No," I answer.

"No?" She repeats my answer. "No to which?"

"No I'm not gonna answer 'til you look at me, and I can answer you properly."

First she peeks over her shoulder to check on a sleeping Peaches. Must be afternoon naptime. After letting out a slow breath, Caitlin gets it all off her chest. "Are you going to keep —um—*being* with the pieces or hot mamas?"

"Being?" I grit my teeth to hold back the snicker that wants to erupt because her saying *being* is cute as hell. But I'm still pissed that she'd even ask. "No. I know how to be monogamous—and yeah, even know your four syllable words."

The woman starts to giggle. "Sorry, sorry... I know you're serious. But I never thought you didn't know multi-syllable words. Actually, you've always struck me as rather intelligent."

Even pissed, that gets her another hand squeeze. I like that she thinks I'm intelligent.

"I guess I'm asking wrong," she says. "What's the differ-ence between being your girl—" She bites her top lip and scrunches up her nose before we finally get to the crux of what's crawled up her ass. "And being your old lady?"

Right. This I can work with. "Seems I gotta explain a few things. You're part of my girls because there's two 'a you. And one 'a you's a little girl. But you became my old lady to the brothers, to the club, when you leaned up on your tiptoes and shoved your tongue in my mouth. And before you open that mouth again, I got more to explain. You been mine since the hospital, but the boys didn't know. Now they know. You don't touch or flirt with other dick. Don't let 'em touch or flirt with you. I don't touch other pussy."

Predictably, she tries to talk, but ain't through.

"So to recap," I say. "You're my girls when I'm talking about you and Peaches. All other times, you're my old lady. We're exclusive. And honey, I'll tell you now. I know you're a doctor so you probably make good money. But I'm not just a man, I'm an old-fashioned type of man. And that means when we're together, I pay. I don't get driven around bitch. —"

"Bitch?" she asks.

"Yeah, babe, bitch. The bitch seat. Where the bitches sit, front passenger."

"Are you calling *me* a bitch?"

"Not right now. But woman seat sounds ridiculous, so it's

bitch. And since I don't ride it, that means I drive. We get there, we get in as deep as I think we have the potential to get, I'll probably tell you shit. Pillow talk that stays between us. Only us. So Doc, you gotta remember I'm the president of an MC. That means I don't get my balls busted in front of anyone, but especially the brothers. You got issue with something I've done or said, you do it at home. Agreed?"

"*Agreed*," she replies quicker than I thought she would, and without a lick of apprehension.

"Who are you, and what have you done with Doc?"

She pulls her hand from under mine, on my thigh, to punch me in the shoulder. "Shut up," she orders. But it's a half-assed punch that lacks any heat.

"Now we got that outta the way, we need to discuss something else. Gonna have to put me on the list to pick up Peaches at school. Emergencies. You might be on call. Need someone you can trust to help with her."

"Oh, um…okay."

"And Doc, no more trips just you and Peaches. I'll once again reiterate, I'm the president of an MC. We got enemies. And Houdini, that fucker, is still out there. Word gets out I got an old lady, it might make you a person of interest, because I ain't had an old lady since Dawna."

She gasps. "We won't be safe? Jade won't be safe?"

"Honey, you and Peaches will be fine so long as you take a man with you when you leave town. Even to patients in the high country."

Her back snaps straight.

"I can't have men with me *on house calls*."

"They won't come in, won't get in the way. Just an escort, honey." I try to reassure her, but this is something I can't budge on.

"Just an escort?" Caitlin repeats as a question. I nod.

Then she thinks about it for a minute. "Sure. I guess I can do that."

"Piece of mind." I tell her.

With a chin dip, she places her hand back on my thigh. Though I scoop it up to kiss her knuckles, and then place it back, holding tight again. Then she sighs. "Peace of mind. I can give you that, Chief." When she turns her head to face me, *shit*. Her smile. "Peace of mind for a new relationship," she says. "Not too much to ask so long as the men stick to their boundaries. Maybe you can send Jesse along with us."

"*The fuck?*" I bark out, louder than I mean to. My grip on the steering wheel tightens to a stranglehold.

"What? He's cute, but he's too young. Nothing says I can't enjoy the view of my escort, right?"

"You just ensured the fuckwad never gets his patch."

"No." She gasps. "You can't do that to him. He's never—"

I shut her up by pulling her neck close to me and kissing her hard and deep, never taking my eyes off the road.

Two and a half hours after we left Thornbriar, I take the exit ramp from the interstate, taking us to a smaller two-lane highway. Right off the smaller highway, I turn to park in front of a dilapidated white chapel. And when I say dilapidated, I mean a beam in the roof needs to be propped and pieces of siding have been ripped off from age and weather. But we're here for the big plumes of gray smoke rising from behind the chapel. Not because the place is on fire, because of the best damn barbeque in the state of Tennessee.

My mouth waters from the fucking fantastic aroma of smoked pork wafting through the vents of the truck. A glance over to Doc, I watch her eyes glaze over and a smile spread across her face. Then I run my thumb along her chin. "Got a little drool there," I tease.

Before she comes to her senses, I switch off the engine

and have the backdoor open, unbuckling Jade from her booster. "Hey Peaches, you hungry?" I ask softly.

"Badass biker Duke Ellis cooed at my daughter," Caitlin mumbles under her breath. God damn, it turns me on when I stump her.

That's when Jade snuggles down to answer. "Yeah," she says. Though she says it through a yawn.

"Good sweetheart, you like mac and cheese?"

She nods against my cut.

"Because they make the best mac and cheese here." I shut the door and beep the locks, joining Doc, my hand to the space between her shoulder blades, I glide it down to rest against the small of her back. Then give a little push to get her moving. I only remove my hand to open the door for my girls to pass through then drop it back into my claiming spot to steer us over to the counter where today's menu is written on a whiteboard in green marker.

Every dish comes à la carte.

"I'll have the pulled pork. Mac and cheese. The greens, and the sweet potato-marshmallow casserole. Then we'll both have the lemonade to drink." Caitlin gives her order. Then she winces. "That's not too much, is it? I don't want to overstep."

Her words, whispered like a secret not meant for anyone else's ears, pisses me right the hell off.

"*Overstep?*" I grumble. What's with her throwing that shit my way? Make me look cheap. "You want twice as much, you order. Don't ever ask that again."

"Sorry," she says to me, then turns to look at the teenage girl behind the counter. "It appears I've pissed him off. He's not cheap. I don't even know why I asked that." Her thoughts spill from her mouth in a rambled flow, and it' cute enough for me to feel the anger begin to ease up.

"Except for—" She uses her eyes to point to Jade, laying

her fingertips rest on the counter, and leans her body way in for the counter girl to hear when she drops her voice. The poor counter girl looks confused but keeps her mouth shut. Which I wish Doc would do. But no. She goes on. "Her... um... *father*." She mouths '*father*', no sound. "He was the last man I was with and he always told me I overstepped, that I took advantage of his generosity."

You've got to be fucking shitting me? Cute be damned. An unexpected rage burns through the cute, reigniting the anger and amping it. I grab hold of her arm, trying best I can to control my barely controlled temper. My ears fill with it thumping against my eardrums. My eyes, blinded by it.

She looks scared. Last thing I need is for her to be scared of me, so I turn her into me. "Honey." I grit through my teeth, then gentle as possible, kiss her to show my anger's on her behalf, and to hold my tongue because I still got Peaches in my arms.

I suck in a long breath to calm myself, hold it, and then slowly breathe it out. Some head-shrink taught me that technique years ago to deal with my anger from Dawna's illness. Apparently, it works for listening to a woman I'm coming to care about relate a shit situation with an asshole ex, too. Good to know.

After we pull apart and I place my order, I hand Peaches over to her. "Get us a table." I direct her with a push over to the seating area.

"Overbearing man," she mumbles. "You could at least say please." And there she is. My sassy Doc back, not scared. And not moving. Instead she looks me dead in the eyes and repeats the word, *"Please."*

Fuck if I don't have to turn my head away, dropping my chin to break off eye contact, in an attempt, albeit a failed attempt, to keep from laughing. "Please?"

"Yes, you forgot to say it. As in, 'get us a table, please.'"

"Manews awe impowtent, Duke." Jade corrects me, and damn if it ain't just as cute as her mama.

I stop trying to contain my laughter, since with these two, I know now it ain't ever gonna work. "Please take Peaches to get a table." This gets me a cheek kiss from both my girls at the same time. Each taking a cheek.

Cute.

7

CAITLIN

With Jade in my arms, I walk over to a booth covered in brown butcher paper for a tablecloth. Two white squeeze bottles of a red, tomato-based barbeque sauce and one white squeeze bottle of a vinegar-based barbeque sauce, a squeeze bottle of specifically Heinz yellow mustard, Heinz ketchup, salt and pepper shakers, and a napkin dispenser sit at the end of the table closest to the wall.

Jade begins to rearrange all the bottles, giving them voices as if playing with dolls until Duke shows up at the table with a tray of white Styrofoam to-go boxes and three paper cups, two large and one small, all with plastic lids and straws. He sets the small one in front of Jade, a large one in front of me, and a large one across the table from me.

Then he opens up the first box, handing it off to me. The second, he sets in his spot, and the third, he opens and sets in front of my daughter. Each to-go box has a plastic fork and knife rolled in a white, paper napkin inside, resting on top of the least messy entrée.

Duke glides into his spot and immediately digs in to his meal.

The linoleum has cracks. The dingy walls could have used a new paint job about ten years ago, but hands down, my new man has brought us to the best barbeque I've ever eaten in my life.

And he watches my mouth chew and swallow every bite I take. It's as unnerving as it is sensual. With each of his bites, sauce clings to his overly shaggy mustache and some drips onto his goatee, saucing some of the silver hairs red. Far from what should be considered sexy, I can't help the urge to lick every drop off his face. But as my little girl is here, that urge gets checked pretty quickly. I'm doomed with this man if I'm finding his messy beard sexy. It's sauce. Sauce isn't sexy.

After I ball up my napkin and toss it in the box, he collects all our trash to throw away, and we leave to take on Nashville.

We drink in every family-friendly sight Nashville has to offer. The Adventure Science Center. I thought we were going to have to take up residence in one of the interactive exhibits the way Jade fought us leaving, which she only relented because Duke whispered something in her ear. What he whispered quickly became apparent when he led us to the largest candy store I'd ever laid eyes on. It put *Willy Wonka* to shame. And my daughter reacted like, well, like a kid in a candy store. Duke was next to her the entire time, her partner in crime, filling bag after bag.

They got candy, I got coffee. Eventually. After we walked off our food truck dinners, we made our way to the Starbucks for Frappuccinos. The icy drink went down smooth, a nice reprieve from the Tennessee heat. Though Duke is a badass, manly biker, and apparently manly bikers don't drink cold coffee drinks, as I found when he ordered his Grande Americano. At my eyebrow raise, he shook his head and uttered one word. "*No.*"

Pit stop over, we took on Nashville again.

The lights of the city brighten the streets. The sky has purpled from the sun setting. We stop, I think our last stop of the day, in front of a street corner cowboy crooning out a country song, just him and his guitar. I'm not much for country music, but the guy has talent... and then there's the ambiance.

Jade has her arms wrapped around Duke's thigh, leaning into it. And he has a hand resting on her shoulder. He drapes his other arm around my shoulders, and pulls me close, dropping a kiss to my temple.

Tucked in his arms, we look like a family. I feel like a family. Aiden never made us feel like a family. I guess because he'd already started up with the woman from Australia. He never wanted to go on any family adventures, and rarely went with us for the obligatory *'he's her father so he should be there'* appointments. But here's Duke, not her father, treating us as a family. The kind of family I always wanted for my daughter.

Those are exactly the kinds of thoughts I shouldn't be having so early on with the man. I'm torn. Torn because I have to look out for Jade, but I don't want to alienate Duke if this really turns out to be something between us.

It's time to get going back home when Jade begins to drag her feet every step. Duke, who's been holding her hand the whole way, scoops her up into his arms, and grabbing a hold of my hand, tows me behind him.

We don't head back to the parking lot where he'd parked the truck. Instead, he walks us down to the crosswalk to cross the major thoroughfare, and back up the sidewalk to a towering, semi-fancy hotel, pushing me through the automatic double doors, then right up to the reception desk where he pulls a credit card from his wallet—connected to his belt loop by a thick chain—to buy us a room for the night.

Duke stops in the gift shop to buy Jade a little Nashville nightgown, pink with a Stetson hat and an acoustic guitar on the front, and I add a package of pink, princess pull-ups. Jade can be a hard sleeper when she's really exhausted, and with all the walking we've done today, she's exhausted. Which means as a precaution, she wears the pull-up.

Up the elevator lined with rich, dark wood and forest green-gold thick-striped paper, we stop on the fifth floor, turning left from where we've stepped off. And we move down a hallway, again of rich, dark wood. But the walls had been papered in a gold with pinstripes of forest green. Gold sconces for the light fixtures, gold kick plates on every door along with gold door handles.

Seven rooms down from the elevator, we reach ours. Duke swipes the key card. The light flashes green, and he pushes open the door to an amazing hotel room. Unlike the greens and golds of the hallway and elevator, we're met with lush creams and copper along with the dark wood. Only one bed, a king. But the room has a pullout sofa. Which after locking up, I walk over to pull out, tossing the cushions on the floor in front of a circular, dark wood table holding a lamp and the obligatory hotel room service menu.

He lays Jade down on the mattress. I remove her clothing, drape her nightgown down over her body, where the hem hangs to her little calves, and then help her out of her star panties and into a pull-up.

Once I tuck my girl in, I lay down next to her. Jade is out before her head hits the pillow. Right as I close my eyes, I feel myself being lifted and open them back up to see Duke's stunning silver-gray eyes meeting mine. He carries me to the big bed where he drops me and proceeds to strip my shorts down my legs.

"What are you doing?" I whisper-yell.

"Getting you naked," he grumble-whispers as if the idea should have been common knowledge.

"I can't get naked with you here." Being a mom, I've mastered the whisper. This being a panicked whisper. "She's in the room with us."

"She's sound asleep, Doc. Ain't nothing waking her up." He's probably right, but I can't tell him that because it will only encourage him to strip me more.

"We can't here."

"Honey, I need to taste you again. Need it."

Oh damn. I want him to do that, too. What that man did to me in my living room was nothing short of magical. My magic man. "Let's go in the bathroom." I offer as an alternative.

"Fuck no. First time I have you, I want you in a bed, not pushed up against a wall or on the floor like we're a couple 'a teenagers."

"Well how about you taste me, that is... um... put your mouth on me, and I'll return the favor?"

"I'll give you that. But when we get home, you and I hit a bed. Peaches has friends or day care, or wherever the fuck she goes. We'll pick her up when we're done."

I start to nod but—*oof*—my gut hits his shoulder because he throws me over it and clomps softly into the bathroom. The motion sensor light flicks on when we enter, and he sets my bottom to the sink's vanity, intent on making me lose my panties. But I want to give him his first, and so I slide off and drop down to my knees while at the same time, go after the buckle on his belt. I undo the button, pull the zipper, and tug his jeans to just below his hips.

Thankfully, Duke is not the kind of man to bother with boxers or briefs. He stands tall and proud, thick and beautiful in front of my face. Something I'd known about him since close to my first visit to the clubhouse. Having seen the outline on several occasions over the past year, when he'd been turned on by one of the pieces, shortened from pieces of ass, because that's exactly what they are. Women who show up to the club for sex. They aren't anybody's girlfriend, showing up on weekends and party nights for a good time.

The pieces shouldn't be confused with the hot mamas who live semi-permanently at the clubhouse. They cook and clean, and take care of the brothers who live there in exchange for that place to stay. And again, they have sex with the brothers. Somehow, it always comes down to sex with the brothers.

Dammit, now all I can think about are pieces and hot mamas, and I don't want to think about either. Because they've had a lot of sex, and me? I haven't gone down on a man in so long, and I know he's used to the professional talents those girls have to offer.

Bad time to face a bout of insecurity and nerves. But I'm here. I'm doing this. After I suck in a few deep breaths and release them slowly to try to calm the bubbling anxiety, I wrap my hand around his base and suck in something else, until my lips hit my hand. He's huge. Bigger than he looked before I took him in my mouth. My eyes water to the point I have to squeeze them tight and try not to gag.

I will my throat muscles to relax. It's easier to do than I thought it would be, the way Duke sifts his fingers through the back of my hair, massaging my scalp as he does. I melt into his touch and begin to suck and lick like I'm enjoying the best melty popsicle of my life. With my other hand, I gently massage his balls. Our noises, the pop from the suction, my little mewls and purrs, and Duke's much louder grunts, not to mention his much, much louder "Oh fuck me" and "Fucking fuck me, honey" fill the small room, spurring me on.

As I chance a look up, his eyes are closed, head tipped

back, ecstasy written over every feature of his face. He locks his arms straight, hands holding the edge of the vanity to keep himself standing when his knees begin to buckle. Is this something that happens every time he gets a blowjob or does he really enjoy it that much?

The muscles of his abdomen pull tight. I know what that means. Though even if I didn't, the "Doc, *honey*," he grumbles and the way his fingers go from gripping the vanity to grabbing a fist full of hair, warns me he's close. I've never done what I'm considering before, but know men like it, and I don't want Duke to miss his skanky pieces, so instead of pulling away, when he growls a second, more forceful, *"Doc, honey—"*

I ask, "Are you clean?"

"What the fuck?" he grunts.

"Are you clean?" I ask again.

"Fuck honey, yeah. I'm fucking clean." On the word clean, he lets go hard and long, my mouth on a down glide. And I swallow. Some dribbles down my chin, but I keep up the swallow and don't quit sucking until I've milked every drop from him. Every drop.

His chest heaves heavy and rapid as he stares down at me, eyes glistening—still hot, but full of something else. Something... beautiful? I don't know what to do with such a look. It's satisfaction, longing, appreciation and even peacefulness, with maybe a few others mixed in there. But from my position on my knees, on the floor, those are what I can pick out. No man that I can remember—even Aiden, especially Aiden—ever looked at me with that expression before.

Wearing an open reverence, his eyes glisten with it, lines around those glistening eyes crinkle with it. Duke pulls me up to stand in front of him, one hand he brings to rest on my hip, stroking his thumb back and forth lightly along the bare skin between my shirt and panties. For such a simple act, it's almost too much for me to handle.

He turns to pluck a tissue from the tissue dispenser then shifts back to wipe the dribble from my chin. His mouth descends until it covers mine.

Hell yeah.

Oh, hell yeah.

He touches the tip of his tongue to the tip of mine, a move done so tenderly, I melt into him. In response, he glides his hands up to rest at the hem of my Tee and takes the kiss deeper, so much more than the tongue touch. A kiss I feel down to the tips of my toes. We support each other, my arms around his neck, his around my waist.

Duke twists and backs me up to lean against the vanity, the place he'd been only minutes before.

Not once this morning, not once did I think I'd end the day in a swanky hotel in Nashville. Especially not after I crashed my Jeep, *especially* not with this man, my 'old man'. He hitches my leg around his hip, moving one hand from my waist to slip into the leg hole of my panties, through the folds of silky wetness, where he zeros in on the spot. Not a direct hit, because he's not trying to hit it, circling my clit, teasing me with the light pressure. I can already begin to feel my body tense up in the best way.

Then because this is my life, there's a tapping on the door followed by a, "Mama? I gowtta potty," in a tired little girl voice. I tear my lips away from Duke's, laughing not because it's funny, but because I'm so turned on its either laugh or cry. And while I help him do up his jeans, pin him with a '*see, I told you*' glare. The very reason I wouldn't let him take me in that fluffy, king-size bed.

When I open the door, she has her little fist rubbing the sleepiness from her eyes, and she turns her head from Duke to me. "Why you in the bafwoom wiff my mom, Duke?"

His hands rest back on my hips, lightly biting his fingers into the flesh there. It's claiming, even if only to a four-year-old. "Your mom and I were talking, Peaches. And we didn't want to wake you up."

"Okay." She readily accepts his excuse. "But I weally gowtta potty."

Duke and I move at the same time, he stops for me to go out first, following closely behind. Jade pushes past us and snaps the door shut.

"So you mighta been right," he says. "Don't know how I'm supposed to return the favor now." His silver-gray eyes dart to the bathroom, then back to me, face showing clearly thanks to the nightlight I'd left on for Jade, for that exact reason. In case she needed to use the bathroom or a drink.

"It's not going to happen," I murmur, blowing strands of hair that had fallen over the bridge of my nose, away from my face.

Duke reaches over to tuck those strands behind my ears and then for some reason, pulls off his T-shirt.

I told him it's not going to happen tonight. *What's he thinking?* His intent becomes clear when he pulls mine off me to drag his down over my head. "Climb in bed, honey. You in my tee, Peaches won't think it's weird that her mom's sleeping next to me in her underwear."

"I thought I'd sleep next to her."

"You thought wrong. You're my woman now, and that means sleeping next to me. She'll get used to it."

Normally the idea would freak me out because I've never been one of those women to parade men in and out of my daughter's life. I will *never* be that mother. But somehow, with Duke, even though we're new, I know it won't be like that with him. He'll have a mind to me and Jade. I don't know how I know, I just do. The biker and the doctor. Who would have ever thought we'd have anything in common?

The sound of the toilet flushing comes at us through the bathroom door. A few minutes after Jade appears, still sleepy, rubbing her eyes. She walks over to me and presses her face against my thigh.

"Night, Mama," she says through a yawn and kisses where her face rests as I bend down to kiss the top of her head. To my surprise, she moves over to Duke and repeats the same action, pressing her face against his thighs. "Night, Duke."

And an even bigger surprise, although by this point it probably shouldn't be, he does the same as me and kisses the top of her head. Then one upping me, he picks her up to walk her back over to the sofa sleeper and tucks her in snuggly under the blankets.

I unfasten my bra and do the old *slide it out through the armhole of the T-shirt* technique every girl learns in like, seventh grade, because it's not comfortable to sleep in an underwire, and with tatas four years post pregnancy, I don't wear anything but underwire. Then I lift up the comforter, climb onto the bed, and let the fluffy, cream blanket fall back over me. I love the coolness of getting into a freshly made bed.

Not two minutes later, Duke slides in next to me. Now with the Jade drama over, my mind begins to reel with the fact that not only have I given him my first blowjob in years, but that I swallowed. I'm simultaneously proud of and horrified with myself.

What did he think of it? What does he think of me?

Maybe I tensed or maybe it's the look on my face, whatever allows him to read me, he reads me well enough to want to ease my mind. The way he rolls us to our sides, face to face, so mine rests against his chest. The way he folds his arms around me. The gentle way he squeezes, not a goodnight, but a *'welcome to life with me'*. It all speaks to me.

"Not sure what you did different, Doc." He whispers in a soft tone unlike anything I've heard out of the man. "But never been sucked 'til my knees give out before tonight."

"Is that good?" I chance.

"The fucking best," he says. "And I don't know how to feel about that."

Because of Dawna. He had a wife. She died of cancer. We haven't discussed her yet, but Elise filled me in on what Boss had filled her in on when I'd started fishing for information about the sexy biker president.

He doesn't know how to feel about it, which means he doesn't know what to feel about me.

I choose to let it go for now, instead choosing to sleep. We've got time. His arms loosen, and his breaths even out, which means he's fallen asleep before me. I listen to his light smoker's wheeze and let it lull me under.

8

CAITLIN

In the morning, Duke and I wake at the same time to Princess Jade jumping on our bed.

"Shit, Peaches. Thought Tennessee was having an earthquake." Then he looks at me. "And we don't get earthquakes in these parts. Not ones that register, anyhow."

I laugh, about to admonish him for cursing in front of Jade when first, I remember Duke is a biker president. It doesn't make sense to take up with *any man* intending to change him, but especially not a biker, so especially, especially, not a biker *president*.

Then second, Jade blindsides Duke with a pertinent little girl question. "Why you sweeping in the bed wiff my mama?"

His eyes go wide, to the point it would be comical if she weren't standing on the bed, hands to her hips, waiting on a reply.

"Well," he says, low and grumbly, because even in a good mood, Duke grumbles, and looks over at me for help. Maybe it's bitchy for me not to offer a hand, but he instigated this adventure, so I feel the need to see how he handles himself in the face of a curious four-year-old, because four-year-olds tend to be curious by nature. I bite my bottom lip, waiting expectantly.

When I offer no help, Duke continues. "Your mom's my wo—" He stops himself, and sucks in a breath. It looks like he's thinking. Then goes with, "my girlfriend." Giving Jade an answer she can understand.

My daughter nods, though she waits like she wants him to give her more. So he gives her more. "See, there are two kinds 'a girlfriends, Peaches. The first is a girlfriend a man likes to spend time with, but not one who'll stay around for a long time. She *doesn't* share a bed. She sleeps in her own bed. Then there's a girlfriend a man likes to spend time with, so much that he knows she's gonna be around, be his girlfriend for a good, long time. Maybe forever. She's the kind to share a bed, because letting her go, even for a night, is an unbearable thought."

I—I almost can't breathe. Swallow. Think. We've known each other for months, close to a year. That whole time he acted like he couldn't stand me. Now in the span of a week, I'm the kind of girlfriend who will be around for a good, long time? And this, after he told me just last night that he didn't know how to feel about the blowjob I'd given him, which in essence, meant *me*.

"Well, she's a good mama. So I bet she's a good gurlfwiend." Jade answers him.

I still don't know that I've breathed.

And Duke must notice. "Breathe, Doc," he whispers with a little laugh.

That's when I take in a breath I'm aware of taking.

Duke pulls my girl down onto his blanket-covered lap. "We had a tradition growing up. Whenever we spent the night out 'a town, we'd get delicious, but not good for you fast food breakfast the next morning. The only day my mom would let me and my brother have it." He turns to me. "What do you think, Doc?"

"The only time?" I ask suspiciously.

"Promise. The only time. But—" He sneaks in. "Every Sunday, Mom, Rex, and I would eat doughnuts and orange juice for breakfast. Sundays were the only days all three of us could be together growing up, and even after we'd grown. Did it right up 'til Rex died. And that was after Mom passed."

My heart falls for him and all he's lost. So without thinking first, I ask a question on a subject we haven't discussed yet. "You didn't—uh—do doughnuts with your wife?"

He wraps one arm around Jade to pull her closer, kissing the top of her forehead. The other, he wraps around my middle. "No. Dawna took her treatments Sunday mornings. She didn't want me at the hospital while they happened. Only to pick her up after. So I went for doughnuts. Just me, my brother and my mom. That was our tradition."

How could I say no? Sharing his family tradition with me and my daughter.

We lay in the bed like a real family. And again, logic tells me it's too soon to think that way. Letting him close to Jade is probably a severely stupid parenting move. But the way he moved one arm around her and one arm around me, to hold the both of us like we're something precious to him, I realize that we are. At least for now. This morning means something to him.

"So, what do you say we get up and go find some delicious, not good for you breakfast?" Duke asks as he sits up.

"Yeah." Jade giggle-screeches.

"The greasier the better," he says as he tickles my girl causing her to giggle-screech even louder.

Great.

As none of us brought a change of clothing, there's really no need for any of us to shower seeing as we'd be putting days-old clothes on our bodies. But I do rake a comb that I pull from my purse through Princess Jade's curls and pull it back in a quick French braid, secured with a rubber band from a different pocket of my purse. Then rake the comb through my hair, leaving the curls to bounce around my shoulders.

Duke gives his hair a simple finger comb, and he's ready to go.

He holds us, a hand in Jade's and one to my back until we hit checkout, then he drops the hand from my back to hand off the key card and take his receipt. The hand goes right back as he leads us outside. Although morning, it's already hot and humid out, making me regret the choice to leave my hair down. We walk to where he'd parked the truck yesterday. He stops to pay the attendant the additional fee while Jade and I continue on. We're both buckled in when he joins us. Even before he climbs in, Duke walks to my daughter's door, opens it, leans in to drop a quick kiss to the top of her head and then folds himself behind the wheel.

I'm occupied watching Jade and her giddy, little girl smile when in a sneak attack, he wraps his large hand around the back of my neck and draws my head to his. He kisses me deep and long. The kind of kiss to leave me breathless. The kind of kiss no man has ever given me in front of my daughter before. Not even her father.

When I stiffen because Jade is watching, Duke takes it upon himself to once again, blow my mind. "Good for her to see this, honey. Good for her to see how a man should treat a woman because eventually, she'll be a woman who'll most likely have a man."

Then he starts the truck, shifts into gear, and pulls out of the parking lot. As if he hadn't left my mind a gooey mess of brain matter splattered on the blacktop. I mean, from blowing it.

We end up eating the greasiest fast food breakfast. Mine, sausage, egg and cheese on a croissant. And these little cheesy hashbrown tots available for a limited time only, according to the sign in the window. Jade ordered those same cheesy tots and French toast sticks. One upped by Duke again, he orders everything both Jade and I did, plus a second sandwich and these mini cinnamon rolls.

We both drink coffee. Jade, an orange juice. I refuse to acknowledge the amount of fat and calories we consume. Not that I'm normally a calorie counter, but I could pretty much feel my arteries clogging. Though I have to admit, it tastes delicious.

Before we leave Nashville, Duke makes a Frappuccino run for me without my asking. And we head home—his hand never leaving my thigh except the one time he has to down-shift because of a traffic backup. An accident already mostly under control. The looky-loos, not the accident causes the backup.

After three and a half hours—the half because of the accident—we roll back into Thornbriar.

"Gonna head to the shop, Doc. You'll need a loaner 'til we get your Jeep sorted."

Stupidly I turn to him. "A loaner?" I ask. "How much will that cost?"

I know it's stupid when he pins me with a *'really, Doc?'* which clearly states it's stupid.

"Well it ain't so much a loaner. I bought me a new truck. This one works, but it's got high miles. Don't have all the bells and whistles 'a the new ones."

"Bells and whistles?" I ask.

"Yeah." His eyes search out Jade in the rearview mirror. "Gonna be carting around a little one, figured I needed an upgrade. Got the text last night, dealership left it at the shop."

"When... um... when did you order a truck?"

"After I dropped you and Peaches off at home when she got outta' the hospital."

For some reason, hearing him tell me he bought a new truck with bells and whistles a week ago, it gets me. Gets me to the point I find it hard to blink back the tears rimming my eyes.

When I know he's not looking at me, I use the inside of my Tee to dab the wetness away. Though, I hear him chuckle and clear his throat, and look to see him glancing at me out of the corner of his eye. Grin visible even through his unruly mustache and goatee.

"Shut up," I mumble.

That only makes him laugh harder. At least he lets my girl moment go without any further discussion on my said girlieness. Maybe I need to adopt one of those bitchy, biker old lady personas that I've seen on television or the movies.

A stop sign and two turns later, we pull into Ellis Auto & Towing, where he stops next to a shiny, new silver pickup.

"Didn't know if you could drive a stick, so the new truck I got automatic. Four wheel drive, standard. You use it on the Jeep?"

He pauses for an answer.

"Ah, *yes*. I have," I say, it still not really registering what he's told me.

"Good."

Then we both climb out of his old pickup *without* all the "bells and whistles".

While I attempt to process, well, everything, it occurs to

me that his shop is a bustling hub of activity. Men, most of them brothers, move cars in and out of the five bays. Five. That's huge for a garage.

I recognize the brothers from my times at the clubhouse, but also because each one wears his cut visible from under greasy blue and pinstriped coveralls. Proud. Elise had explained some of this to me, but it's something else to see the proof in front of my face. They work so hard to earn their cut and it means so much once they have that they wear it like a second skin.

Chin lifts and, "brother" or "Prez" greet Duke. And then it happens. I get my first, "Hey Caity." From Sly of all people.

"Caity?" I ask.

"Yeah, Caitlin sounds too formal. So we decided last night, it's official. Caity."

"You—uh—decided last night?" I ask. Though he doesn't answer, apparently because he already had.

What I get instead is a smiling Duke—which a smiling Duke is almost as dazzling as watching a solar eclipse—move in my space, deep in my space. Fingers of one hand splayed over my face from jaw to chin, the other pressing against my back to press us together. And his chin drops, his head descends, and then his perfect lips cover mine. One of his all-consuming kisses, his tongue dances around the inside of my mouth, his teeth nip my lip. His hand at my back, drops to my back*side*. Because of this, I melt.

"*Fuck*...shoulda' gone for it."

Both Duke and I pull apart to see Sly watching us. Until he sees us pull apart, then shaking his head, he walks away.

"Is he going to be a problem? Should I go talk to him?"

"Nah. He'll be fine. Won't make a move on you. Plenty 'a brothers drool over Trish, even more over Liv, and even more than that, over Elise. Not uncommon for a brother who ain't got a good woman to lament not going after that good woman first. But that's all it is. Wound licking."

"*Duke*," I whisper, because I don't know what else to say, and grip his cut, pressing my face against his chest.

"Right." He clears his throat. "You head on home. I got Peaches, get her in the truck. Few things I gotta get done here, then I'll join you."

"Sure thing, Chief," I respond. One more quick kiss, and he swats my bottom to get me moving. Which I do, moving to the driver's side of the new silver pickup to wait as Duke jogs inside the office to presumably grab the keys and then he bleeps the lock so I can climb in.

Once Jade has been buckled securely in the backseat, he kisses me one last time when he drops the key in my hand and shuts my door. I roll down the window and wave. "Later guys."

To which shouts of, "Later Caity," sound behind us.

The mountains are beautiful all the time, but especially this time of year with all the greenery covering the limestone, lush and thick. And Thornbriar, tucked in the middle of it, sitting cute and quaint. I knew when we rolled into town it would be the perfect place to raise my daughter. Even though they don't recognize the truck, the waves I get from residents —only some of them patients—because they see me sitting behind the wheel, makes me feel like after years of wandering, that I'm finally home.

With a town the size of Thornbriar, it only takes us five minutes from Duke's shop to turn down our street, and only a minute longer before we're parked in my driveway.

A wide-awake and full of energy Jade unbuckles her seatbelt then she leaps into my arms when I open her door. It might be just a rental, but we live in a nice rental. Two story, stonework on the bottom, tan siding along the top. Brick and stone paved driveway, and the same for the walk leading up to the stoop. Maybe after I pick up a few more patients, we'll look into buying a house. One with a big porch where I can sit and sip iced tea while Jade plays outside. I have a patio out back where I placed a nice umbrella table and chairs, but no porch at either the front or back.

After I unlock the front door, Jade pushes in from under my arm to open it. She rushes inside, and for some reason I reach out to grab her. The hairs on the back of my neck stand on end. She evades my hand and I drop it, realizing how stupid I'm being. Then I shake my head to clear it and follow more slowly behind her, shutting and locking the door the way I always do.

MY PURSE DROPPED to the coffee table, keys tossed in the decorative sweetgrass basket I bought during our trip to Charleston before we settled in Thornbriar sitting in the center of the coffee table, I flick on lights and adjust the temperature.

It's been a good day. A relaxing day. One that I plan to continue at least until Duke shows. Then who knows? I walk into the kitchen to pour myself a glass of ice water. After pulling a glass down from the cupboard, I stand at the refrigerator water dispenser filling the glass when a giant black bug on the patio door catches my eye.

I walk over and bend down to get a better look. I have no idea what kind of bug it is, either. It hasn't moved, but who can look away from a giant black bug? I bring the glass up to my lips to sip my water while willing the bug to move and notice the latch on the sliding patio door flipped *down*. Unlocked. Here I thought Jade was upstairs playing.

The bug certainly moves when I throw open the patio door. "Jade?" I call out to her.

"Yes, Mama?" She calls back... *from inside the house.*

Um, no. If she's inside, how is my door unlocked? I did not, *would not*, leave the backdoor *unlocked*.

Checking doors is one of my rituals before I leave the house. We're two girls living on our own. Nothing is more important than my girl's safety.

"Nothing sweetie, never mind." I call back up to her.

For safety, I do a onceover of the entire house, checking every room upstairs and down. Not one thing of value seems to be missing. Not our televisions. Not my laptop. Not my copper pots from the kitchen. Not even the prescription meds they sent home for Jade after her discharge.

With that said, I don't know if I should call the police. They'd probably think I'm just some silly woman who *thinks* she locked the door. What if this one time I really hadn't?

I bring my hands to rest against my hips and bite my bottom lip while standing in the threshold between the living room and kitchen, unsure if I should feel scared or stupid. The time for water has passed. I need a beer and move back to the refrigerator to grab one.

The home phone rings as I pull a cold brew from the bottom shelf. So I close the door to answer. That's when I see it. The missing thing.

How had I missed it before? Jade's preschool picture, the one I keep in a magnetic photo frame on the upper freezer door so I can look at it whenever I walk to the fridge. It's not in the magnetic frame.

The phone quits ringing by the time Jade runs it over to me, her face clearly says she's confused as to why I didn't answer.

Someone broke into my house. Someone. Broke into my house. My house. Where I sleep. Where my daughter sleeps. And they *took her picture*. Literally took her picture from my house.

"*Oh god.*" My hand shoots to my mouth. I stumble back a

few steps. My whole body begins to tremble as what Duke said to me yesterday comes back in a rush. Being with him might make Jade and I persons of interest. And Houdini escaped capture. The same Houdini who targeted women attached to the club. I mean, it couldn't be him, could it? Duke has hardly spent any time with us. Unless he's watching Duke. This is crazy, absolutely bonkers. Why would Houdini want a picture of my daughter?

Duke would know.

I need to call him.

Calmly, so as not to worry my girl, I walk into the living room, over to the coffee table to fish my cell from my purse then immediately hit Duke's contact. "Doc?" He answers without a hello. "Just need to get a few more things done before I can make—"

"Someone broke into my house." I cut him off.

"What the fuck?" he barks.

"The… the latch on my patio door was unlocked, and Jade's school picture is missing from the refrigerator."

"Get Peaches. Get out to the truck. Now."

"No one's here, Chief."

"Lock the doors." He talks over me. Not listening. "I'm on my way. Calling Tommy. Doc?" He prompts, when I say nothing, then, "*Caitlin.*"

I jolt. "Yes. I'm here."

"Know you're there. Where you should be is in the truck. Now." He reiterates.

"Okay," I whisper. "Jade, sweetheart. Come here."

Since it's only been the two of us for so long, even though she's young, she reads me and doesn't argue, knowing I mean business.

Grabbing up my purse and the keys, I swing my girl into my arms and move outside into the, thankfully, bright sunshine to the cab of the truck. Where I lock the doors and wait. Houdini took a picture of my daughter. My daughter. I'll die before I let him hurt her. My Hippocratic Oath be damned, he'll die by my hands if he tries.

It takes everything in me not to vomit, swallowing back the bile rising in my throat about once a minute. After six swallows, Tommy's cruiser rolls up to the curb in front of our home and only seconds after that, the rumble from pipes cuts the air. Although Duke shows up in his old pickup, not his bike. The pipe rumbles come from all the brother's rallying.

I jump out of the truck, a trembling Jade still in my arms, and rush to him. The closer we get, the more I can't control the fear or my rapidly beating heart. A stupid sob rips through me as we collide, and his strong arms wrap around us. And maybe that's why the sob comes, because in Duke's arms, my daughter and I are safe. Nothing can touch us, not with his strong hands holding us to him, stroking up and down my back. So big, he engulfs the two of us. A mountain of muscled power.

"Shh…" he coos, so soft. "I got you. I got you both."

I hiccup then laugh at my own stupidity. And face-plant against his shoulder.

"Doc." Although his tone remains soft, he's put more power behind it to get my attention. I don't respond verbally, but look up so he knows I'm listening. "Here's what's gonna happen. You and Peaches pack a few bags, 'cuz you're coming to stay with me in my house."

"We can't stay here?" I ask, lamely. Clearly the fear making me not think straight.

"My house is on the compound. It'll be safer for you. At least 'til we get that patio door replaced. The easiest doors to break into. Jesse's driving my old truck back, so I can ride with my girls. Your escort starts today. If I ain't with you, Jesse's carting you around. He's a good man. A good recruit. You can trust him."

I open my mouth to agree, but Duke mistakes my intentions. "Please don't argue. I need you and Peaches safe."

He *needs* us safe? *Needs,* not wants.

"I wasn't going to argue. Actually, I was about to say, 'okay.' I need us to be safe as well."

9

CAITLIN

"Try to only touch what you need to touch." Tommy orders us after he's taken my statement. "We need to dust for prints. Though, if this is Houdini, which I hope to god it ain't, we won't find any."

Both he and Duke follow me around upstairs and down as I pack a few bags of essentials for Jade and me. I left her outside clinging a death grip in the arms of Jesse. Hero, Sneak and Carver check out my backyard for any more signs of Houdini's presence.

After I've packed two bags for each of us, Duke hefts them over one shoulder, and taking my hand, leads me back downstairs. "Need anything else before we leave?"

"No. Thank you. My purse is in the truck."

"Good deal. Tommy, you need any more from Doc?"

Sgt. Tommy Doyle gives his head one sharp shake then squats down to open a kit he'd set down on the front stoop when he'd arrived, to fish a pair of blue latex gloves out and shove them over his hands.

We leave Tommy and his police brethren to search my house.

The brothers ride off, some in front of the pickup, some to the back like a convoy. A different recruit mans the gate since Jesse's been promoted to protection detail. He opens the gate for us, then as the bikes drive straight, Duke turns to the right to park his truck under a carport attached to a gorgeous painted white wraparound porch off the pretty blue doublewide. Flower boxes and hanging baskets overflow with red and pink perennials.

Several other double and singlewides dot the grounds, but this one is by far, the cutest. My umbrella table and chairs would look great on the back stone patio, an extension off the covered porch, with a clear view of the woods and mountains.

Plenty of room for a little girl to play.

Without thinking, I admiringly tell him what his yard screams for. "You need a swing set."

"Sorry?" he asks.

Thankfully I start thinking once more, enough to realize my faux pas. "Oh, nothing." I reply. "I was overstepping again."

"Something you or Peaches need?" He stares out to the open acreage, along with me.

"No. Nothing we need. Just me being foolish."

"Then let's go inside."

We climb out of the truck, Jade in my arms because Duke once again, hefts all four of our bags over his shoulder as we walk up the steps to a side door which opens into a large utility room. He has a nice, front loading washer and dryer and a couple wicker hampers with probably a week's worth of dirty laundry stuffed inside. A dusty blue washer and dryer. White wicker hamper. I'm sensing a theme.

From the utility room, we emerge into a huge, open plan kitchen. Smack in the center is a ginormous butcher-block island with an attached bar along the back where four white barstools sit snuggly pushed under the lip. The stools are white with dingy from use, flowery chintz fabric covering each. Not the fabric a biker would choose.

All the cabinets have been painted white, the upper ones fitted with glass fronted panels. All the doors, to the utility room and I assume a pantry, are white as well as all the appliances. A short curtain made from the same flowery chintz fabric of the stools, hangs from the window over the sink, which looks out into the backyard.

Next to the kitchen he walks us through the dining area. More white on the rectangle table legs with a varnished tabletop, the same blond wood as the butcher block. A variation on the flowery chintz, although using the same colors, each high-backed farm chair has a cushion. And long chintzy curtains drape from a rod, framing each side of a set of double French doors.

Very pretty. Very girly. Again, not at all where I'd expect a biker like Duke to live. Too much flowery, even for me. My denim covered sofa would fit in nicely in this space. Something hearty, but with class. That's what Duke needs.

First we stop at a smallish room of four white walls and a window with standard, white horizontal blinds, no curtains. There's a twin bed with a faded, navy blue comforter and two pillows in white cases. A guest room, which will work as a temporary room for Jade, although I know she'll miss her pink princess room back home. Though, he has an older television and a DVD player. So she should be happy.

Duke drops her bags next to the bed. I'll get her settled after the rest of the tour.

There are two more rooms the same smallish size of Jade's, but without bedding. One he uses for storage and for bike parts. And one, stark empty. Those three share a decent sized bathroom with a large tub-shower combination and double vanity, along with the commode.

At the back of the home, last room in the hallway, he leads me into the master suite. I'm not sure why one man would need so much space. Granted, he's filled it with a king sized bed. The headboard pressed center to the main wall opposite the door we entered. There's a walk-in closet as big as the room Jade will sleep in *and* a master bath with a swimming pool for a bathtub, complete with hot tub jets, a separate two person shower, double vanity and a separate, sectioned-off "room" for our other bathroom needs.

My heart breaks even more for Duke as I walk around the place. He'd set my bags down in the closet and now just watches me, arms resting at his hips. A single man with all this room. In a house made for a family. The man has so much love to give. He's already given glimpses. But has lost his world.

Thus, I walk over to him, wrap my hand around the back of his neck to pull his head down, as I go up on tiptoe for us to meet in the middle, and place the tenderest kiss I could imagine against his perfect lips.

Duke being Duke, he takes over the kiss.

Duke being Duke, it quickly turns from tender to heated. He lifts me, both hands hold my bottom as he urges me to wrap my legs around his hips, but he doesn't move to the bed. Only holding me there in that spot, making out in a room I presume we'll be sharing. Making out *hot* and *heavy*.

When the kiss comes to its natural conclusion, still panting like I'd just been making out hot and heavy, I ask the most mundane question in the world. "What do you want for dinner, Chief?"

Two slow blinks and stares at me, then barks out a beautifully boisterous laugh.

"You cooking tonight, honey?"

"Absolutely. You like stuffed peppers? I make an awesome Italian stuffed pepper. Even Jade eats them."

"Should probably make enough we have drop ins. Men find out a woman's cooking here, bound to make 'emselves at home. At least the men without women at home to take care 'a 'em."

"Boss is out on a run. We should invite Elise and baby Gun over, too."

He starts laughing again, downgraded to a snicker, though it still makes me smile.

"What?" I ask.

"Been here ten minutes and your already planning a fucking dinner party."

"I don't... we don't..." I sputter. He squeezes me again.

"Just giving you a hard time, honey. Be good to fill the house again."

Oh.

My burly biker wants to fill the house again. Foolish as it may seem, it makes me happy to be the one to give him that. A night hanging out, no pieces, no pressure to be or act a certain way. Just friends eating and maybe enjoying a few beers together.

Then, because he must sense my feelings, Duke hugs me. "Make a list, Doc. Everything you think your gonna need, 'cuz chances are, I won't have it. Don't do a lot of shopping. Go up to the clubhouse and eat whatever one 'a the women makes."

We walk back into the kitchen, and he shows me a drawer where he keeps a scratch pad and pen. I write down, one by one, all of the ingredients I'll need for the peppers, and the dessert I decide on the spot to make. Then Guinness. Milk. Breakfast and lunch options, and other sundries such as sugar, flour and butter. Sundries most people keep standard in their pantry.

Once I hand him off the list Duke phones Jesse—because Jesse has Caitlin duty and Caitlin duty apparently involves all things Caitlin, which in this case would include grocery shopping—to come grab the list. Which he does right away. And takes the keys to the old pickup.

While my bodyguard shops for us, I unpack Jade. Clothes hung up in the closet and moved to the one dresser in the room. Then take her body wash, shampoo, toothbrush and toothpaste to the bathroom across the hall.

I can hear Duke on the phone again, but his words are murmured. So I move to the master to unpack myself. After I'm done, I sit on the bed and stare out the window, watching the leaves of the trees blow in the soft, summer breeze.

Not knowing how long I've sat here, I know it has to be a while when Duke calls into the room. "Honey, Jesse's back."

When all the groceries have been put away, leaving out what I need to start dinner, I take note that Duke needs canisters. For flour. For sugar. They keep the bugs out. He needs newer pots and pans, too. Copper or cast iron. Like I have at my house.

Come to think of it, Duke needs a lot of new. And that's when it hits me. His home life stalled when his wife died. He'd thrown himself into the club to compensate for her loss. As such, his home turned time capsule. Not even a shrine to her, but a representation of how his life stopped when hers did.

Which makes the fact that he brought me and my daughter here to stay, even temporarily, mean even more than it otherwise might have. At least for me.

I pull a pot for rice from the pot shelf in the pantry, fill it with the appropriate amount of water per the rice directions, throw in a Jade-size handful of salt, replace the lid securely and set the pot on the back burner to come to boil.

From there it's a whole lot of chopping, grating, sautéing. Dicing to chiffonade. Not to mention measuring, zesting, mixing and pouring for the gooey Limoncello cake I'm preparing for dessert.

The house smells amazing, if I do say so myself, from the lemon and Italian herbs and sweet sausage.

"Where'd you learn to cook?" Duke surprises me by asking.

"When I was a girl, I spent every summer in Ireland with my grandma. She was a wonderful cook. Lived a glamorous life, lived all over. Had lots of affairs before she settled down with my grandfather. Some even with famous men. Actors. Producers. She'd tell me saucy stories about her life while we cooked and canned and baked. Stories my parents would have freaked out if they'd known she shared. As a parent, I'd freak, too." As I talk about my grandma, a hint of accent comes through, as it always does. Maybe because I hear her stories spoken in her soft Irish lilt, in my head.

"Sounds wonderful."

"Some of the best times of my life. My grandma was my best friend. When I cook, even things we never made together, I think of her for the simple fact that she's the one who taught me. Though... you'll be happy to know..." I huff hair from my eyes, not wanting to touch it which would mean stopping my work to rewash my hands. "The stuffed peppers are mine. But the Limoncello cake is hers. Something she picked up when she lived in Rome for a summer. With a famous Italian producer, I might add."

"Lips," he says bizarrely non sequitur.

"Come again?" I ask, pulling my brows together.

"Lips," he says again. This time sounding more like an order.

As he stares, pursed perfect lips waiting for it to click, it clicks.

Oh, *lips*.

I stretch my body over the island to lean in and give Duke my lips. I guess he likes my sharing.

Our moment gets interrupted when we hear a female voice say, "Knock, *knock.*" At the same time hear the double rap of a fist against the front screen door. Duke has central air, but opened the windows and doors to let the breeze flow through the space.

Elise, with baby Gun in a carrier, stands waiting and I don't mind one bit she interrupted. "Will you get that, Chief?"

He brushes his thumb over my cheek before walking over to the front door and holds it open for our first guest to pass through. "It was unlocked," he says, and grumbles.

"But it's rude to just enter someone's home." Elise protests.

"You just enter the clubhouse."

"But that's not your home." She continues to argue her point.

"She's got you there, Chief." I decide to chime in.

And that's when Jade who'd been watching movies in her room and most likely heard voices thus came out to be nosey, spies Gun and screeches. "*A BABY!*" Then she makes a beeline straight for Elise and her son.

"Oh my gosh, Caitlin? Is this Jade?"

I nod.

"She's your mini me." Elise finishes.

"Yes. She most definitely is. I'm so glad you two could come over," I say, pointing to her and her boy. "Too bad your husband couldn't make it."

"Yeah, well..." she trails off.

And I understand why, because he's still not home and from what she'd explained, no plans have been made to bring him home. So I change subjects promptly. "I hope you like stuffed peppers."

"Are you kidding? I like anything I don't have to cook right now. Although I *like to cook*, cooking with a baby attached to your hip isn't the most fun experience. Oh, but my boy started rolling over."

"That's exciting. Did you bring a blanket? Lay it out on the floor, then you can set him down. Jade will look out for him. She loves babies."

Elise walks over to the living room area to drop her diaper bag down on the—yet again, dingy from use, chintz fabric sofa—to retrieve Gun's blanket. "Jade," she calls. "Would you like to hold Gunner while I get him set up?"

My daughter, meanwhile, in her little girl exuberance, climbs up next to Elise and the baby carrier, knowing it's alright to talk to Elise because she's here in the house with us and so has registered her as a friend.

"I'm Elise Hollister." Elise introduces herself. "This is my son, Gunner. But we call him Gun."

"Dat's cute." Jade giggles, clicking her sock-covered feet together as she reaches a gentle hand out to stroke Gunner's head. The excitement of her feet juxtapose the calmness of her hand. I love my little girl.

"Your mom's my friend, but she's also the one who delivered baby Gun, because she's my doctor."

"He's da pwettiest baby I evur seen."

"Think you can hold him?" Elise asks.

"Oh yes. I helwp Miss Jenny wiff da babies at school."

Then I watch as Elise unbuckles Gun from his carrier and sets him in Jade's waiting arms. Not needing direction, my daughter carefully cradles the boy, taking care with his head. Then she begins to sing to him. My heart might explode from the cuteness factor, while Elise moves the coffee table out of the way and lays the blanket out on the carpet, then spreads some soft baby toys around on the yellow and gray baby elephant blanket that I'd given her as a gift when he was born.

"How about we lay Gun on the floor, and you can play with him?"

Jade vigorously shakes her head yes, while Elise takes her son and waits for my girl to situate herself on the blanket. After, she places her boy down next to Jade and steps back watching, like me and Duke, as Jade picks up a squeezy toy and squeezes it to get Gunner's attention. Once Elise seems satisfied my girl will be gentle, she walks back over to us and slips onto one of the barstools.

"Beer?" I ask.

"That'd be great," she answers.

I look to Duke expectantly and wait.

Then he gripes. "Damn woman in my house not even a day, and she's already bossing me around." But, I will add, he does it going to the refrigerator to grab Elise's beer. "Doc?" he rasps, his back to me while grabbing bottles.

"Yes, please."

He sets them down. Twists the cap off the first and slides it over to Elise. Does the same with the second, but sends it my way. And the third, he keeps for himself, taking a long pull. When he sets the bottle on the island, he has a smile on his face that I know isn't from drinking beer.

"You got company, Imma head up to the club. Got some work to do there."

"Okay, Chief." I don't mind.

"Call me when dinner's ready?" he asks.

"You know I will."

"Good. Lips," he orders. And this time I don't have to think about what he wants, and walk around the island to kiss my man. Quick and closed-mouth, but as always, satisfying.

When he turns to leave, we all hear, "Duke?" And turn to

look at my girl who has set Gun's toy down, and is resting her hand to her hip.

Her face looks hurt, her lips pursed.

"Sorry, Peaches." A red-faced Duke walks over to her and bends down, where he kisses her cheek and allows her to kiss his.

"Oh. My. God." Elise mouths.

"I know," I answer verbally. Then I turn back to dinner prep.

10

DUKE

"So? Dr. Brennan." Scotch, who'd been sitting at the bar sipping on a double malt when I walked in, turns to talk to me but continues to keep his ass planted on his seat. "She's a right fine lass. Glad to see you finally manned up and went after her."

Manned up? Who the fuck does Scotch think he's talking too?

"Unless you wanna shit that glass out after I shove it up your ass, watch yourself, brother." I pull a cigarette from the pack and light it, then take a long drag. The first smoke I've had since I jumped outta the pickup at Doc's house. Fuck if I don't need it.

"You think you got it in you, old man." Scotch teases. "Come at me. But come at me knowing that we all know you putting the no touch order on Dr. Brennan—"

"Caity," one of the other brothers calls out as he passes us.

"Caity," Scotch continues, "had fuck-all to do with Elise or Gun." Then he slams back the rest of his drink and stands to walk over to me, grabs a cigarette from the pack I offer, and lights it. "Heard Houdini's back?"

"Yeah. That's what I'm here about." To the rest of the room I bellow, "Brother's rally, *now*."

All the brothers, despite what they might 'a been doing at the time, stop to walk into the rally room, the room where we hold club meetings that we don't need old ladies, hot mamas or pieces overhearing. Only Carver and Sneak, of my lieutenants, sit around the oval table. Boss, Chaos and Blood are out on a run. The rest line the walls and wait for me to take my seat at the head. It's a respect thing. You don't sit the table unless you've earned that spot as a lieutenant.

"I'm sure you all heard by now, 'cuz you gossip like a gaggle 'a women, Dr. Brennan, which, Caity to you, I claimed her publically as my old lady."

Laughs, and "'bout fuckin' time" ring out around the room. Guess all the brothers knew I was hot for the good Doc. Shit. Here I thought I was keeping it low.

I suck back on my smoke before continuing. "Don't know if you heard, she's got a little girl, Jade. I call her Peaches. They're staying at my house right now 'cuz hers got broken into while we were in Nashville.

Another chorus of "fuck" and "shit" travel the men.

"I'm afraid Houdini's back." The room goes stark quiet at that motherfucker's name. "Last time he went after our women. Now, it shits me to say this, he might be going after the kids. All that was missing was a picture of Peaches from a magnet frame on the refrigerator. All that was fucking missing."

"Kids?" Sneak is the first to ask. "Should we bring the women in? Mine ain't born yet, is it safe?" All the shit he gave Boss about Gun, the man sits at the table practically pissing his pants with concern. Gonna have to tell Boss that one, let him rip a little on Sneak.

"He caught us off guard last time. Don't want to overreact, but don't wanna under either. Elise's already here with Gunner. She's staying in Boss's room while he's gone. Maybe you and Trish should stay here for now, 'til we get a handle on the situation." After that, I look to all the brothers around the room. "We got those singlewides on the property sitting empty. Any brother with kids, move 'em to one 'a those. Better safe, brothers."

I dismiss them with a wave of my hand. But before Sneak and Carver leave, I stop 'em. "Doc is cooking dinner. Italian stuffed peppers. And she made this lemon cake thing for dessert. I'm just gonna say the house smells fucking fantastic. Anyway, the two 'a you and Trish wanna come to dinner, Elise's already there."

"*Dinner* at *your house*?" Carver snickers.

Bastard.

"Ayeah. But all she drinks is Guinness, so you want something else, bring it."

"You're fucking a woman who only drinks Guinness?" Carver keeps it going.

I'm about to punch him in his fucking face.

"She's Irish, for Christ sake. Lived in Ireland. What'd you expect her to drink?"

"Don't get your panties in a twist over some pussy, Prez. But I'd be happy to drop by," he finishes, and barely escapes my fist from the punch I'd thrown to shut him the hell up. Who knew Carver could be so damn annoying?

"Me and Trish'll be up after we pack. She'll be glad, not cooking after a long day at work, or worse, eating what *I* cook."

"Well, it'll be done soon. So hurry."

His back to me, he calls, "Will do." Then pulls his phone from his back pocket. Before he leaves the room I hear, "Hey sweetheart." Man's gone soft.

My phone rings next. I look at the screen, Tommy calling. I swipe to answer. "Whatcha got?" I give as my greeting.

"Well hello to you, too." Tommy teases. "What we got is a lot of nothin'. I don't like it, don't like it one bit. Elise at the compound?"

"Yeah, she's fine. Hey, Doc's cooking. You and Maryanne should stop up."

"That'd be good. I'll call her now. But, so you know, I'm callin' Boss too. He needs to know."

"You can, or I will."

"I'll do it on my way home," he says. "Got some other stuff to talk to him about, non-Houdini related."

"Good. Get your wife then come on up." Then I ring off, set my phone down on the table and rub my hands vigorously over my eyes. The last fucking thing we need is Houdini sniffing around again.

My phone rings for the second time. This time the display says Doc's calling. I answer her with a, "*Honey?*"

"Hey Chief," she says, and insanely, all the shit 'a the world melts away. Just from hearing her voice. I'm so screwed.

"Whatcha need?"

"Dinner's ready. You said to call."

"Good. Carver, Sneak and Trish, Tommy and Maryanne'll be around soon. Be there in a few."

Once I hang up with her, I walk out into the common room of the clubhouse. There's hot mamas hanging around, doing their thing. And the pieces have started to show. Including Viki-Lee. Always enthusiastic, especially with her mouth, Viki-Lee. Knows exactly what I like and how I like it. Though, she ain't got shit on Doc. That's for damn sure.

"Hey Duke, baby." She brushes her hand along my chest. "I'm in the mood to suck some cock. Where you been? It ain't nice to deny your cock from Viki-Lee." Then there in the common, she drops to her knees to begin unbuckling my belt.

I pull her up. "Not anymore, Vik. Got me an old lady now."

"I don't mind sharing." The bitch don't get it and drops back down to her knees.

"*No*. Get the fuck up or get the fuck out. My old lady ain't the type to share."

"Just one for the road, Duke." She sounds as if she's pleading.

Fuck. This bitch needs to go. "Hey Blaze?" I call to one of the younger brothers, newly patched in after he helped save Elise and Liv during the first Houdini crisis.

"Yeah, Prez?" He turns from where he'd just taken a shot at the pool table.

"Vik's in the mood to suck cock."

"Well, it just so happens I'm in the mood to be sucked." Then the cocky little bastard hangs his pool cue up to walk over to Viki-Lee while unbuttoning and unzipping his fly. The man's got his dick hanging out when he reaches us. "I'm all yours babe."

Knowing she ain't gonna get it from me, she shrugs then drops down to her knees again to begin sucking off Blaze. Before I leave him to it, I pat his arm. "Elise's at my place right now, so take advantage, because with all the women and children showing up, you gotta take this show to your room 'til we get the club back."

Though, I'll probably have to repeat myself. Don't think he's much paying attention to me, not with his grunt as reply.

As I cross the forecourt of the compound back over to my house, I see Doc holding open the door to let Tommy and Maryanne in. She catches my eye and smiles, lighting up her whole face. God she's gorgeous.

Inside, Gun's back in his carrier, the coffee table righted and Elise and Maryanne sit on my sofa while Tommy reclines in my chair. Doc's at the fridge pulling out five bottles of beer. Two in one hand, three in the other, holding the necks between her fingers. She sets them down on the island. I walk over to twist off the caps.

"Thanks," she says.

But before she can deliver 'em to our guests, I stop her. "*Lips.*"

She presses against me, hand to my chest, and lifts up on her tiptoes to kiss me. Fuck if I'd ever want the likes of a skank like Viki-Lee touching me again when I got Doc who's got skin of peaches, smells of vanilla and right now, tastes like lemon, probably from that dessert she made. Vik's a nice woman, but she's a skank and proud of it. Sure as hell don't smell like vanilla, and she's never tasted like lemon. My old lady's pure class.

When I pull back, I feel the eyes on us. And sure enough, every pair stares at us wearing various degrees of smiles on their faces. That's when, thankfully, Sneak and Trish show. Sneak don't knock or wait for me or Doc to offer 'em inside. He plows in, holding his lady's hand.

"Fuck, it smells good in here."

The women jump from the sofa to greet them, laying a hand on Trish's belly because apparently that's what's done to pregnant women.

Doc calls to our newest guest. "Hey Sneak, beer?"

"Yes, ma'am."

"Trisha, juice? Water? Tea? It's herbal."

"Juice will be good." She laughs, rubbing on her own belly. "I can drink it from a bottle and not feel so left out. I miss beer."

I grab up my beer and one for Sneak. Doc takes hers and

the bottle of juice for Trish, then we join our guests in the living room. The last to arrive is Carver.

"Don't get up," he says to my old lady. "Beer in the fridge?"

"Yep," I answer for her. Though she gets up anyway to pull the peppers from the oven. Along with those Pillsbury breadsticks. She's also made a salad, and in squeeze bottles that I know I didn't have, so she must have put them on the list for Jesse, it looks like three different salad dressings.

Then she sets out my plates, flatware, and napkins.

"Okay, everybody. Time to eat. We try not to eat a lot of processed foods in our house because Jade has allergies to some preservatives, so it's just easier to make my own. The dressings are buttermilk and Italian. And, of course, creamy cucumber, because that's Princess Jade's favorite. So please, help yourself. Jade, sweetheart, sit at the table, and I'll fix you a plate."

Peaches kisses Gun's forehead and runs over to the table with her bottle of juice and waits. Doc slices a cooked pepper in half, putting half on Jade's plate, along with a breadstick and a small pile of salad, which she squeezes creamy cucumber dressing on top.

"Fank you, Mama. Will you sit wiff me?"

"Well sweetheart we've got—" I know she's gonna say we've got company. But Trish picks up her plate and juice to walk over to the table, and sits down next to Jade.

"Look," she says, "We've got matching drinks."

"Mama, me and Twish got matching dwinks."

The women congregate at the table, while the men take their food back to the sofa and chairs. Gun starts to fuss, and Elise puts her fork down mid-bite to go to him, but she's stopped by Sneak, who puts his hand up. "I got him. Bottle in the bag?"

"Yes," a stunned Elise answers, watching Sneak fish a full

bottle of formula from the diaper bag. He pops the cap, then positions the boy in his arms and feeds him.

We all watch him in silence, about as stunned as Elise. That's when he looks around the room at all of us and asks, *"What?"* Sounding affronted. "Got me a kid coming. Figure I should get used to this."

"Right." The brothers start on him.

"You gonna have one of those joint baby showers?" Carver asks.

"We'll get him one of those Snugli front wearing baby carries like we got for Elise, so he can keep the baby against his chest while he works." Tommy teases.

"Whoa, whoa, whoa." Elise cuts in. "I'll have you know, Tommy Doyle, that Beau wears that just as much as I do, if not more. So leave poor Sneak alone."

"What?" Tommy asks, unbelieving. "Someone facetime Boss. I need to hear this for myself."

Carver puts his plate down on the coffee table to pull his phone from his front pocket. He hits a couple buttons, and we hear his phone ring. After about four times, Boss answers with a, "Whatcha need, brother?"

"Hey Boss," everyone but Elise calls out. Hers is a, "Hey baby."

"That my wife?" he asks. "Where the fuck are you?"

Carver turns his phone so Boss can see all of us. Then turns it back. "We're at Duke and Caity's for dinner."

"Caity?" Boss asks.

And fuck if I don't like the sound 'a that. Duke and Caity's. Shit. Shit, shit, shit. I look around to find my woman, who's turned as strawberry as the lip gloss she usually wears, tastes.

"Dr. Brennan," Carver continues.

"I thought her name is Caitlin. I always call her Caitlin." *That's* what throws him, not hearing Carver call it Doc and

Caity's place? Tommy must have explained some things when he called earlier.

"Boys voted, it's Caity now."

"Okay. Well we're about to ride, got to find a place to stay for the night. So whatcha need?"

This time Tommy answers. "Sneak's feeding your kid."

"He probably should get the practice. Just keep him off your tit, Sneak." The brothers and Tommy, and all the women laugh. It's good to hear so much laughter in my house again.

"Elise here says you wear that Snugli carrier more than she does," Tommy says.

"Sure do. She carried him the first forty weeks. Can't wait to get home, so I can fuck my wife then snuggle with my boy. He loves Westerns."

"*See*." Sneak shouts, startling a half-asleep Gun. He points around at all the men, then presses one of Gun's ears against his chest and covers the other with his hand. "Fuck all y'all."

"Gotta go." Boss chuckles. "Night baby girl," he calls to Elise. "I'll call when we settle."

"Love you, Beau." She calls back.

Carver ends the call then shoves his phone back in his pocket and picks up his plate to dig back in eating.

Everyone but Trish and Peaches continue to consume beers, the peppers, salad and breadsticks get decimated. And the dessert. Fuck. I ain't ever tasted anything like it. She's a goddamn culinary genius.

Tommy goes back for his, like, third piece, which also happens to be the last piece, which means I'm ready to kick his ass. Doc must see me glaring 'cuz she struts over to slide onto my lap, wraps her arms around my neck and whispers in my ear, "Don't worry, Chief. I made a second pan."

Hearing that just might be sexier than any dirty talk she could throw my way.

At the end of the night, after Elise, Gun, Trish and the

brothers head back up to the clubhouse where they're staying, and Tommy and Maryanne head for home, Caitlin picks up a passed out Peaches from the sofa.

"I'm just gonna get her in bed, then I'll come clean up."

I walk over to kiss my girls. "You cooked, I'll clean. After you get her down, go on to bed. I'll be there in a bit."

"Right," she says. Then heads down the hallway to Jade's room.

Good friends. Good food. It's easy to forget the reason everyone's here. I pull the note from my wallet. The note Houdini left for Elise along with the roses. And I stare at it for several beats. My gut clenches. "What shit are you gonna pull this time?" I ask the paper. Then before Doc can see it, I fold it and slip it back inside my wallet.

Well, one positive to come from Houdini messing with Doc and Peaches. I got my girls. Under my roof.

Ain't no way he can get to them now.

11

CAITLIN

The moon shines so bright tonight that even with the curtains drawn, they're sheer enough to allow the blue hue from the moonlight to filter inside the bedroom. Everything is washed in translucent blue. Even me.

Goosebumps prickle my skin when I feel him come up behind me. Not from cold, although he turned the central air on once he closed up the house. But because Jade is asleep in her new, temporary room, and I'm standing in my satin nighty, the color of mauve, in Duke's bedroom. My new, temporary bedroom.

He runs his fingers up and down my arms, both calming the goosebumps and creating more from his whisper-soft touches.

Who would have ever thought a badass biker could have whisper-soft touches? His hands travel from my arms to the hem of my nighty where he grips the sides and tugs up, stopping just below my navel to gently push against my pelvis, grinding his hardened cock through his jeans against my bottom. I lose all rational thought, my free will gone at the feel of him, and where he hits. I sit, an empty vessel ready to be filled however he wants to fill me.

And I reach up behind me to run my fingers through his hair while he licks and kisses my neck.

As he continues to grind, he dips a finger inside my panties going right for the golden spot. He hits it dead-on, because he means to, and begins the sensual, torturous rub. I was already wet from his grinding and neck kisses, with the way he uses his finger, my sex weeps for him, and I find it hard to stay standing.

"Come on, Doc," he whispers in my ear, shoving me forward toward the bed. Before I climb on, he pulls the nighty from my body and drags my panties down, kissing the small of my back, my bottom and each thigh before helping me step out of them completely. "Lay down," he orders, then.

I do, watching him undress all the while. His cut tossed on a chair, the rest of his clothing dropped to the floor. Tonight is the first I really get to look. All that sinewy mass covered in a lifetime of tattoos. The ridges and valleys of a twenty-year-old on a man more than fifteen years older.

I've never seen anything like him in such an intimate setting before. Never have I been with a man his size, with his strength.

Duke climbs on the bed, trapping me underneath his powerful body to kiss me again. I already can't catch my breath.

"Gonna let me fuck you how I want to?" he asks.

I nod because I can't find my voice.

"Good," he says and rolls me to my side, where he fits himself the length of my back. If we were sleeping, we'd be spooning.

"On the pill, Doc?"

Over my shoulder, again, I can only nod. Then I watch, mesmerized, as he grips his rock-hard cock and runs it through my wetness several sweeps, then feel the intrusion of the tip inside me. He pulls back and pushes a little more, the whole head stretching me. I might have had a baby, but it's been several years since I've had a man between my legs.

And so I pinch my eyes shut and try to adjust to the feel of him. That's when he pulls out again, kisses my jaw, and slides back in, giving me more. But he's teasing now, even if he doesn't mean to.

Not nearly enough, I need him to give me enough.

"More," I beg.

"Sure you ready for that?"

My response is to push back against him and repeat, "More. Please."

To honor my request, Duke moves my top leg over his to open me up more, spreads my opening with his hands and positions himself, then he slams inside me, not a gentle glide, though not rough. Hard. I gasp, as he begins to thrust.

His hand moves to my breast where he rolls the nipple between his fingers.

"More," I beg louder.

Switching hands, he moves to my opposite breast and begins to roll that nipple. This, after moving his first hand down to between my legs to stroke my golden spot again. The feeling so primal, as if intrinsically downloaded from every coupling since the beginning of mankind.

We move in time together. I jerk my hips back as he thrusts forward. It's unbelievable. Sex has never felt this good before, and I become greedy, wanting, no *needing* more.

"Harder," I demand.

He thrusts harder.

Oh hell.

Oh hell yes.

I need him to go harder. The fuse is lit. If he'd just give me the, "harder," I demand again.

"Okay, Doc." He moves his hand from my clit to fling his arm across my waist and pushes on my back. "Bend over my arm," he commands.

A command to which I comply immediately.

Then Duke slams into me. Brutal yet beautiful in its power.

Oh hell.

Oh hell yes.

"Yes," I shout, though it's whispered. "Yes, yes. *Yes.*" I keep repeating as he continues to slam into me. Slam after slam after slam. Punishing me with every thrust.

He runs kisses down my back. Then I feel it. I'm like a carbonated beverage he's shaken up and ready to explode.

I feel his cock grow thicker, harder inside me on his final thrust. And he hollers, *"Oh fuck."* Then clamps his teeth into the tender flesh of my back as he releases, and I cry out. No words, just the sounds of pure ecstasy as we come together.

With our breaths heavy, I stay bent over his arm, while he presses his forehead against my back, avoiding the bite mark.

I've never been bitten during sex before. Of course I've never been with a man who brought on such an intense orgasm that my legs won't move before either. But here we are.

"Did I hurt you, honey?" he finally chances to ask when he moves us so our heads both rest on pillows, and he's turned me to face him.

"If by hurt me, you mean make me come harder than I have ever come in my life? Then yes."

He chuckles. The sound resonates from his broad chest in the quiet room. "Didn't mean that kind of hurt, but good to know." He rolls me again so he can tuck me under his arm, my head against his throat. "Need a smoke, but came so hard, don't think I can get up."

"Just go later. The cigarettes will still be there."

"When you first took Elise on as a patient, smart, independent doctor struts her ass into my club and doesn't even blink at what she sees. Did you ever think you'd end up here?"

"You mean in your bed? No. Because I thought you didn't like me. But I noticed you that very first day."

"Every brother in the compound, aside from Boss, Chaos and Sneak wanted to fuck you. But I told 'em you were off limits, because 'a the two doctors in town, you were willing to do house calls here. But honest to god, Doc, I couldn't stand the thought 'a you hooking up with one 'a the brothers."

"Well that won't be an issue."

"It sure as fuck won't be."

We don't speak again for several long moments. The drowsiness moves in to replace the sex high, and I feel myself begin to drift. Only then do I give him my final commentary. "You better stop being so nice to me because I could really fall for you, Chief."

The last thing I feel is Duke's arms tightening his hold on me.

When I wake, it's to the soft glow of morning sun. Duke's side of the bed, empty. I'm sore in all the right places, including my back where he bit me. I get up and head for the two-person shower, only to find it also has jets shooting at me from three sides.

The hot water feels wonderful. Massaging all my muscles. The next house I get has to have a shower like this. I wash then condition my hair, rinse, then turn off the water. After I wrap one of Duke's old bath towels around my body, I find a second to dry my hair. He needs new towels. These work, but the terry is worn and the one I use for my hair has a big rip in it.

I pull my blow dryer from the storage cabinet underneath

the sink to blow out my hair, then twist it up into a bun. Next I moisturize, add a layer of foundation, blush, eyeliner, mascara and I set it with translucent press powder. The finishing touch, a neutral lip stain.

Then I move back to the closet inside the bedroom to pick a work outfit. I like to mix business and casual when meeting patients. So I pair a nice pair of dark wash jeans and a white button-down with three-quarter length sleeves that have a wide cuff on each. I pair that with a pair of brown loafers, small gold hoops in my ears, and finally my lab coat.

Some days I wear my scrubs, but on days when I'm going to make a lot of house calls, I prefer this style of dress. And since I've been off work for a while, and the other doctor doesn't make house calls, I know I'll be playing catch-up all day.

I leave the bedroom to get Jade up when I hear her out in the main room talking with Duke. He's at the stove preparing what looks like oatmeal, while she sits on a bar stool with a glass of milk.

"What's going on here?" I ask. A big smile on my face because a beautiful, burly biker man who fucked me how he wanted just last night, which equated to the best lay of my life, is cooking breakfast for my daughter. Like a real family.

"Duke's making me oatmeaw."

"Got enough for me and your mom, too, Peaches. Wanna give her some grapes, Doc?"

"What's in the pan?" The pan next to the pot of oatmeal he's stirring. "It smells like… butter, brown sugar and—"

"Pecans." Duke finishes for me. "She said she ain't allergic to pecans and those are the kind 'a nuts Jesse bought."

"No, she's not allergic." I answer, my face in the refrigerator as I pull the crisper drawer to get to the grapes.

Washed yesterday before I put them away, I simply break off a vine and lay them down on a napkin.

"You going to want some, Chief?"

"Sure. Coffee's done. Get a cup."

I break off a vine for myself and one for Duke before putting them away and grabbing a mug from the upper cupboard, having to reach on my tiptoes. "This house is made for giants." I fake whine. Duke and Jade both snicker.

He turns off the burners and reaches inside the lower shelf of the upper cupboard to pull three bowls where he lines them up and spoons in oatmeal. Then he spoons on the butter, brown sugar, pecan mixture on top of each.

Because I stand watching him instead of getting coffee, he grabs my mug from my hand and swats my bottom. "Sit," he orders.

So I sit. He slides a bowl and spoon in front of Jade, then one in front of me. But before he begins to eat, he pours me a mug of coffee and then reaches inside the fridge to get the flavored coffee cream, a crème brûlée flavor I'd made and stored in an empty water bottle when I put the groceries away yesterday. He pours some in then looks to me. "How blond you like it?"

"Sandy blonde?"

To that, he gets it and pours just a bit more into the mug. A perfect sandy blond. "Never met someone who makes their own coffee creamer before."

"It doesn't take much time. Pretty easy, actually. Try it."

He nods and pours a couple glugs into his mug, then refills the rest of the way up with more coffee. Then he sips. His eyes grow huge. "Holy shit, honey. If you're as good a doctor as a cook, ain't nobody gonna die in this town ever again."

Although I shouldn't be smiling at the thought of people dying, his comment makes me smile at least for the moment.

Leaning against the counter, his feet crossed at the ankles in a relaxed pose, bare feet and everything, he picks up his bowl and shovels a hearty spoonful into his mouth.

"So Chief, if you give me the address here and your driver's license number then I can sign you up as a pickup person for Jade."

"Will do." He sips on his coffee.

"Do you think you could pick her up today by six?" My stomach does a little clench. I hate not being the one to pick her up. I've always been the one, *always*. But this is what I've wanted for us, isn't it? Instead of freaking out, I take a napkin and lean over to wipe oatmeal from Jade's chin.

"Not a problem. Where you gonna be?"

That's funny. *Where am I going to be?* Only leaving my daughter alone for the first time since she'd been injured a week ago. Since my home had been broken into where only a picture of my girl was stolen. Maybe I spoke too soon about not freaking out.

"Working, unfortunately," I say, and try to sound chipper about the whole crappy situation. "Since the other guy doesn't do house calls and I've been off since Jade went to the hospital. I'm going to be playing catch up."

"Time you think you'll be home?" *Home.* He didn't say here. He didn't say his house. But *home.* "Do I gotta get Peaches dinner without you?" The man has accepted our intrusion in his life surprisingly well.

"Yes. You and Jade should eat. I'll try to be here by eight, okay? There will be some late days for the next couple of days. Jesse and I can grab some dinner."

Well that might have been the wrong thing to say by the way his body jolts and straightens, and he sets his bowl down on the cupboard harder than the situation requires. Or the way he walks around the island to where I'm sitting next to my girl, pulls the spoon of oatmeal I'd been about to shovel into my mouth away and drops it back into the bowl then wraps his arms around my shoulders.

"You *do not* grab dinner with Jesse. He's a prospect. Your guard. Need to eat, you eat with me, Doc. I'm your man."

Wow.

I swallow the lust lump formed in my throat from him giving me that, and nod. "Okay. Feed Jade. We'll eat when I get back here."

"Home." he corrects me. "When you get home.

"What?" Still caught up in the whole eating dinner with him thing, it doesn't register.

"You said here. I said home. 'Til further notice, this is your home, honey."

Oh man, I like that too.

"Sure Chief, when I get home. Because for the foreseeable future, this is my home. With you. And you don't mind us invading your life?" *There*. I put it out there.

Duke pulls me even closer, which I didn't think possible, in order to whisper into my ear, a whisper Jade can't hear. "You ask something that stupid again, I'm gonna drag your fine ass into that bedroom and fuck you 'til you know for a fact I don't mind, making you really late for work. Understand?"

Oh, I understand. Understand in a way I have to fight the urge *to let him* make me late for work. Well one thing's for certain, he knows how to distract me from an impending freak out.

"I understand, Duke," I whisper back. He leans his head down to kiss me, clean enough for a four-year-old to see, but dirty enough for me to know he means business.

Saved by the escort, Jesse raps his hand against the back door leading into the utility room to announce his intrusion.

"Don't mind me," he mutters and heads to the cabinet to

grab a bowl, then spoons in oatmeal and butter, brown sugar and pecans on top.

We all return to eating with minimal, light conversation until we've finished.

Clearing our dishes to the sink, that's the first I notice men in the back yard building something. "What's going on out there?" I point to the men.

"Jungle gym." Duke shrugs his shoulders like it's nothing.

"A *jungle gym*?" I ask. Stunned. Because those are expensive.

"Yeah, well, you said Peaches needed a swing set. If a swing set is good, a jungle gym is better. She'll have stuff to do, and with the families moving onto the compound for a while, she'll have kids to play with, too."

"Oh-*kay*." And because I don't know what else to do to say thank you or express how much him doing this for her means to me, I launch myself at him. The bear-est bear hug probably ever given by a woman to a man.

He holds me right back. Then Jade, feeling left out, hops off her stool to wrap her little arms around our legs until Duke bends to pick her up.

Yes, he has to stop being this nice or I *will* fall for him. I fear I'm already falling. One more quick kiss for Jade, and one not so quick kiss for me, then he leads us out the back through the utility room to the carport where he flings open the backdoor of the new truck to hook my girl into her booster.

"Be there by six, Peaches."

After a tweak to her nose, he turns to me. "Alright woman, don't wear yourself out."

"I'll try not to, Chief."

Leaning his forehead against mine, he doesn't really hug me but grabs my bottom with both hands, eyes closed, he breathes in deep, as if he's breathing me in. He lets me go and lifts me into the passenger seat.

"Ah Chief, wrong side."

"No it ain't." He tosses the keys to Jesse. Freaking *Jesse*?

"I can drive, you know?"

"Yeah, but I don't ride bitch," Jesse answers. "No real man gets carted around by a chick, hot or not."

Did Jesse call me hot?

I look to Duke. "Is this one of those biker things Elise told me I'd have to get used to?"

His reply is to laugh, one of his rich ones from deep in his belly, which I take as his yes. Jesse laughs too, but as his voice isn't as deep as Duke's, it's not as rich as Duke's.

I lean in to Duke. "Keep my girl safe," I whisper.

He sobers. And nods.

12

CAITLIN

My biker bodyguard drives us to Jade's preschool where he opts to stay in the car and wait because some screamo song he likes, by some artist I'll never listen to and therefore, never remember the name of, comes on the satellite radio station he'd picked.

If he thinks I'm listening to that all day, he's got another thing coming.

Per her usual, Jade beats me inside the building but stops at the check-in desk.

"Hi Miss Jenny." I hear my daughter greet her.

"Jade, sweetie, you're back. How are you feeling?" Miss Jenny asks.

"Good. Duke's gonna pick me up by six."

That's when I reach them, and Jenny greets me. "Hey Dr. Brennan, Duke?" Then she cuts Jade a curious glance. "Just a moment," I say. Holding my finger up. "Jade, go put your stuff in your cubby, baby. Then come back and give me a hug." My daughter runs off to do as I asked.

"Duke?" Miss Jenny asks a second time.

"Yes, where do I sign him up?"

She walks to a file cabinet next to the check-in desk and rifles through the second drawer until she finds a paper in a file folder and hands it to me to fill out. I take one of the pens from the pen can sitting on the desk, bend over to place the form on the desktop for a solid place to write, and begin to scribble down my answers, careful to use my best penmanship because doctors have notoriously bad penmanship.

As I write, I explain the situation to Jenny. "His name is Duke Ellis," I tell her as I write it out. Address. Phone number. Driver's license. All things I had Duke give to me before I left. He knows he has to present it when he comes to pick her up. It's policy. "Of Ellis Auto & Towing." I finish. "We're seeing each other. It's sort of serious."

"Really? *Serious, huh?*" Jenny asks.

"Well, I'm letting him pick up my daughter, and we're staying with him while we have some work done on our house."

"*Wow.*" Jenny's excitement makes me excited. Wow is right. "Good for you." Good for me is right.

"Thanks." I smile at her.

"We're getting a new girl, so you know. Come in one day this week to meet her. She's training afternoons because Em's going on maternity leave soon."

"Sounds good." I agree as Jade skids to a stop, hugging but pushing me toward the exit at the same time.

"Go Mama, if you don't go, Duke won't pick me up."

"I guess she likes him, too." Jenny chuckles as I move away from her.

"He calls her Peaches," I give as my answer. Which any woman who knows anything about single mothers knows what it means when a man gives her child a special nickname. Miss Jenny not only knows about single mothers, she is one. A good one.

The glass door swings shut behind me, and I scurry to the

truck. Jesse starts it while I climb in. "I have to stop by the office so I can pick up my box of toys and my files, so I know who we're visiting today."

He shifts into drive and turns out of the parking lot. Five minutes after we turn into the parking lot of mine. Well, mine—I'm in family medicine—A pediatrician, and a chiropractor. All of our offices are in a strip not too far from the center of town.

Once again, he waits while I go in to meet Shirley, my office manager who's been keeping me from hitting a paperwork backup the time I've been off. She and my RN, Carol, who has been funneling appointments and transferring priority cases to the other guy, have kept this place afloat. My staff is amazing.

"Dr. Brennan? Glad you're back," Shirley greets me. "How's our girl?"

"Better. Much better. I'm going to be out all day today, tomorrow and probably Wednesday, making house calls. You can start making office appointments for Thursday."

Then I walk to my personal office in the back of the office and pass Carol along the way. "Hey, Carol. Who did we send to Dr. Dimwit?" I stop her.

She laughs. "Willow's mom called about strep. Mrs. Grady, Tom Heinlein and Grace Stanley all needed to be seen. I can get you the complete list."

"Okay, have it here by Thursday. I'm going to be out."

"House calls?" She asks.

On a firm head nod, we part. I gather my roller cart of toys and pile my folders on top, then wheel the whole thing out to the truck. Jesse gets out to heft the cart into the truck bed, the files come up front with me.

Then we take off to visit my first patient.

AFTER VISIT *NUMBER FOUR*, which means five hours later—there's a lot of drive time with house calls—we stop for lunch, grabbing a couple of messy Everything burgers from the Whippy Dip and a couple orders of onion rings, which we eat in transit.

My phone rings. I pull it and answer. Elise. I assume she's calling to find out how my first day back is fairing. "Hey lady. What's up?"

"He followed me into the bathroom." She speaks low into the phone.

I shift mine on my ear to keep Jesse from hearing. "What? Who?"

"*Houdini,*" she says. Well more like hisses. I know it's her fear talking.

"Are you sure?" I ask.

"Yes. I'm with Blue at the grocery store. Gun needed a change, so we walked to the women's. Blue stood right outside the door. I don't understand. I don't know how—"

"Calm down, sweetie. Are you safe now?"

"I think so. I set the diaper bag on the pulldown changer. Then Gun and I popped into a stall to grab some toilet paper. I like to wipe those changers down with toilet paper before I use the wipes. I didn't hear anyone come in. But in that couple of seconds, *he came in*. There's a silver baby rattle sitting on the diaper bag. A piece of torn paper says H. That's all it says, just H."

"Elise, listen to me. You need to tell Blue and then you need to call your husband."

"I will," she replies. But the ways she says it, I don't know that I believe her.

"I'm serious. You don't, I will."

"*You can't, you promised.*" She's right. I did. Though, I promised when she only *thought* he was watching. The situation has escalated. Still...

"I'll give you time to tell him. But not much. I'm scared for you, Elise."

We ring off. I shove my phone back inside my jacket pocket. Then I turn to Jesse. "I promised Elise I wouldn't say anything. But since you overheard my side of the conversation, maybe you should call Duke."

Jesse nods, then fishes his phone. A second later I'm in the clear. "Prez," he says, and I can breathe again.

FIVE HOURS AFTER LUNCH, we pass through the gate of the compound, and Jesse parks the truck.

"No offense, but glad the day's over. That kind of sucked."

"It wouldn't suck if you were inside helping patients. But yes, I'm sure it sucked sitting out in the truck waiting on me all day."

"That, and not knowing what the hell is going on with Houdini. Tell Duke to call me, but I'm heading inside for a beer and maybe a blowjob."

"Wow, TMI Jesse." I laugh while I watch him walk toward the clubhouse. Houdini found my friend in a grocery store, yet I still find something to laugh about. I guess that's life.

Then I head inside the house through the utility room. Duke and Jade sit on the sofa together, well, she sits on his lap as they watch a movie. I set my purse and the files on the island, then bend to slip my shoes off my feet, stand straight, remove my lab coat to toss into a bin in the laundry and rub a kink in the back of my neck.

"Hey Doc." Duke stands, sets Jade down and walks over to me. "You look tired. Have a seat." He makes no mention of the Jesse call.

"Jade needs to go to bed."

"I'll get her down. You sit your ass on the sofa and put your feet up."

Who am I to argue? I wouldn't mind being comfortable before discussing Houdini, but first I walk over to drop down next to my girl and slide her onto my lap to cover her in kisses. "You and Duke have a good time?"

"He made me chicken noodow soup for dinnew. And biscuits. He makes weally good soup." I don't remember seeing any cans of soup in the cupboard. I guess its fine, not like she can't breathe from the preservatives. Some light sniffles and watery eyes won't kill her. I'm thankful for his help.

"Alright Peaches, let's get you ready for bed, yeah?"

"Okay," she sing-songs, bobbing her head as she skips to her room.

Before he leaves to get her sorted, he bends down to kiss me. "Honey, why don't you get comfortable. Go change into your pajamas or whatever, then I'll feed you."

Instead of answering, I hold my hands out to him so he can help me up. I peck a kiss to his cheek, pat his bottom and move down the hallway. Last night, I wore my satin nightie in honor of our first night here because I knew we'd end up doing what we did. Although I had no idea it would be as mind blowing, as life altering as he made it. Tonight I opt for comfort over sexy and pick my pink nightshirt that hangs to just above the knee. It's T-shirt material, though it's fitted and has a slightly deep V-neck. So I guess there's a hint of sexy. After I drop my clothes into the hamper, pull my hair from the bun and wipe the makeup from my face, I head back out to the sofa, stopping first at Jade's room to kiss her goodnight.

Half her bedroom from our house is in her room. Her toys. Her comforter. Her pink, princess flat screen and DVD player. "Is this what you and Duke did today?" I ask her.

My half-asleep daughter yawns. "Yeah. He said I needed

my stuff to make me feew at home." I bend down, push her hair back then place a kiss to her forehead, each cheek, her nose, and finally, her lips. Our usual bedtime routine.

"Night baby."

"Night Mama."

Duke is at the stove ladling out big bowls of soup. From a big pot. There's a folded fleece throw on the sofa now, too. I walk over, shake it out, then sit down and tuck the throw around me. And my man, bless his beautiful heart, walks over with a tray for me. On it is that big bowl of soup, a hot buttered yeast roll, not a biscuit as Jade had suggested, and a Guinness.

Egg noodles. Rounds of carrot. Dices of celery. Kale. And large chunks of chicken. "She said you made her soup. You *made* her soup." I inform him of something he clearly realizes, because he *made soup*.

"Eat honey," he orders. Then he turns to me. "Got some shit to discuss before we settle in. Know Elise called you. Smart not sitting on that, honey. Not sure what was in Elise's head not calling Blue in right away. Anyway, debriefed him. Says no man went into that toilet. Only a woman. He don't remember much about her, wasn't guarding against a woman. So now we know he's getting others to harass her for us."

"What does that mean, then?"

"Nothing for you to worry about right now. Stay diligent. Stay with Jesse. And do *not* ever fucking hesitate to call me or tell Jesse about any potential threat, yeah?"

Immediately I answer. "Yes."

"Good." He sifts his hands through my hair until it reaches the back of my head. He grips it to pull me forward, and kisses my forehead. A quick kiss. Then he drops his hand. "Eat." He orders me again, which means the Houdini talk is over.

I take a bite and almost orgasm while he watches.

"Shit, woman. You keep making faces like that, you won't get the chance to eat because I'm gonna fuck you on the sofa."

That idea has merit. After the day I've had, the day we've had, I'd welcome his fucking. But we need sustenance first.

Duke walks back into the kitchen, ladles his soup, grabs his beer and rolls, then walks back in to sit next to me, placing his beer and saucer with two rolls onto my tray. He flips the throw up, settles beside me and flips the throw back over the both of us. Though, he doesn't eat right away, pressing the remote to find another movie. A thriller new to pay-per-view that I'd been wanting to see, but with no one to watch Jade for me, I never got to see when it was in the theaters.

Only after he hits buy and the opening credits start, does he tuck the remote between us and begin to eat. When we're both finished—he'd gone back for seconds for the both of us because his soup was that good, and he'd grabbed us a couple fresh cold ones, too—when we're both finished stuffing our faces, Duke sets the tray on the coffee table and shifts us so we lay on the sofa, my back tucked against his front, under the throw. His arm draped around my waist, our heads share his other arm as our pillow.

The movie is incredibly scary, but I'm ready for him to fuck my day away. So I shift around on the sofa to face him and kiss my man. Slow and long. Slow enough and long enough for me to feel him harden.

"On your back," I order him, for once.

Then I stand and shimmy out of my panties. My night-shirt, I whip over my head so I stand buck naked in front of him. He rolls on his back. While I unbuckle his belt, unbutton and unzip his jeans, he rips off his Tee, then together, we shrug him out of his jeans so he's lying on the sofa buck naked in front of me.

Thank goodness he's hard, and has been pressing himself against me the whole time we've been watching the movie. Thank goodness women come with a self-lubricating function, because I don't have any foreplay in me tonight. So I mount him, holding myself above his straining cock, gently grab hold to position him and glide down, taking him to the root.

We both groan. I have to take a moment before I move because he's just so big. Only after my moment do I ride him, rocking front to back. Sliding up and down. Not fast tonight. Though, with every downglide, I grind hard.

Oh lord, he feels great. And he makes me feel greater when he digs his fingertips brutishly into my hips, stinging the flesh there from the pressure. Pain and pleasure. The man has mastered the art of pain and pleasure. I bite my bottom lip to keep from crying out too loud, so as not to wake Jade.

My muscles tense. The first orgasm of the night hits on one of my downward glides. He growls, digs his fingernails in harder and thrusts upward to impale me as he throbs inside me. I guess we're going rough tonight. And I'm plenty okay with that. My head falls back. I close my eyes. My body begins to shiver from his raw power.

Duke inside me is totally consuming, all encompassing. Every sense in my body becomes overwhelmed by all that's him. He won't let me come down, drawing out one climax into the next to the point that even that teeters on painful. Right when I feel close again, he flips us so my back is to the sofa. My calves rest against his shoulders, and he goes at me with such ferocity, I swear he moves the sofa with every thrust.

The shivers turn to shaking, and the shaking intensifies. I

know it's going to happen. Soon. Now. The hardest. My muscles don't tense this time, but seize up completely, all while he keeps up the thrusting. I open my mouth to scream his name, but no sound leaves. And I break apart.

Still high off my orgasm, he keeps slamming into me until I feel his neck, shoulders, back and abdomen pull taut and he buries his face against my throat, exploding inside me. He slows way down, stroking in and out a few more times before he stops moving to kiss me, sweet.

"Woman, I think you're gonna be the death of me," he says, looking in my eyes.

"No. I'm as good a doctor as I am a cook," I reply.

He chuckles, and it's such a new sensation because he's still inside me, so through our connection, I feel his laugh. I've never had that with another lover, not that I've had many of those.

This man, my man, might be a sexual demigod. And as he's managed to fuck the last of my energy out of me, or maybe I did that to me seeing as I started it, he scoops me up in his arms the way a groom would carry his bride on their wedding day, and walks us back to the master. He sets me down inside the bathroom to take care of business and is waiting when I open the door to exit. Back in his arms, he carries me to sit on the bed, folds back the blankets, scoots me over the sheets, then flips the blankets back.

After helping, he leaves the room only to come back a few minutes later carrying all our discarded clothing.

"Didn't wanna chance her waking up before us and seeing our clothes in a heap by the sofa. Hard to explain away a pair of panties."

I've never had a man take care of me, not since I became an adult and left home.

Even in the dark, the man carries himself with such power and confidence. I watch the patch tattooed on his back shift as he moves. It's the same flaming devil head as on his cut. The symbol of their brotherhood. The ideals they hold most dear. But unlike on his cut, the flames on his back seem to flicker and dance as he walks to my side of the bed to hang my nightshirt over the headboard, then tosses my panties and his clothes in the hamper before crawling back in the bed next to me.

Both still naked, he lays flat on his back and rolls me to tuck against his side with my head on his chest, arm slung over his middle and my bent knee resting on his thigh. Lying in the dark next to Duke, this is where I'm most comfortable. This is when I feel safest. And he deserves to know it, despite how tired I am.

"Thank you, Chief."

He gives his is arm around my shoulder a gentle squeeze. "For what?"

In the following silence, listening to him breathe, I can almost forget about the evils of the world outside the compound.

"For taking care of me," I say, finally settling on an answer. "I've not had a man take care of me since my father when I was a girl."

"Not even Peaches' father?"

"Especially not him."

His arm squeezes me again, but this time tight. It feels more out of surprise. "Explain," he orders.

The last thing I want is for Duke to learn how foolish I'd been when I was younger, but he deserves to know about the woman he's sharing his bed with.

I suck in a lungful of air, let it out slowly, and explain. "We met when I was in medical school. He was going for his Ph.D. in research virology. So a few of our science classes overlapped, in the sense that he was the one teaching the classes on virology.

"I thought he was smart, funny and charming, those qualities made him handsome in my eyes. Plus, he was from Ireland, grew up only a county over from where I spent my summers growing up…"

Duke bends down to kiss the top of my head. A sweet gesture to let me know he's listening and once again, that it's safe to go on.

"We had a fling for the last semester he was in our country. He told me if I found myself in the old country, to look him up. Well a couple years later, my grandmother got sick and I arranged to do my residency program over there, so I could take care of her, too.

"I looked him up. And we fell back in to how we'd been pretty quickly. But this time, my schedule kept me from being the doting girlfriend I'd been when I was a new med student. Apparently he wanted a doting girlfriend, someone who took care of him. I guess the two-way street concept was foreign to him. I could be on a twenty-four hour rotation and get bitched at because I didn't have dinner on the table for him and he had no clean socks."

"*Doc.*"

Whatever he's about to say, I cut him off because it feels too good to get this off my chest. "Forget about when I was pregnant. They had me working nights in the ER at a class-one trauma center and I was sicker than I'd ever been in my life. I couldn't keep food down, and survived on PediaSure.

"The *smell* of food kicked in my gag reflex and I'd get home dragging, and have to make him breakfast before I went to sleep. He seemed to love Jade, though, when she was born. He doted on her. Right up until the day he told me he just wasn't ready for domesticity. He needed Aiden time. He needed someone to give all her attention to him. And that he'd met that woman online, and he was moving to Australia.

"Oh, I forgot to add, my grandmother had taken a turn for

the worse and passed away two days before he left us." I laugh, though none of this is funny.

"Jesus, Doc. Good thing he lives in Australia because I'd kill that motherfucker for treating you the way he did. But then I'd give thanks over his dead body because he was stupid and threw away the best thing to ever happen to him, and I got Peaches down the hall and you in my bed. *Jesus*," he repeats himself, then bends to kiss my head again.

I'm so overcome by his words, and at too high a risk of blurting out something neither he nor I am ready for me to say, that I force myself to change the subject completely. "Will you take me on your bike?"

"Honey, this weekend. You and me are going on the bike."

"What about Jade?"

"I'll figure something. And Caitlin, don't you worry."

Don't worry. If it were only that easy.

13

DUKE

My fucking phone rings, or at least I think it rings. I sit bolt-upright for *some* reason. My woman hasn't moved in her sleep, still turned toward me, half on her pillow and half on mine. I blink my eyes and look at the clock. Three-thirty in the morning. Her vanilla smell fills my nose, and rub my hands over my face, using my fingers to swipe my hair back.

Then I hear it, my cell. It rings and lights up.

I get up, tuck the covers around Doc, and answer it.

"Better be good," I say into the line.

Tommy answers. "Sorry, Duke. I just got a call on Caity's break in. They found some photo albums, things she wouldn't have thought to look through. One of them is a baby book. Says 'My First Five Years' on the cover. It's Jade's book, and several pictures from the back of the book are missing."

"Missing?"

"Missing," he repeats.

"What the fuck does that mean?" I whisper, so not to disturb Caitlin.

"It means he has more than just one photo, and we don't know what he wants them for. So keep diligent."

Christ, gotta fight Houdini on two separate fronts now. Can't call and let my VP, Elise's fucking husband, in on any 'a it until we locate Liv because he's gotta keep Chaos from going off the rails worrying over her. Add to that, the Horde have kept low these past several months, and I don't trust it one bit. The fuse is lit—explosion is imminent. I just wish I knew how long the damn thing ran.

I sigh into the line. "I'll keep diligent."

"You gonna tell her?" he asks.

"Don't know. Keep this between us for now."

"Will do. 'Night Duke."

"Same," I say, and end the call.

I set the phone down on the nightstand, walk to the closet where I pull a pair of sweats off the shelf to shrug on, then I leave the bedroom, stopping to check on Peaches before I make my way back over to the coffee table where I'd left my cigarettes earlier today. I grab up the pack and my lighter then walk out back.

It's a warm night, black sky full of stars. Don't see that too often. I lean against the porch railing, pull a smoke from the pack and light it.

The clubhouse is lit up and the dregs of loud music reach me. Soft enough not to wake up my girls. Poor Elise and Trish. The boys must be partying tonight. I'll talk to 'em tomorrow. With each drag on my cigarette, I feel myself get a little calmer.

Why the fuck does Houdini need photos of my Peaches? What's he got up his sleeve?

A burst of laughter disturbs the quiet when a piece and one of the brothers stumble outside. I can't see 'em, but after a couple minutes, I begin to hear the grunts and moans of early sex noise.

Even though I'd love to have Caitlin let loose with me at a club party, what I had tonight, one on one time with Peaches and then a different kind of one on one, fantastic one on one, with her mama, was one of the best nights of my life. Higher on the list than the night we spent together in Nashville.

As the sex noises get louder from outside the clubhouse, I take the final drags from my smoke, snuff the still bright butt in the sand of my outside ashtray and walk back inside. I lock the door, check on Peaches once more, then head back to the bed and my woman.

When I slide in, she readjusts and groggily asks, "Everything okay? Phone call, then you left."

"Sorry I woke you. Call was club business. And I left for a smoke."

She yawns. "Okay, Chief. You'd tell me is something was wrong, right?"

My body gets tight, even though I don't mean it to. "What do you mean?"

"Just that you listen to me, but I'm a good listener, too. You can trust me. I want you to know that, that you can trust me with anything."

"Know that, honey. Nothing to trust you with right now, though."

"Okay," she says, the corners of her mouth drop, she sounds almost hurt. Fuck I gotta give her something, but I can't tell her 'bout the photos yet, not 'til we know more. Got Peaches covered. She's safe, no need for her to worry unnecessarily.

So I tell her something else, something I thought on out there on the porch. "I was never gonna have a family." I give.

Caitlin rolls to her side, elbow to the bed, chin to her hand, she waits patiently.

"Married Dawna knowing that would never happen for us. But you know, I had her, so I had enough. Loved her, Doc.

She needed me, I stepped in and took care 'a everything for her. Then one day, I didn't have her."

"Dawna was your family," she whispers.

"Yeah. She was, mean kids. After she left this world, I knew aside from my club, I was destined to be alone. And then I meet you. Maybe you'll think it's too soon for me to feel this way, and maybe it'll scare the crap outta you, but honey, with you and Peaches, I got my family."

She bursts out crying. Did not expect that reaction. She launches herself at me, her arms around my neck, she takes my mouth. I feel her tears, taste her tears.

"We're... your family... Chief." She stutters through her crying.

Giving her that, right thing to do. I hold her, her head resting on my chest and hand to my belly. Hold her the rest of the night. Neither of us speaks, and eventually, we both fall back to sleep.

The next few days go as the first. We eat breakfast together, Doc and Jesse drop Peaches off at school, I head to work, then pick her up by six. Feed her, feed Doc when she gets home and then we end up naked in bed.

Peaches loves playing out on her jungle gym. Several kids come to play with her.

Since it wasn't getting any use sitting in a backyard without a family, Peaches and I drove the truck over to their place to load up the patio set, then moved it back to my back patio. And because now we had this patio set, Peaches and I drove to the home store about half an hour away where she and I picked out a gas grill with an attached wood smoker. Huge. Burners and a prep station. Then we stopped at the store to grab some steaks, corn on the cob and a few other groceries for dinner. Finally we headed home.

Now she's swinging from one of the swings next to a little girl named Teeny. Her dad, Brutus, got out 'a the joint two years ago. His old lady has the other two kids up at the singlewide. Twins born nine months after his release.

"Another?" I ask Brutus, shaking my empty beer bottle so he knows what I mean, and stretch over to the outdoor fridge Peaches and I also picked up.

"Sounds good," he says in his slow drawl, and twists the cap from the full one I hand him. He takes a pull, swallows, then pauses. "This is the life." Brutus keeps watching his daughter play. She's seven now. Only a baby when he got sent up. "Rex was a good man, but I like where you've led the club."

Well *shit*. This comes from left field. But maybe not, when he goes on. He sounds like a man who's done a helluva lot 'a thinking.

"I can't go back. Missed the first five years of my girl's life. Made my wife a single mother all that time. Now I know the club kicked in financially, but I promised her, she sticks with me, never again. Was gonna quit the club when I got out."

Hell. My brows furrow. "What stopped you?" I ask, then take a swig from my own beer.

"You. Boss. Chaos. Brothers taking us legit with real businesses. I fix cars. I'm proud of what I do. For the first time in my life, I feel like I'm giving my girl a good role model. Boss is married with a kid. Sneak's got one on the way. And now you, the man at the top. Hooked yourself a doctor, and with that comes the privilege of playing daddy to that little girl." He pauses to take another pull. "The wife and I talked just last night. She's going to school to be a medical assistant. Something she really wants to do. So long as you keep our noses clean, we're staying. Just thought you should know."

"Glad to hear it, brother."

"You gonna adopt her?" He points the neck of his bottle toward Peaches.

"Adopt her? Never thought about it."

"Well here's a little something for you to chew on then. I were you, I'd get my ring on the doctor's finger. Adopt that sweet little girl, then give her a brother or sister and sit back and finally enjoy the good life you've created for all of us." Then he yells, "Come on, Teeny. It's getting late. We gotta go spend some quality time with your mom before you gotta go to bed."

"Awe, Daddy..." The little girl whines.

"We can come back another day."

He sets his empty bottle down on the table, pats my shoulder, then takes his girl's hand when she runs up to him. They walk out through the grass to the trailer they're staying in for the time being.

Dusk turns twilight and the first stars begin to show. I set my beer on the table and walk around the perimeter of the yard, lighting each citronella candle, twenty-four in total. Then pull my steaks from the outdoor fridge and get those on the grill.

Adopt Peaches.

The corn, I pull from the water they boiled in and toss them on the grill, too. Give 'em some nice marks.

Live the good life.

"What's all this?" Her melodic voice asks. And I turn to see that sexy woman, my sexy woman, leaning against the corner of the house, watching us. A peaceful, if not tired, look crosses her face.

And in this moment, I know Brutus was right. Don't matter we don't got a lot 'a time under our belts. This is my family, dammit.

"What are you still doing up?" she asks Peaches.

"It's Fwiday, Mama. I'm eating wiff you and Duke."

"Lips." I order her, no hello.

She smiles, shakes her head, but walks over to give me

those lips. Slow and sweet. Fuck, she tastes like strawberries again. Holding my face as she brings the kiss to its conclusion and rests her forehead to mine. She breathes out. I wrap her tighter in my arms.

"Missed you today," she says. "A patient went into labor. That's what took me so long."

It's like the woman can read my mind. Though, her showing up home wearing scrubs and a lab coat, of course I'd ask.

"Why don't you go inside and change. Then come join us."

Doc don't answer, but drags herself inside and closes the door.

"Okay, Peaches. Wash your hands. It's dinner time." She runs inside, much faster than her poor mama, to wash up.

After a few minutes, mother and daughter stroll out together, hands locked, arms swinging, matching smiles which reach a set of matching, twinkling eyes that take my breath away.

Fuck if I ain't the luckiest son of a bitch on the planet. I shake off the thought and clap my hands together. "Alright. Let's get this dinner started." Then I turn to them. "Only my girls get to sit at the table, so if you're my girl, sit."

Both my girls race to the table, a blur 'a red hair, as each 'a their ass's glide onto a patio chair.

I pull the bowl of salad from the outdoor fridge along with couple dressings Doc made. The creamy cucumber for Peaches and the blue cheese for us, and place 'em on the table.

Two ribeye and a filet for the squirt hit the plates. Corn next. Then I deliver three to the glass-top.

Without thinking twice about it, she proves why she's the best mom in the world. Before ever taking a bite off her own steak. Even knowing how hungry she's gotta be. Doc reaches over to cut up Peaches filet into tiny chunks perfect for little fingers to pick up, and dunk not in ketchup, but more 'a that creamy cucumber dressing.

Put a ring on her finger and live the good life. Fuck if that ain't the best advice I've received in years.

After making sure her girl was set, only then does she saw off a hunk of ribeye and tear it from her fork. She sighs, and rightly so. I'm a man who knows how to cook a steak.

Peaches' little legs kick back and forth underneath her chair, I know this because her foot makes contact with my shin several times.

"Boys finished your backdoor, but honey, since we brought the other families in, I need you to stay here. Now before—"

"Okay," she cuts me off.

"Okay?" I ask. "That's it?"

"Yeah, okay. Families are here. Houdini is a lunatic. We stay."

We keep eating, Peaches almost has her plate cleared when she face-plants into what's left of her dressing.

"If Peaches would be more comfortable with her room painted pink, do it. Do what you gotta do to feel comfortable."

14

CAITLIN

There's a knock on the front door.

I lay the roller down on the tray to rest in the rich, almost copper-hued tan paint the home store labeled "suede". A flat color, it looks like suede as it dries. And I pull the rag tucked into the waistband of my old sweatpants to wipe what wet paint I can from my hands while I move to answer.

Why would one of the brothers or their old ladies use the front? From the time Jade and I started staying here *all* our guests use the side entrance. That first dinner party we threw being the only exception, and really, that one is on me. I greeted our guests from the front, holding the door open to welcome them.

Paint had already dried in my hair and dried in patches on my face, seeing as before I started on the living room, I gave Jade back her pink, princess bedroom just as Duke had decreed.

Yesterday couldn't have been anymore special. I woke up to my first Saturday in Duke's house naked with him holding me, different from the rest of the mornings since we'd been here because on those days, I woke up naked and alone in bed. Those days he'd gotten up with my daughter to make her breakfast.

I stretched then snuggled even closer to him when I felt his eyes on me. Tilting my head to look at him, his silver-gray eyes smiled with crinkled lines around the corners as he ordered, "Lips."

To which I happily obliged. Long, sweet and even tinged with morning breath—delicious.

After I pulled back he bizarrely ordered, "Mouth."

Mouth? But I'd just given him that.

"Huh?" I asked, blinking several times.

"I ain't had your mouth on me since Nashville. My dick is hard and twitching, and I need you to suck me Doc. Suck me like you did that night."

So I did. But unlike Nashville, he gave me mine *while* I was giving him his.

When we finished, he kissed me deep again. Duke, I found, liked to kiss. And he was good at it. So good. Incredibly good. "Best I ever had," he whispered against my cheek, lips moved to press there.

From there we commenced showering, dressing and heading out to the kitchen where I made him and Jade my special Belgian waffles with Bing cherry compote and whipped cream.

I found it odd, what with it being almost June in Kentucky, that he ordered me to wear jeans. Since I figured Duke had a reason for that, I had. As well as Jade.

While my little girl and I were finishing the breakfast dishes, I heard a loud thump like a box plopped on the island, behind us. When I turned, I found I was close. It was two boxes stacked one on top of the other. The top one being smaller.

He handed the smaller box off to Jade, the bigger one to

me. We pulled the tops off to reveal black, leather boots for me. Sexy, flat three-inch heel biker boots. For my girl, he'd gotten her leather boots, oh yeah. Pink, little girl Harley boots.

She.

Squealed.

Who even knew they made pink leather boots?

"What's this for?" I asked. Because I knew leather boots would not come cheap.

"Put 'em on." Was his answer. "Follow me."

Both Jade and I pulled our boots on and scurried outside to join Duke next to the carport. Not next to his truck, though it was there. Or what I'd come to think of as my truck, thought that was there, too. But his Harley. Now I know nothing about models, all I know, it was a huge black and chrome monster with one of those sleek, black sidecars attached. Inside the sidecar sat a Jade-sized pink leather jacket to match her boots, and a pink helmet with *'Harley Princess'* scrawled in a pretty periwinkle script across each side.

Commence squeal number two.

He had a black jacket and helmet for me.

I started to ask when he'd done this but he shut me up by cupping the back of my head with one of his enormous hands and pulling my face in for a quick lip touch.

Without her even having to ask, when he finished with me, he bent over to give my daughter her kiss as well. She was training a big, burly, *badass* biker.

And further, he went on to pluck her up in his arms and drop her inside the sidecar where he got her situated and buckled.

He lifted me to set me on the back of the bike, climbed on in front of me where instinctively, I wrapped my arms tightly around his middle, and we spent the whole day out riding. Duke and his girls.

That brought us to this morning, early this morning. Duke got called away on some club business, leaving us to putz around the house. I got the brilliant idea to head to the home store. With Saturday having been so perfect, I should know better than to expect a carryover into today. When will I learn?

I open the door to find an older woman with gray hair but brown eyebrows fidgeting with the red leather hobo bag resting at her hip. She's thin, age undetermined, as she suffers from permanent sad eyes. I've seen these a lot in my line of work. And a general look of constant suffering about her. That, I've also seen a lot in my line of work. Sad eyes and constant suffering age harsher than time ever could.

"Can I help you?" I ask, tucking loose hair that had fallen out of my ponytail behind my ear.

"Where's Duke?" The woman asks, sharply. Confused.

"He's out on club business. *How*—did the prospects let you in?"

"They know to let me in. Who are you? Why are you —*what are you doing*?" She shoves me out of the way to storm inside. "This is Dawna's house. Who gave you permission to change Dawna's house?"

Confused now myself, I answer. "Duke…did."

"Bull. I don't know who you are, but Duke would never let some strange woman change his Dawna's house. The love of his life, this is how he keeps her. So you need to go."

Now starting to lose my cool—*hello*, redhead after all. Fiery hair, fiery temper—I raise my voice to almost a yell. "I will not leave." Although, it hurts to hear her say Dawna was the love of his life. As he's still quite alive, that would encompass all his remaining years to come. So where does that leave me in this hierarchy?

Jade comes running out from her room. "Mama, why you yelling?"

"A kid?" The strange woman asks incredulously. "Seriously? You pieces bringing kids around now? I should call child protective services, but I don't know where you live."

And that's when my beautiful preschooler, only trying to help, pipes up. "We live heew."

If a person's head could actually explode, I'd be covered in brain matter about now. Which is when I put it together, that this is Dawna's mom.

Phone in hand, she punches a contact and puts the device to her ear. After what I would guess to be about four rings, no hello, she shouts into the receiver. "There's a whore in your house painting over Dawna." She pauses. "You get her gone, Duke. She's ruining Dawna's home, everything she built for you." More pause. "No. I'm not going until she does."

"Please don't talk like that in front of my girl." I order through gritted teeth. My lip pulls thin as I try my best to check my temper.

"Shut up, whore." She replies.

Not good. "Jade, your room. Close the door."

My girl knows me, hears the seriousness in my voice and does what I ask without hesitation or complaint. Then I turn to the unwanted bitch standing in the living room. "I told you, don't." I shove her chest, not super hard, but hard enough for her to take a step backward. "talk." And I shove again. "like that." A third shove. "in front of..." Shove number four. "my girl." The last shove she stumbles out the door and down the stoop.

"Duke will hear about this." She threatens me.

"Fine. Let him hear it outside because you're not coming in again."

I shut the door in her face to a whole lot of, "You can't

treat me like this." Repeated over and over. Loud enough that I start to think she'll strain her vocal chords, and I will not be doctoring her after she called me a whore. Loud enough that I wonder why none of the brothers at the clubhouse have come to check out the situation.

Finally, she shuts up so I go back to my painting. Besides, if the woman bothered to pay attention, the color I picked freshens up the room, is manly enough for a guy like Duke *and* compliments the chintz in the fabric on the sofa.

The last wall just about finished, her screeches pick up again. The front door opens then Duke strides in, a smug, still loud but not screeching any longer woman on his heels.

"Look." The woman points to the paint on the wall. "She's ruined your house. Dawna's vision gone."

"Mamie, that's enough." Duke grumbles at the woman. "Doc, why'd you paint in here?"

What? He told me to. "You said to do what we had to get comfortable."

"I told you to paint Peaches' room."

"Peaches? Who's Peaches?" The Mamie woman shouts. "Duke, I want her gone. This would break Dawna's heart, seeing her home destroyed."

"I hardly destroyed it," I defend myself. "The walls needed a fresh coat of paint. Duke?"

"That's not something a whore decides," she fires back at me. "That's for the lady of the house to decide. And you aren't her."

"*Duke?*" I repeat myself, questioning why he hasn't spoken up in my defense. When he says nothing, only stands with his hands on his hips, I decide it's time to stick up for myself. "I told you not to call me a whore. I'm a doctor. I worked hard for my degree, my practice. And that *never* included spreading my legs for money."

"*Doc*," he says sharply. "That's Dawna's mom. Show her

some respect."

"Show… show *her* some respect? She called me a whore. More than once and in front of Jade… You know what, never mind." Then I stomp to Jade's room. "Come on sweetie, we're leaving."

She hardly has her sandals on before I'm grabbing my purse and heading out the back. Duke swears and calls after me, but I just found my place. And it's sure not where I thought it was. I tug Jade by the hand over to the clubhouse, but make her wait outside by the wall because who knows what we might walk into?

"Jesse?" I call. "Is Jesse here?"

"Here, Doc." He strolls out from the kitchen with a sandwich in his hand. "Whatcha need?"

"I need to go. Now."

"What? Why?" he asks around a bite-full of food.

"Duke's mother-in-law showed up and doesn't like me being at her daughter's house."

"Fuck."

"Duke took her side."

"*Fuuuk*." Jesse repeats low and slow, for effect. But he grabs his keys from his pocket and asks, "Where's Jade?"

"Outside. I didn't know if it was blowjob hour or not."

He snickers around a mouthful of food. "Let's go."

Back out the front, I grab up my little girl in my arms, and we walk over to Jesse's truck. Since he'd been put on Caitlin guard duty, he'd put a booster between us for when Jade came along. Though, the middle doesn't have a shoulder harness, only a lap belt, so I sit in the middle and put Jade by the door.

My phone rings four different times in just the short while I've been collecting Jesse. They've all been Duke. Duke can kiss my ass. Or keep on kissing his mother-in-law's.

"Where we headed?" Jesse asks.

"I don't know. We haven't eaten yet. Let's take Jade to Fun Zone."

"Caity, that's forty-five minutes away."

"Then just drop us at our house."

He glares at me. Then, turning out of the compound onto the street running along the fence, he decides, "Okay. Let's do Fun Zone."

God, I love this kid. I lean my head on his shoulder. "You smell good," I tell him. "Not interested in older women by chance?"

He laughs a hearty laugh. "Not as much as I want my patch." But then he drops a sweet, almost older brother type kiss to my forehead.

Jesse only took his eye off the road for a brief second on an empty country road.

It happens so fast, like a scene from a movie. I'm suddenly aware of a black SUV. I'm suddenly aware when it comes out of nowhere to ram the tail end of Jesse's pickup. Jesse swerves, but gains control. Then he speeds. The SUV speeds up behind us, ramming us again. I pull my phone from my pocket to call for help when we're hit for a third time and I drop it.

I drop it.

Jade is screaming, "Mama!" and she's crying so hard as Jesse fights to keep control. His truck is old and can't outrun the SUV which rams us a final time. Jesse swerves a final time, hitting the shoulder and skidding on loose rock.

We skid right over the steep cliff edging the right side of the road, our side of the road coming down the mountains. The truck hits tree after tree until it all becomes a blur of green. Then we hit solid. With only my lap secured, my upper body is thrust forward, slamming my head into the dashboard.

That's it.

15

DUKE

"Mamie, shut the fuck up." God, the woman won't give me a chance to think. And Doc taking off, *shit*. What did I expect? I told *her* to stop. "Why'd you come here? You know you're supposed to call first."

"Who was that woman?" She says woman the same way someone might ask, "Who was that monster?"

I didn't want her to find out about Doc this way. "She's *my* woman, Mamie. She and Peaches are mine."

Dawna's mom stops her ranting dead, mouth gaping open. Fucking stunned. "No… no. The pieces. You promised, Duke. You'd stick with the pieces. You'd never replace my girl. She was the love of your life. You said that, over and over. At the hospital, you told me… her body was still warm when you made me that vow."

"We both know it wasn't fair for you to even ask 'a me. To spend my life alone."

"*No.*" She throws her hands to cradle her head as she cries. "What's not fair is my baby cold in the ground. If not the one you made to me in that hospital room, think of the vow you made to my daughter."

"It's not fair that someone as beautiful as Dawna left us so early. But I fulfilled my vow to her. 'Til death do us part. Death parted us, Mamie. I met Doc. And fuck, I ain't even told her yet."

"Told her what?" she asks, but damn if it ain't accusatory.

"That I fell for her."

Mamie gasps, then drops to her knees crying. I feel bad for her, but I need my family. My girls. While she continues to cry on my floor, I pull my phone and attempt to call Doc yet a-fucking-gain. And yet a-fucking-gain, it goes straight to voicemail.

"Come on, sweetheart. Get up." I help Mamie stand and lead her to the sofa. She ain't a hefty woman by any means, but when she plops down on the cushion, the whole damn thing lists to the right and hits the floor. Both legs on that side broken off.

I think it happened when I fucked Doc on the sofa that day. We went at it so hard we moved the damn thing. Mamie starts crying harder. But I think it has more to do with the fact that I'm gonna have to replace the sofa now. And that's another piece of her daughter's life gone.

After getting her a bottle of water from the fridge, I start to leave my mother-in-law on the broken sofa to head up to the clubhouse.

"Stay 'til you're composed. Then I gotta ask you to leave. Sorry, but the way you treated Caitlin, can't have you in my house, she gets home."

"Home? No. This... this is my Dawna's home. *Your* Dawna's home."

"Don't gotta explain myself, Mame. Not gonna."

Then I turn to leave, but she stops me. "You forgot."

That stops me.

"It's today, Duke. Four years ago, today."

I squeeze my eyes shut, reach inside my pocket to pull my

pack of smokes, but remember I don't smoke in the house anymore so I don't light up. "Living life again is the best way to honor her memory."

"Aren't you lucky you can do that," she says snidely.

"No. It ain't luck. It's Doc. Peaches." And that's all I'm willing to give, because I gotta make this up to my woman.

Finally outside, I light up and suck back the calming effects of the nicotine while I walk across the forecourt to the clubhouse. I walk inside and look around.

"Where is she?" I ask Hero. He's the brother sitting closest to me.

"Who?" he asks.

"Who the fuck you think? *Doc.*"

"I haven't seen her."

"Anyone seen her?" I call out to the other brothers.

Blaze walks from the back hallway. "She grabbed Jesse, and they took off. Don't know where."

Immediately I press his contact and wait… and wait…

Fuck. The punk don't answer.

I hang up and call again.

Still nothing. That little fucker not answering *my* calls? His president. Oh hell no. Demote his ass back to puke duty.

"I'll be in my office." I grumble to the brothers and stomp off. At least she was smart enough to take her guard.

Behind my desk, I get caught up in paperwork. A shit-ton of it. Though I keep calling my woman, and she keeps ignoring my calls. So I decide fuck it, she has to come back eventually. Then bury myself in work.

Finally, *finally*, my phone lights up. I grab it and answer, not bothering to look at who's calling. Four hours since she took off. Four fucking hours. "Talk," I order.

"Duke, man." Sneak. "I'm about three miles from the compound."

The severity in his tone makes my body seize up tight. "And?" I prod.

"Something didn't look right. Skids, broken branches. Got out to check, Duke, I think… is Jesse there?"

Suddenly I can't breathe. But I gotta breathe. Hand to the back of my neck, I force in the calming breaths that won't come on their own. Then I stand and walk back out to the common. "Jesse back yet?" I bellow to any brother who's in earshot.

"He's been gone for hours, prez." That was Blaze again.

"Call him."

Blaze quickly pulls his phone and calls. "Not answering," he says.

"He ain't answering." Don't mean to, but my answer comes out a bark at Sneak. "What you got?"

"Jesus," Sneak mutters. "Prez, it's got to be his truck at the bottom."

"Blaze, call 9-1-1," I order. Running. "Three miles out. Need ambulance. Jesse went off the cliff." Then turn to Sneak. "On my way."

On my bike, I speed up the road. It don't take long for me to ease up on Sneak and Trish pulled off to the shoulder. Sure enough, that's the ass-end of Jesse's truck sticking up about halfway down the gully. I try Doc's cell again. Voicemail.

I'm about ready to lose it when the shrill of the ambulance sirens and flashing lights cut through the dim lighting caused by the canopy of tree coverage. Along with the ambulances, two police cruisers speed ahead. Behind the racing ambulances, one of Ellis Auto's big towers.

After another forty-five minutes, we get the truck back onto the road. Too steep to send rescuers down, our only option was to harness up one of the officers experienced in repelling to repel down and hook the winch to the rear axle. Once we hauled the truck up, we could get to the occupants.

Oh fuck. *Oh fuck.* We all hear it, the desperate low, painful whimpering of a child. They wrench her door open. The paramedic extracts my Peaches. She looks okay, but'll have to be checked out.

Not thinking, I run over to her. She sees me and her eyes go big. "Duke," she cries. "Duke. Duke. My mama. Duke... my mama." Fat tears spill down her cheeks, and it takes everything in me to keep standing. I reach her, my Peaches. One medic begins checking her. The other goes after Doc.

They lay her, my woman, on a gurney. She's gray. That peaches and cream skin drained of color. They check for signs of life. *Signs of life?* "We've got a pulse, but it's weak." The medic calls and both load her into the back of the ambulance.

The other medics for the second ambulance have to wait as Sgt. Tommy Doyle and one of his officers cuts the driver's door with a power saw. They pull Jesse out with much less haste. Not a good sign. I hold Peaches' hand and force myself to look.

No.

God no.

This can't be happening.

Half of Jesse's face is hanging off. And Peaches had to see that for how fucking long? They lay him flat on the road and one of the medics drapes a wool blanket over top of the kid, covering his head.

The ambulance with Doc speeds off. Once they give Jade the all clear, I take her into my arms and hold on tight. She hasn't stopped crying. I ain't cried since Dawna left this earth, but dammit, if those tears don't streak my face.

"Duke..." she cries. "Mama..."

"I got you, Peaches. Shh... I got *you.*" My voice hitches on the *you.* Shit I need to get my shit together.

Sneak walks up to me, staring down at the blanket covering Jesse. He places a hand to my back. "Go," he says.

Though that one word comes strangled. He pauses. "Get to the hospital. I'll stay, call the boys. We'll take care of things."

No. I can't let him do that. Jesse is—*was*—my responsibility. Fuck. *Fuck.* "Appreciate it brother, but I'm the president. He's mine to take care of."

"Not now. Now you're a man who has a woman in bad shape. Take care of your family, prez. Consider this a mutiny."

My little Peaches, her tears still flow just as strongly, though she's silent now, snuggling closer against me. And I know Sneak is right. My club, my brothers are important, but I got a woman who needs me, who don't get how much I need her because I was an asshole. Time to take care of my family.

"Thanks, brother." I tell him. "We're heading out now."

He nods, acknowledging me, but never takes his eyes off the blanket as he pulls his phone from his pocket. Knowing he's got this, he has my back, I walk over to my bike and have to peel my girl from the death-grip she has on me to set her into the sidecar. Only now does she make any noise again, a whimper.

"We gotta get to the hospital, Peaches. Check on your mama. But I won't leave you. Promise." She lets me put the helmet and jacket that I kept stored in the sidecar on her, then buckle her in. After a final glance toward Sneak and Jesse's lifeless body, I climb on my bike and thunder down the mountain to get to my woman.

After a ten-minute drive, with my girl in my arms, clinging, her arms tight around my neck, I stomp through the sliding glass doors into the emergency room of County Medical, the same hospital where Peaches stayed after her accident.

This part of the emergency room ain't like how it is on all those medical dramas on TV. A bunch 'a people, some look sick, some stressed, some downright worried sitting in chairs, watching the silent television, checking their phones or stopping anyone in scrubs who looks like they might be able to help 'em.

I walk up to the check-in desk.

"How can I help you, sir?" The receptionist asks.

"Ambulance just brought an injured woman in. Caitlin Brennan. I'm her—" Fuck, how do I identify myself to this bitch? Quick-like I decide on "Man, partner. We live together. This is our daughter."

Compassion spreads across her face. "Sure Mr.—"

"Ellis," I tell her.

"Mr. Ellis," she repeats. "Let me see what I can find out." Then she starts typing on a keyboard. "Take the doors to the left. When you get there, I'll buzz you through. Go down that hall and turn right. There, you'll find the surgical check-in. They'll be able to tell you more."

"*Surgical?*" I shout, making Peaches jump. So I try to calm myself down at the same time taking off in a run toward the doors on the left. The buzzer rings before I reach it, letting me yank open one of the doors without waiting, and continue down the hallway. A right turn leads me to the surgical check-in station, just as the receptionist directed.

Out of breath and needing a cigarette real bad, I rush out to the nurse. "Caitlin Brennan?"

"You're family?" she asks.

"Yes."

She begins typing on another keyboard, but I'm met by a deep voice, "Mr. Ellis? Is that correct?"

I turn to see the doctor who treated Peaches. "Yeah, that's right."

"Karen," he says to the nurse behind the desk. "This is Dr. Brennan's partner." Then, to me, "Not married, right?"

"Not yet."

He nods his understanding. I finally have time to think, with it all happening so fast. But what Brutus said to me about wifing Doc and giving Peaches a brother or sister makes sense. Knowing that things might get complicated, what with medical decisions and Caitlin being a single mother. I could lose Peaches, too. Her parents would never let some tattooed, Harley riding man raise their grand-daughter.

I follow close behind as he leads me to the surgery waiting room, which holds much fewer people, and tells me he'll be right back.

My turn to nod. About five minutes after he leaves, three women and one baby storm the waiting room. Elise, Trish and Maryanne Doyle, Tommy's old lady, come right at me. Tears and puffy faces.

"How is she?" Elise speaks for the group.

"Don't know yet. The doctor went to check."

"Right," she says back. "Beau, Chaos and Blood are on their way home. I hope you don't mind." She walks over to one of the chairs to drop Gun's diaper bag. "But I stopped by your house and grabbed a few things for Jade. Change of clothing, because she'd been stuck in that truck for a while."

It's not 'til she holds up the bag that I realize my girl smells of piss. Shit. She'd spent all that time soaked in her own piss.

Loosely, I come out of my head enough to hear her still talking. "...her blanket, for comfort and her tablet and headphones."

I clear my throat. "Thanks sweetheart." And reach my arm to cup her neck, I give it a squeeze so she knows what this means to me.

"Hey Jade, sweetie. You want me to change you?"

"No," my girl cries. "Duke. My Duke."

Elise starts to speak, but I stop her. "It's okay. Do this at home."

"You *do*?"

That gets a laugh. "Sure. She's my girl, ain't you Peaches?"

"Your gurl," she whispers against my cut.

Slowly, Elise sets Gun's carrier down on the seat next to the bag and begins to riffle through it, pulling a pair of cotton shorts, little girl panties and a T-shirt to hand me.

I nod my thanks. "Come on." We walk out into the hallway across from the waiting room, the hospital has a men's, women's and family restroom. For obvious reasons, I walk straight for the family restroom where Peaches only lets me set her down long enough to help her change.

She waits as I pull several paper towels from the dispenser, wet them and douse them with soap, then hand them to her. And like I always do, because I don't know the laws with this stuff, I turn around for her to wash her legs and other parts, and change into her clean panties.

"Done," she whispers.

I turn back, help her with the elastic waist that always gets turned under, help her with her shorts and T-shirt, and hold my arms open for her to climb back up. No saving her other clothes, I toss them in the trash then head back to the waiting room.

We only just get back inside, when the doctor, his badge says Talmouth, walks in. "Can I speak with you? He asks me, real business-like. Too business-like.

"Just a sec," I answer, then look down to Peaches. "Gonna set you in the chair. Elise brought your blanket and tablet. We'll put your princess on."

"No."

"*Sweetheart.* Gotta talk to the doctor. Okay?"

She sucks on her bottom lip, but after a moment agrees. "Okay."

With Peaches in the chair next to Gun, I tuck her blanket around her legs, then let Elise take over setting up her movie so I can find out what's going down with Doc.

"Talk to me," I order Talmouth.

"She's in surgery to repair tears causing significant internal bleeding. And she's sustained a concussion, ruptured spleen, which they're also removing, from where the seatbelt cut across her abdomen. Two fractured wrists from where it looks like she covered her head, and hitting the dashboard caused her left lung to collapse."

My hands rest at my hips, I drop my head. "Fuck."

Talmouth pats my shoulder. "It could've been much worse."

Don't I know it. I think of Jesse. One seat over and she'd be gone, too. Or instead.

"We'll let you know when she's out, then once they move her to a room."

Moving a hand from my hip, I rub the back of my neck. "Thanks," I tell him, then turn to the women.

"How is she?" Trish asks.

"Hey, you should head home and rest." I offer up first. "She's still in surgery. We're gonna be here a while." The woman is pregnant. She's gotta take care 'a herself.

"I'm good." Trish insists. Brother's done good choosing wives. "What are we looking at?"

I run down the list Talmouth gave me for the women, Caitlin's friends. All three listen while holding back tears. So I repeat Talmouth's other words. "It coulda been worse."

"You want me to bring Jade back to the compound? I'll sit with her at your house." Though Elise's offer is kind, I need my girl safe with me.

"Nah, thanks. I got her."

"That little girl is lucky to have you. Will you keep an eye on Gun? I'll run and grab some coffees. What would Jade want?"

"No soda." I clear my throat, thrown from Elise's comment. "Her mom don't like her to have soda. Juice, or chocolate milk or even a hot chocolate if you can find some ice to cool it off."

She smiles, which I choose to ignore because that woman thinks she knows me so well. And what she thinks she knows is probably right. Boss has got his hands full with that one.

I wait next to a sleeping Gunner until his mom returns with a tray of coffees, then I move to the chair on the other side of Peaches. She seems content to watch her movie, but leans her head against my arm as she does. Damn if that little girl don't carve out another large piece of my heart with such a simple act.

These Brimstone old ladies—even by association since Tommy ain't a brother—prove just how brimstone they are, settling in for the long haul with me and Peaches.

My brothers' text updates on the Jesse-accident situation periodically, and inquiries as to Doc's condition, others. After several hours, a doctor different from Talmouth, walks into the waiting room.

"Anyone here for Caitlin Brennan?"

"Here." I stand, walking over to her.

"We've moved her to a room. She's sleeping but you're welcome to go see her. Follow me."

"Hold on." I order. She pauses, but don't look happy about it. I don't give a fuck what she's happy about and pluck Peaches and her blanket from the chair, up into my arms. She still has her headphones on and tablet in hand. Only then do we join the doctor.

Out of the corner of my eye, I see the other three women,

Elise with Gun, of course, scramble to follow us. And I should wait for 'em, but I got to see my woman.

To say it's a shock to see her laying unmoving, eyes closed, only slightly less gray than when they pulled her from the truck, fuck, that's the understatement of the day. Guess I figured once they stopped the bleeding, she'd pink back up. Well, as much as Doc pinks without embarrassment.

Seeing a woman I care about looking lifeless in a hospital bed, it could be four years ago. "*Fuck*," I whisper, stumbling a step back, held up by three other amazing women.

Maryanne lifts Peaches from my arms as Trish orders points her finger toward the door. "We got her. Go have a smoke."

16
CAITLIN

Since Jesse had no family, the brothers arranged for him to be cremated. We've all gathered today up on a mountain bluff overlooking a valley. It's a beautiful spot to hold a memorial service. It's the best we could come up with right now, seeing as Houdini is still out there somewhere.

The Lords have a tradition, one last ride for a fallen brother. They'll sprinkle his ashes along the open road. Freedom in death. But as Houdini *is* still out there somewhere, neither Duke nor the other brothers would leave yet. So Jesse's final ride will have to wait until it's safe for them to leave us women and children alone.

Not that I have the right to be here, Jesse would still be alive if I hadn't dragged him out of the clubhouse to take me and Jade to Fun Zone. All Duke's pain, the new lines formed around his normally bright eyes, the tired weariness that accompanies him even in his sleep, all my doing. And I'd know, since I left the hospital sleep hasn't been my friend. I lay in bed at night and watch him struggle.

So much struggle. So much heartache. I woke up for a few minutes what I assume was that first night in the hospital or it could have been any night as I'd stayed unconscious for two and a half days. That night, Duke held my hand. His eyes were closed, head downcast, but even in the dark, I could see his pain. *Feel* his pain. "You fucking owe me," he'd whispered. "Today of all days, let her be okay."

I'd never seen a man so broken. Part of me wanted to squeeze his hand, to let him know. But the casts on my wrists felt awkward and he looked like he needed to be alone with his thoughts. Then, I passed back out so quickly, it had probably been good that I didn't.

They waited the week for me to be released and the second week convalescing at home, before holding the service. Duke helped me dress this morning, a simple black sundress. Trisha showed up to help with my hair and makeup, seeing as with two broken wrists, I'm pretty much useless.

All that's left of my friend, that beautiful man, rests in an industrial strength cardboard box. No chairs except for the one Duke brought for me and Sneak brought for Trisha. Elise leans against Boss, who holds their sleeping son against his chest.

I have my arm around my girl as she stands with her head resting on my shoulder. Duke stands before all of us, a pillar of fortitude for the men and women gathered today. As he begins to speak, stoic emotion filling his words, I feel myself begin to shut down.

Back erect in the seat, as I continue to hold my girl, dark shades cover my eyes. Duke's voice washes over me. The words become a jumble of sounds. When he moves from the front of the gathering, I'm the first to stand, move my girl back a step, because no matter how much she wants me to hold her, I'm still weak and recovering, and slowly walk over to the urn where I place my hand and whisper my apology.

An apology, which will never reach his ears because he's dead. Gone.

My daughter whimpers as she trails along behind me. She knows we're all sad, and she feels his loss. Jesse was her friend, but death is a hard concept for a child as young as Jade to understand. I wish to any god that would listen, that she didn't have to understand it now.

I'm heartsick.

Though being the president's old lady, the brothers and their women won't see me cry. It's a time to show strength, even if I don't feel strong. Others follow me up to the urn. They also try to engage me in conversation. That I can't handle right now, and excuse myself and walk back to the truck with my daughter in tow.

Once secured in her booster in the backseat with her blanket, I turn on a movie for my little girl. None of it comes easy with two casted wrists, but this is the least of the penance I deserve for taking that beautiful life.

Jade and I wait until the last of the mourners has moved to a bike or truck, and Duke slides in the driver's seat. He tries to take my hand as he drives us toward the compound, but I pull away, clasping my hands in my lap so he can't try again.

Neither of us speaks.

When we reach the house, he parks and moves to get Jade. I don't even tell him thank you, walking into the utility room through the main living space, down the hallway into the master where I immediately head to the bathroom and lock the door. Only then, only then do I allow myself to cry. Sinking down to my knees, I close my eyes and let the sobs rip through me.

"*Jesse.*" I cry to no one. "I'm so sorry. I'm so, so sorry. Please... *please...*" I beg him, though I don't know for what.

Forgiveness? To have this all be a practical joke? A nightmare? "I'm so sorry..." I continue to cry.

The doorknob jiggles and there's a soft knock. "Doc?" Duke calls. When I don't answer, he knocks harder. "Doc, honey let me in."

No. He'll only try to comfort me. I don't want his comfort.

A couple minutes pass. The doorknob jiggles again and then the door pops open. Duke, my Chief, looks haggard as he bends to pull me up. His touch almost stings as he tries to hold me.

"No." I ball my fist and pound on his chest. "Don't touch me. We killed him. *We did*. I took him with me, but you took her side." My accusation comes out a yell as I pound on his chest again, needing him to hurt as badly as I hurt. "You took her side. Now Jesse's dead. *I hate you*." I used both fists now to pound, and he doesn't attempt to stop me, taking everything I throw at him until there's nothing left, and I sag against him.

Then his arms wrap to hold me.

Scooping me up like a bride, he moves us to the bed and lays me down, spooning against me. No space between us. Between the crying and still recovering from my surgeries, the tiredness engulfs me. My wrists throb bitterly, and I'm achy all over from the exertion. My skin pulls especially tight along three incision marks. I can only hope my insides have healed enough to not reopen.

Hitting him was stupid. For so many reasons.

"You might hate me, honey," comes his gruff whisper. "But somewhere along the way, I fell for you. It's my fault. I shoulda told Mamie to shut the fuck up right then and there. *Fuck*."

God, I'm such a bitch. The way he's taken care of me, of

my daughter while I recover. What a terrible, heartless thing to say.

"No." I sniff, then whisper back, "I don't hate you. I could never hate you Duke." I sniff a second time. "I just hurt so badly, I needed you to hurt too. I'm sorry. He was just…. He was like the brother I never had, you know? We spent so much time together, and now he's gone. What am I supposed to do?"

"You lean on me," he answers without a hint of hesitation. "Just lean on me. I've got you." And he does have me. His arms wrap even snugger around me, his body practically cocoons me. But if I allow myself to fall into his protection, I just might break down again. And my head hurts too much to cry anymore. Which leaves me only one option, to change the subject.

"Any leads on the black SUV?" I ask. Monotone. Business-like. Drained.

"Houdini's gonna die," is his only response.

Eventually exhaustion carries me under. Thankfully, I don't dream. A welcome reprieve from the heartache to heal, even if just for a night. When I wake, Duke's side of the bed is cold. Jade plays with her Barbies scattered all over the rug on the living room floor, and Hero sits on my blue jean sectional watching a program on the television.

How had my sectional ended up here?

Before I can ask, Hero beats me to it. "Since Duke's sofa broke, we brought it over this morning. You want some coffee?" He asks.

Coffee. Yes. I look down at my feet, and that's when I realize how I must appear. Still wearing the black sundress from yesterday. My hair and face must look a fright. "Yes, please." I answer him, then turn for Jade's bathroom.

Sure enough, mascara tracks have dried in streaks down

my face and my hair, a frizzy mess, sticks out all over from the once pretty bun.

Using one of Jade's moisturizing wet wipes, I scrub at the makeup until I can pass for human again. And I'm able to pick out the hairpins holding my disheveled bun in place. But the dress, I can't do the zipper. And I need help with the shower.

"Where's Duke?" I ask when I make my way back out to the kitchen where there's a steaming mug of coffee, sandy blond, on the island. I raise an eyebrow at Hero. "How'd you know?"

"Before he left, he told me you like the crème brûlée, and it should be sandy blond. So I guessed." But I'll note, he doesn't tell me where Duke is.

"You draw the short straw?" I ask, then.

He cocks his head, face wearing his puzzlement.

"Guard duty," I finish.

"Volunteered." He counters.

What? "Why on earth would you do that? Jesse's dead."

"And that would be why. You and Jade need protection. I don't have an old lady, but if I did, I'd hope a brother would step up to help protect her when I couldn't be around. And our prez has enough to worry about. So here I am."

"Elise loves you," I blurt. "She says if she hadn't met Boss first, that she'd have gone stalker over you."

He laughs at my assessment of the situation. "Yeah, so she's said. But as she did meet Boss first, and those two are head over heels for each other, I won't get my ass handed to me for you saying that. Did she tell you before or after you and Duke hooked up?"

"After. When I told her I had a crush on…" I exhale slowly. Bringing his name into the conversation hurts. "*Jesse.*"

His face falls, and we both remain quiet for a minute

before I voice what needs to be voiced. "I should leave here, shouldn't I?"

"Excuse my language, but *fuck no*. Duke needs you here. I wasn't around when his wife was alive, but from what the brothers say, you've changed him. Given him back something he was missing in his life."

Of course, I open my mouth to dispute him, but am once again cut off by a sexy biker.

"And before you argue, one thing we know about Houdini, if he's got a taste for you, he'll hunt you down. Learned the hard way with Liv and Elise. Especially Elise. Your ass needs to stay put where we can protect you. None of us knew how he was gonna strike, so he took us off guard. That was his one chance. One."

"But maybe—" I protest.

"One, Caity." He cuts me off.

Because I know he expects me to, I nod once. Though the jury is still out if I exactly believe him or not. I mean, weren't they already supposed to be vigilant? So how did he take them off guard? Yet somehow now I've got a psychopath after my daughter, and he tried to kill us.

And if that isn't enough reason to grab my girl and run away, to a different continent if necessary... or have a nervous breakdown, hell maybe just be out-of-it drunk for a month or two, there's yet another problem to deal with as a result of this hopeless situation.

"I'm going to lose all my patients," I tell Hero, holding up my casted wrists so he gets the gist of what I mean. But it's not just that. After having to take that week off after Jade's injury, I was back for a week before the accident, and my subsequent week stay in the hospital. And still recovering, I haven't been cleared to go back to work. Not that I could with casted wrists.

"Wouldn't bet on it." He offers with a knowing smile as

he rounds the island, mug in hand and stops in front of the coffee pot. He pours himself a refill, then turns to lean his bottom against the edge of the counter, feet crossed at the ankles and an arm across his stomach. With the other, he lifts the mug to his lips, takes a sip and winces because it's hot coffee, then goes on. "Not if all the flowers and cards dropped by the front gate or all the casseroles from those brave enough to approach Duke mean anything."

To prove his point, he leans over and pulls open the door to the refrigerator. The completely full refrigerator. Every shelf stacked with glass or aluminum casserole dishes. Then to really drive his point home, he opens the freezer.

"Those are all from—"

"Your patients." He cuts me off. "My count, you and Duke are gonna be eating tuna noodle casserole and lasagna for a year." The jerk laughs as he shuts both the refrigerator and freezer doors, and then resumes his spot against the counter sipping hot coffee while I stand stunned into silence.

My patients aren't mad that they have to deal with Dr. Misogynist-who-doesn't-do-house-calls again? And for who knows how long?

"Jesus, Caity. You look constipated."

So Hero's a hot young biker who works a tight pair of jeans like a workaholic, could easily grace the cover of a romance novel and has a smile that could induce an orgasm just from aiming it at a girl. I walk over to him, over my stupor, and knee him in the boys. Albeit, my movements are slow and choppy due to my injuries and thus easily defendable. Thus, causing no pain except for maybe the one in his side from laughing at me.

"Mama," Jade calls over to me. "Can I pway outside?"

Bad mom award. With all the heavy and latter not-so-heavy tête-à-têtes happening this morning, I forgot my girl was sitting in the living room, probably soaking up every bit of our conversation. "Sure Princess Jade, we can go out back. But first, you have to help Mom unzip her dress. I need to take a shower."

Jade jumps up to help me but is stopped by Hero. "Sorry. Breakfast first, then shower." When I roll my eyes at him, he holds his hand up for me to stop. "Duke's orders. He said you'd argue about eating, but I wasn't to let you out of the kitchen until you ate something. So sit your ass down, and I'll fix your breakfast."

Breakfast? Is he serious?

Jesse *is dead*, while Jade and I walk around with big, neon targets painted on our backs inviting Houdini to take his best shot. My man left me alone in bed, cold and casted, to go off doing God knows what, which means it probably has to do with the accident. Although, no one will explain a god dammed thing to me about the case. Do they have any leads? Are they planning a counterattack? Would it be safer for me to take Jade and visit my parents for a few weeks?

Because, I will repeat, Jade and I have big-freaking-neon, Houdini-inviting targets on our backs.

And they're worried about breakfast?

I love that these men want to take care of us. Though I could live without the not listening to me because I don't wear a patch or because I have a vagina, part. I don't have the strength to fight it out today, which leaves me one choice. "You and Jade eat anything you like, but I'll just have some yogurt and fresh fruit."

17

DUKE

We'd lucked out, though we didn't know we needed to luck out. But shit, I ain't looking this particular gift horse in the mouth. The Department of Fish and Wildlife had motion detection cameras hooked high to several trees around the area, tracking the habits of some endangered bat. The cameras automatically snap photos every couple seconds when movement's detected.

They contacted us this morning because in the distance on several of their photos, beyond the bats, they captured a car running Doc and Peaches off the road the morning we ended up in Nashville. Because Tommy Doyle's police cruiser is visible, and he knows better than to keep me in the dark concerning anything having to do with my woman or Houdini, we both got calls. That is, they called him. He called me.

So now I'm standing in some stuffy office with ugly brown carpeting and even uglier nineteen-seventies utilitarian office furniture—ironically with no view of wildlife in sight—of some environmentalist, perusing grainy black and white photos.

"You gotta be shitting me," I whisper when I spy exactly why they called us. This DFW officer would have no reason to understand the significance. He just thought he'd been doing a good deed, calling us in after an apparent hit and run.

Except, except the hit and run ain't about some punk kid texting and driving as Doc had initially suggested. It's a black-fucking-SUV. A black SUV matching the one that killed Jesse.

Enlarging the picture, we're able to recover a partial license plate. Tommy leaves to call it in in his official capacity. I call Blood.

My gut physically aches. Houdini, that asshole targeted Doc and Peaches. *My girls.* But what's his angle? Why Doc? Why fucking Peaches? She's just a kid, for fuck's sake.

"Can we make out the driver?" Blood asks me.

"'Fraid not. They're grainy black and whites. All we can tell is that the guy's hair ain't black or dark brown. He's got a beard. Which last time we saw Houdini, he had not black or dark brown hair and a beard."

"Not a lot to go on, prez."

"You've worked with less."

"True that. Anything else?" he asks.

"Just get me something to catch this fucker. He won't walk away breathing again."

"On it," Blood answers, then hangs up.

There ain't anything I like less than feeling helpless. I felt helpless with Dawna's cancer. Now this fucker messing with my woman, with my little girl. My family. After all this time, all these years, I got me a family and he's trying to take 'em away from me.

"Thanks for calling." I bite out to the DFW officer as he hands off a manila folder to Tommy, shoot Tommy a chin lift to let him know I was out and then leave them to it. Tommy will call with any more. Me, I gotta shoot.

I mount my bike freed from the sidecar, and as I'm about to spark it to life, my phone rings. It's my second in command. My right-hand man, Boss. "Blood call?" I ask instead of hello.

"He did. But not why I'm callin'."

My body goes tight. What could have gone wrong now? "'Sup?"

"Wanted to make sure you're alright."

Well that got me. "What do you mean?"

"With all that's goin' on. Jesse. Caity."

Don't usually make this kind 'a small talk with anyone. Well, except for Doc. But she's Doc so it's different, but I find myself answering him honestly anyway. "Don't know how you did it with Elise. We were with you, going through it right alongside you. But it's different when it's your woman."

"Sure as fuck is," he returned without hesitation. "It was the worst. And I'm still scared, though I don't tell her that. But he could decide to come back after her with more than notes and flowers. Or Gun and that rattle. I'm gonna be honest, I hate that he's goin' after Caity and Jade. But I'd be lyin' not to admit I'm relieved that for now, he's not comin' after *my family*. And I know that makes me a dick. Because I don't want him comin' after yours either."

That comment should piss me right the hell off. But he's right. Had Dawna been alive, despite hating Houdini going after Elise and Liv, I'd have felt the same way. Which makes me a dick, too. Boy, ain't that some shit to think about? And I do, pausing, not speaking.

"*Shit*," he mutters into the line. "You're pissed."

"Actually, no. At all. Because that'd be me, situation reversed. Just didn't have a family to feel that way about when it was going down with Elise."

"So what now?" Boss asks.

"Heading to the range. I gotta shoot."

He feels me. When we get the chance to take Houdini down, I wanna be the one to put a bullet in his brain. I want it *my eyes* he stares into when he takes his last breath. For Jesse. For my family. And for that, I have to be on my game. No chance that my bullet will miss the target. No fucking chance.

"Meet you there," is all he says before hanging up.

My brothers.

This is club life.

This is what people on the outside don't get. Why I stuck with it after my dad got sent down on weapons charges. After my uncle, and then my blood brother and all the club brothers bought it from war with the Horde, why I took my place as president. Why, in the face of losing my wife, I didn't renounce my club. Because when shit goes down, and life is full of shit, we need people we can trust at our backs. And even if I wasn't the president, those men would always have my back.

Only now, after shoving my phone back in my pocket, do I let the bike rumble beneath me, and ride away.

SHOOTING with Boss was exactly what I needed to let loose. We didn't talk, just kept emptying round after round into the targets. Couple of hours we stayed. Yeah, I'm gonna be ready for that son of a bitch, Houdini.

Afterward, we headed back to the clubhouse. Now Boss and I, longnecks in hand, sit at the bar in the dark room. Not long ago I'd have been a willing participant in the scene unfolding all around us.

Not often we lose one of our own. Not since the full-on war with the Horde decimated both clubs. Over what? Drugs? Fucking meth. Always someone willing to smoke, inject or slam it. Kept our pockets fat. Though fat pockets didn't help my uncle or my brother, Rex, or half the damn club. Didn't give us the time to properly mourn our fallen brothers.

At least, even though not a fully patched-in member, Jesse'll get his proper sendoff—eventually. And the brothers can mourn him or celebrate him or hell, just celebrate still being alive, tonight.

The clubhouse is loud, at full potency for music and inebriation. Metallica pounds through the speakers. And with all families barred tonight, the Pieces and Hot Mamas fuck brothers on the sofas and suck cock down on their knees. Sly, for his part, has Vicki-Lee bent over the pool table, pounding her ass while Blue chalks up his cue and takes another shot.

Our parties don't usually get this carnal out in the open, but with the amount of alcohol consumed tonight, it happens.

"You miss it?" I ask Boss, tipping my bottle out to the room to indicate the debauchery before us.

"Not one damn bit. You?"

"Nah," I answer, honestly, and take another pull from my beer.

We both laugh and shake our heads.

"And she's healing, so it ain't like I can even go down on her. Doctor's orders. She can't bend to go down on me, either." Why I feel the need to share, who the hell knows? But I keep spewing this crap. *Sharing* my *feelings* like I've grown a freaking vagina. Fuck, what's that woman done to me?

"How she dealin'?" he asks, levity gone. "With all that?"

"Best she can, I 'spect. We hit a rough spot after the memorial, but she didn't stay mad for long. Yelled at me, got it off her chest. Burned out as fast as she ignited."

"Bodes well for your future."

"Everything about her bodes well for my future."

"So you gonna marry her?"

"You know, you're the second brother to ask that." I laugh again, this time the humorless kind, at him and myself.

The sound of a cue ball cracking against another catches our attention. Both Boss and I look over in time to see Vicki-Lee rear her head back and hit Sly in the jaw as she lets loose a high-pitched moan, the same moment Blue sinks the solid red.

Do not miss it.

"I'm out." Boss drops his bottle back on the bar top. "Gonna go fuck my wife now."

"Yeah," I reply. "Gonna head home, too." I stand then set my bottle down. "Oh, and Boss?"

He turns to me. "Yeah?"

"Thanks, brother."

He dips his chin then walks away. I'm not too far behind him. Since no family allowed inside right now, and that means babies that cry and make your dick go soft, Elise and Gun are with Maryanne Doyle. They'll stay at their own house tonight, then be back here tomorrow when Boss hits work again.

While he mounts his ride, I veer left toward my home and my woman.

18

CAITLIN

"I just don't know how I'm supposed to stay." I tell Hero out of the blue after walking back out from Jade's room, down for her nap. We'd ended that line of conversation earlier before fresh fruit and playing outside. But that doesn't mean I'd stopped thinking about it. Quite the contrary. Leaving here, getting away from Houdini seems all I can focus on.

When he crosses his arms over his chest and glares at me, I continue. If for nothing else than to defend myself. "That truck came barreling around the bend, Hero. Like he'd been waiting to see us leave the compound."

"We figured," he replies, dryly.

"No." I protest as I sit down on the sofa and turn to rest my back against the arm, pulling my knees up, and squeeze a tan and blue striped throw pillow to my chest, curling around it like a rollie pollie bug. "You don't get it. He's watching me specifically. I've been thinking on this. Doesn't it seem odd I get run off the road? My house gets broken into. And then we get run off the road a second time in only a couple of weeks? Whose luck is that bad?"

"I've been thinking that all along, Caity. So tell me why it means you should leave when we've already established *why you shouldn't*." Hero cocks his brow and waits for me to continue.

"I told Tommy I thought it was probably someone texting and driving. But that's not what happened. I'm sure of it. Jade was with me both times. She's his target. The rattle incident with Gunner just proves it. That asshole is going after Lords kids." My eyes water, though I manage to keep the tears in check.

Hero pulls his cell from his pocket after it had chirped with a text, then he looks at me. "Oh shit. You gonna cry? I can't handle crying."

"No, I'm fine. Deal with your text."

But he doesn't text back as he starts to walk out of the room with his phone to his ear. "Blood." I hear him before he disappears to the laundry room.

This is not good for so many reasons. Because it means Houdini has been in town, he's been watching more than just the Hollisters. To run me off the road, he had to have watched Duke take me to get to an injured Jade. Watched as he stayed all night at the hospital with me. Watched him bring us home, and when he brought bags laden with groceries over to my house. And watched when Duke took us to Nashville.

We'd been watched by a madman and never knew. Not until he'd broken into my home. I hate my daughter being the Guiney pig for Houdini's next dastardly plan, but I can't help think it was good Boss had been out of town. Otherwise he could've gotten to Elise again, or baby Gun.

Before he leaves my sight completely, Hero pops his head back in the room. "Just don't do anything stupid, okay? Shit went from bad to really freaking bad when Elise took off. Boss was a mess. And we haven't seen Chaos in... how many months? I don't even know anymore. You're a strong woman. If you weren't, you wouldn't be the president's old lady. Stick, Caity. For all of us, but mostly, for him. Stick." Then just as quickly as he'd shown back up, he's gone.

Stick? Could it be that easy?

No. It can't. Because at the end of the day, he doesn't have a daughter targeted by a psychopath. I have the daughter targeted by a psychopath. Duke loves Jade. I know he does. But he's not her father. He's never made any promises or declarations of his future intensions toward her. Or me, for that matter. He hasn't asked us to move in with him permanently, only to stay until the other families went home.

God, my head is so messed up.

No time to stew on that, though. Not when the man himself strides into the kitchen. He's the handsomest man I've ever laid eyes on in my life. The kind of handsome that sucks you in and forces you to reveal all your secrets. He's the most dangerous kind of handsome there is.

Gruff, gritty, rough around all his sexy, impossibly strong, tattooed edges. Yet he has the softest heart of any man I've ever been with. And the way he looks at me, with so much warmth, he makes it hard to consider leaving.

"Hey honey," he says. But the honey cracks and he has to clear his throat. My heart beats erratically in my chest. "Quit looking at me like that, or I'm gonna fuck you so hard on that sofa, we'll end up breaking it, too."

Defiantly, I continue to stare at him as I have been, taking up the challenge. Because I want him. I want him so badly my entire body vibrates with need. When Duke and I connect, I feel safe. I feel alive. Nothing in the world can get to me. To Jade. When Duke slides inside me, I'm home. And right now, with my head a mess and my emotions prickling my skin, they're so close to the surface... Corny. I know, I know it's corny, but there's no place like home.

"Right," he murmurs. Then, lightning fast, he's across the room. Hands on each of my forearms, he pulls me up off the blue jean sectional to press his lips against mine. Gliding his tongue over the seam back and forth until I open for him. Taking a long pull, he drinks down my kiss as if it's the coldest beer in the cooler on the hottest day of the year.

But right when I'm ready to find home, he breaks the kiss, closes his eyes and rests his forehead against mine. We're both breathing heavily. I couldn't catch my breath if I tried.

"W-why did you stop?" I ask. Shock and disappointment thick in my words and meaning.

"Ain't been cleared yet. Still healing."

I wince because I know how much it cost him to stop. Because there's a physical ache in my heart that only Duke can ease when we're connected. And I can feel his very prominent erection pressed against my belly.

His next words undo me. Make me not care if every healing wound rips open.

"God woman, I wanna fuck you so bad. Fuck you 'til you know down to your bones how I feel about you. But that's why we can't. Because I won't ever risk hurting you. Never."

I close my eyes and breathe him in. It might be lame, but at least it's an attempt to calm my raging libido.

"But I will lay with you," he finally whispers, taking my hand as he leads me inside our bedroom. He pulls off his boots, drops his cut on a chair, pulls back the comforter, then gently helps me down onto the bed, pulling me practically on top of him after he settles. In a last move, he flips the comforter back over the top of us.

In his arms, in his bed, the decision is made. I have to try to stick. Unless Houdini takes that option away completely, I have to stick.

OVER THE NEXT couple of days we'd cleared out three-quarters of the refrigerator and freezer space by sending lasagnas and tuna noodle casseroles up to the clubhouse and over to some of the families living in the singlewides. The thought was nice, but no one needed *that* much pasta.

Funny how those, in retrospect, could be considered the good 'ole days. The trail for Houdini had run cold. Or if Blood had found something, Duke hadn't relayed it to me. My fractured wrists seemed to have healed nicely, so much that I could probably get the casts off, but I hadn't been back to the doctor yet to have it done or be cleared for any other activity.

I'd been living on pins and needles since the accident. As a result, I've become somewhat of a shut in. If we don't leave Duke's house, then my girl stays safe and no other man has to needlessly die on our behalf. One of the prospects or Hero does grocery runs whenever I need something.

Though, I got an earful the time Hero had to buy my tampons. Christ, what is it with guys and tampons? It's a fact of life. Women have periods. Period. That didn't stop Hero from coming at Duke. "I don't care you're my president, you're fucking her, you buy the damn tampons."

Since we haven't left the compound, Jade has gotten to know everyone really well. She's in her element, entertaining compound kids on the jungle gym that *her Duke* bought for her. There are perks to being considered the stepdaughter of the man in charge. In the hierarchy of kiddom, my little girl falls squarely at the top. She's outside pushing her friend Teeny on the tire swing when a news story on the television catches my ear.

I walk over to stand in front.

Breaking news. Child abduction. Thornbriar.

What?

At the same time, I jump as a loud beep sounds from my

phone, startling me. An Amber alert. The picture of a little girl fills the television screen. I've looked on that face so many times since Jade and I moved here. Her name is Laynie Briggs. Even if it wasn't plastered across the screen, I know it. She's Jade's age. Goes to Jade's preschool. And further… worse… all Jade's teachers joke almost every time they see me that little Laynie Briggs could be my daughter's twin.

Her twin.

There, of course, are some differences, since they share no common DNA. But the two little girls really do look startlingly similar.

And then I hear Jade's small voice. "Why is Waynie Bwiggs on the TV, Mama?"

What do I tell my four-year-old? How do I explain that her classmate has gone missing without scaring her to death? Without giving her nightmares? Without taking away her childhood innocence?

Oh god. My chest feels tight. I can't catch my breath. A girl from my baby's school was abducted. A girl from my baby's school, who could be her twin, *was abducted*. As hard as it may be, I fight to calm myself.

The news breaks to a press conference, and I see her scared, grieving parents begging for the safe return of their daughter. Parents who happen to be patients of mine.

The kids see the pediatrician next door because they want *'what's best'* for their children. They only eat organic because they want *'what's best'* for their children. And they enrolled Laynie at Jade's preschool, the same as they'd done their other kids, because they wanted *'what's best'* for their children. And yet, it didn't turn out to be best for Laynie. One of the few places she should have been safe, one of the few places… and she wasn't.

Days like today I wish my grandmother was still alive.

She'd know what to do, what to say to calm my nerves. Hearing her sweet voice always had that effect on me.

I could call my mother, probably should call her. But I don't know if I want to handle my mom's attitude when I tell her the man I'm living with is the president of an MC. Furthermore, she'd be all over me learning that said sexy biker has a murderous psychopath after him and his brothers.

Forget about telling her about the accident and its connection to the psychopath. She and my father would be here next plane out to drag me and my daughter back to Arizona, where they'd moved years ago for the dry climate after my dad's asthma got worse.

But he'd be willing to risk his health for my safety. My daughter's safety. Especially my daughter's safety. And he'd waste no time going off on me and my poor life choices for the rest of my life. Then he and my mother would want to set me up with every polo and khaki pant wearing, golf-loving, church going man they meet.

I don't go to church or enjoy golf, and never, never have I entertained the idea of a stuffy polo/khaki man in my life. Even Aiden wore jeans and button-downs untucked, with the sleeves rolled up. Casual class.

Clean-shaven. Expertly coiffed. I shudder at the thought. I know the kind of men my parents would gravitate toward. If he had any tattoos, they'd probably be one of those unfortunate tribal's preppy frat guys get on drunken party nights.

So not me. I doubt a man like that could engulf my whole body with his sheer size. I'm tall for a woman.

Those kind of men are fine for other women. I'm sure making them perfectly happy. But I've never desired a man like that before, nor do I see myself with one now.

And I'm quite sure no other man could fuck me so hard we'd break the sofa.

No other man would ever be Duke Ellis.

So no, I won't be dialing my mother.

Without a second thought, I pick up my phone from the coffee table and press Duke's contact. After three rings, he answers. "Everything okay?" he asks. It's loud. Like maybe he's by a busy road.

"I'm scared, Duke."

His voice grows hard. "What happened?"

"A little girl from Jade's class. She was kidnapped today from the playground."

I hear his sharp pull of breath when the words hardly finished leaving my mouth.

"She looks just like Jade. No joke, they could be twins."

"Okay," he says. And I appreciate the way he tries to soften his voice. "I'm on my way. Peaches with you?"

Like an idiot, I nod. Realizing he can't see me, I speak up. "Yes. She's right here."

"Good. Right. Make sure she stays in sight, yeah?"

"Yes, Duke."

"So talk to me."

Jade and Teeny get tired of me not answering Jade's question about Laynie and walk off back toward Jade's bedroom. That's a good place for them. Inside her room, inside the compound.

"Doc?" Duke prompts again.

"We can't have sex yet." Yes. That is what I blurt out into his ear, completely non sequitur to the conversation at hand.

The bastard laughs.

"It's not funny. The doctor hasn't cleared me for physical activity yet. You rub up against me every night. I'm horny as hell, and I don't want some expertly coiffed, golf-loving, polo and khaki-wearing, tattooless man."

"Pardon?" He's still laughing.

"Nothing. I suppose you're busy and need to finish up with what you have going on. I'll let you get back to it."

"Never too busy for you. Now talk to me. What was all that?"

Melting from his confession. He's never too busy for me. In response to all that, I lose control of my faculties and tell him what I promised myself I wouldn't. At least not yet. "I'm horny, I'm too scared to leave the house, and I think I love you."

Silence. Complete humiliating silence.

I'm saved from having to endure his reaction when my other line beeps. "Someone is calling, I have to go." Then I swipe to answer the other call.

Trish would be in class right now. Maryanne, at the law firm. That leaves one friend. "Hey, lady," she says softly in lieu of a hello. "How are you today?"

I'd likely still be grieving over Jesse and know I'll go back to it once my fear abates but for now I answer. "Did you get the amber alert?"

"No. Just got out of the shower. Why?"

"Do not go anywhere, but if you do, *do not* take Gun without more than one escort."

That gets her attention. "What's going on? Cait, is Jade alright?"

"Yes. It's—uh—not Jade."

She breathes out heavily.

"But," I continue. "It's a little girl from Jade's school." My chest feels as if it's being squeezed by a giant hand again. Tight. Painful. "She could be Jade's twin."

"Did you call Duke?"

"Yes. I hung up on him."

"What? Why?" she asks, well more like screams as she laughs. Yes, laughs. As if anything I've said is funny.

"Because I have to break up with him."

"Sweetie, I know he made a mistake with his mother-in-law, but you can't really be still holding—"

"That's not it." Do I have the guts to repeat it out loud again? "On the phone, before I hung up, I blurted out..."

Her voice has calmed. "Blurted out?" She draws out the out to make it five syllables long.

"I blurted out that I love him."

She giggles. "That's what I thought you were going to say. What'd Duke say?"

"Nothing. He said nothing. Not even thank you. Just let the words hang between us through the humiliating silence. Then you called, and I hung up on him."

"I can't believe you hung up on Duke," she says, getting her giggles under control.

"It was for the best."

"Well girl, I'm married to a badass biker who I'm going to call right now because I don't want to deal with the fallout from him finding out about that little girl later. But I can tell you, they don't take kindly to being hung up on."

"Yeah..." That's all I have in me to reply.

Laynie Briggs is missing.

Laynie Briggs. *Is missing.*

So what happens when he finds out he took the wrong girl?

19

DUKE

My woman stands in front of the TV with a hand on her hip, staring down at the cell in her other hand. Her hair flows long and curly down her back. Those same navy blue, cotton shorts that she wore the first time I tasted her, barely cover her ass again now. And she's got on one of her ribbed tanks that hugs all her curves. Damn. Fuck. Shit, she's hot. She's so god damned hot my dick don't just twitch, it throbs as it struggles to point north in my jeans.

But she also hung up on me. Drops that bomb over the phone, then hangs up. When you tell someone you love them for the first time, you don't do it over the phone where they can't hold you, hug you and kiss the ever-loving shit out of you.

I hesitate only a second before plowing in like the bull I am, the bull she waved the red flag in front of. She turns around, and I only have a moment to take in the fear on her face before I'm crushing my lips against hers as my arms wrap her in the same crushing embrace. Strawberry. Damn, her lips taste great. And the vanilla scent.

She whimpers against my mouth. I pull back only enough to bury my nose in her hair. Fucking great hair. Silky and soft.

"Don't ever hang up on me again," I order. Knowing she's going to argue, I kiss her again. And when she opens up to me, I slide my tongue inside her mouth, meeting hers half-way. She grips my cut in each fist, pulling me closer so my erection rubs against her belly.

"We can't," she speaks against my lips. "Jade and Teeny."

"Don't give a fuck if the pope is in the next room. You asked for it." I grit out. She wraps her arms around herself protectively. I know one sure-fire way to make her feel better. "You're a doctor. Will I hurt you?" She knows what I'm asking and shakes her head. "Good." Then I pick the woman up, one arm around her back and one under her knees, and head to our bedroom.

We've been laying in the bed for a while now. I don't think I fucked all the scared from her, but at least she's calm and seems contented for the time being.

It wasn't easy taking her the way I wanted to, knowing our girl and her friend were just down the hall from us. Doc kept her face tucked against her pillow most of the time to stifle her moans and out-and-out shouts of pleasure when I done something she particularly liked. But the end result was worth every challenge we went up against. The way I came so hard I thought the tip of my dick might explode in the process.

Now, with her tucked up under my arm, her head resting at my shoulder, hand lightly resting at my ribs and her bent knee laying against my thigh, now I can fully revel in the knowledge that my woman loves me.

She said it. And she ain't taking it back. Ever.

"*Wow*," Caitlin says dreamily, casually moving her hand from my ribs to draw patterns in my chest hair with her finger.

I snicker. Hell yeah, wow. Every lay tops the last with this woman. Don't think I'll ever get enough of her. Hope I don't.

"What was that?" she asks between dropping kisses against the skin of my collar.

"That was my response to you telling me you love me."

"Oh... Well in that case, I love you Duke."

"Give me a minute to regroup, then I'll be happy to oblige you, woman." I give my arm around her a little squeeze. She giggles. "But just so we're clear, remember I said it first."

"You did not," she protests, lifting her head to glare at me.

"Sure did. After Jesse's memorial. You said you hated me. I told you, you might hate me but I fell for you."

Doc lays her head back against my shoulder. "You said it first," she mumbles her amended statement.

No matter I want to spend the rest of the day naked in bed with my woman, that's the fantasy. Reality strikes at the sound of a small knock against our bedroom door and a, "Duke, I'm hungwy."

"Be out in a minute, Peaches." I call out loud enough for her to hear me. She can't get in, I was smart enough to lock the door, but still, there's always that lingering fear that she could.

I roll out 'a bed, walking over to the closet to pull a pair of sweats. Caitlin watches me the whole time. Then after I'm clothed, I walk back over to kiss her. "Get dressed. I'll make those cheese-stuffed burgers I promised. I'll even make the steak fries you love so much."

After twenty-five minutes of prep work, Doc, Peaches and even Teeny sit at the table devouring burgers. Plate in hand, I'm just about to join them when there's another fucking knock. This one, from the outside door to the utility room.

The pounding on the door pisses me off more today than

it probably would any other day, but fuck, can't a man be left alone with his family for just one day?

Just got done making love to my woman after a couple months dry. We need the day to decompress.

Need it.

Some nut sack kidnapped a girl who looks like my Peaches. Don't know how much more Caitlin has in her before she breaks. And not one man would blame her if she did. Becoming a part of my club put her and our girl in danger.

That don't mean I'll stand by and wait for it to happen. Part of her keeping sane comes with decompressing, spending the day doing normal shit.

And yeah, I was smart enough to lock the door when I got home. Though now, I got to walk over to answer it, setting my plate and beer down on the island and move annoyed, swinging the door open at the same time grumbling, "*What?*"

It's Sneak and Boss. Boss speaks first. "Blood got a lead on that fuckwad who took the girl."

"Seriously?" I ask, amazed at the man's skills, and happy he's on our side. It was just after I got Doc's call I sent him on the trail. He's been out hunting Houdini's location since I saw the DFW photos, but a missing child takes precedence. Will always take precedence.

Between Blood, whose name's short for Bloodhound because he can sniff out any trail, and Sneak, who can slip in and out 'a just about anywhere without being noticed, ain't nothing and no one can't be tracked down with enough time.

"He's there now. Rundown trailer off Rabbit Hole road." Sneak offers up.

"Right, be out in a sec," I answer, leaving the door open but turning to make my way back to Doc.

"Everything okay?" she asks. Burger halfway down from her mouth, she'd just taken a bite. There's a drip of cheese sauce I'd rather lick off her chin than have to tell her I got to run.

Her eyes, round, concerned, wait for me to answer. Fuck it, I swipe the cheese from her chin with my thumb then suck it off. Her cheeks pink. I love how a woman her age can still get pinked cheeks from such an innocent act. Though between me and her, we both know it was far from innocent.

Knowing how much she wants me to lean on her, too, I decide on honesty without too much honesty. "The boys got a lead. Need to head out." Even though I raise my eyebrow at her, waiting on the inevitable questions, she proves once again why she's perfect president of an MC old lady material, and nods. She just nods. That's trust. She trusts me to keep her safe and get the job done.

Cupping the back of her neck, I lean in as I pull her forward. "Lips," I whisper. When our lips fuse, even for that briefest moment, all her emotions, all she feels for me shines bright through that kiss. Goddamn if it don't mean the world.

And after I pull back, immediately move to kiss my Peaches. A pat on Teeny's head later and I leave to meet my brothers at the bikes. But we don't leave on the bikes, taking a windowless, white, nondescript van that we keep parked with a tarp covering it until there's a use for it. Registered to a geezer a couple counties over who happens to have died a decade ago. Ain't no one tracing it back to us. Our one remaining carryover from the old life.

She might be ancient, but runs quiet. And quiet is exactly what we need.

Before we get too far out, I call Hero to go look after my girls but he's at the parts store a couple towns over. It'll take a few for him to get to them. "Hurry," I tell him.

They're in the house at the compound. A prospect on the

gate. My girls will be fine until he gets there, and I have to focus on what's going down now.

Half hour later, we roll up to the wooded lot off Rabbit Hole road. The pocked dirt drive has more holes than dirt, so we choose to hide the van in a thick of trees and walk the rest of the way, about two hundred yards back, up to the trailer.

Blood steps briefly from behind a shallow gathering of bushes and Black Walnuts for us to locate him, then steps back right away. We silently make our way over to him.

"He's in there," Blood says.

"Any sign of the kid?"

He shakes his head. "No. None. That's got me worried."

"Okay, boys. Surround the bastard. Count of three, we go in hot. He ain't getting away again," I order.

Head nods from my brothers. Two of us on the front door, and two on the back. I shout, *"Three."* and we plow through the doors, guns raised. The bastard has a band tied around his arm and a syringe dangling from the bend of his elbow. Reflexes not near fast enough, he scrambles for his gun, but we overtake him quick and easy.

Face pressed to the dirty, moldy carpet. Or what's left of the dirty, moldy carpet, I shove the barrel of my gun against the back of his head. "Where's the girl?"

The bastard is so fucked up on whatever shit he injected into his veins, he giggles, not even like a little girl. It's too high-pitched and maniacal. A giggle of pure evil.

Boss punches the side of the blitzed bastard's head. "Where's the fuckin' girl?" he shouts. But Houdini's too out of it to answer. And I'm too frustrated to control my temper any longer. I flip him around to hold him by the neck of his dingy, ripped T-shirt so he can look me in the eyes before I put a bullet in his brain.

"*Fuck.*" I grumble to the same sentiment from my brothers. It ain't Houdini. Never seen this guy before in my life.

"How'd you mess this up so bad?" I turn on Blood.

"Didn't. This is the same guy who ran Caity off the road. He's the one took that little girl. The trail was good." He defends himself.

"Prez," Boss starts. Placing his hand on my shoulder. "He obviously hired this one to take the girl. Probably paid him with whatever he shot up his arm. A druggie like him, even with pictures, wouldn't have known he got the wrong girl."

He sent somebody in for him. Knew we been keeping an eye out for Houdini. That rat-bastard sent someone else to run Doc and Peaches off the road. The only thing I can guess is that the guy had eyes on Caitlin, but not our girl. Reason for the break in. Since getting her that day didn't work.

But where the hell is that other little girl, the one he thought was Jade?

The pit of my stomach drops, becomes nauseous as the rest 'a my gut clenches tight. I got a bad feeling.

Jesus, I got a bad feeling.

Then the situation goes from bad to worse when the junkie begins to seize in my arms, foaming at the mouth and everything. His eyes roll back in his head and he stops breathing. No telling what kind 'a Hepatitis or HIV this guy could have from sharing needles or whatever. Keeping him alive or trying to keep him alive ain't worth risking any 'a our lives from trying to revive him. Not that you could catch that shit from mouth to mouth, but no. Not happening.

Right in front of our eyes, the guy dies clean away.

Dead.

I let the body drop. "Check the place, see if there's any signs that kid's been here."

The brothers fan out, but in the end, come back with a load 'a nothing. Not one fucking trace.

He never brought her here. So then where the hell is she?

We leave him face down on the floor. It's more consideration than he deserves. Anyone comes across him this far out, they'd see the syringes and needle. They'd assume the truth, that the guy overdosed.

On the way back down the mountain, me and my brothers save Sneak, who's driving, are on the phone putting out feelers to all our contacts around the county, reminding them to keep their eyes wide open. Though, since we didn't find her at the trailer, chances ain't good we'll find the kid still breathing.

We're about twenty minutes outside the compound when my phone rings. Doc. She's freaking out. So much I can hardly understand her.

"Calm down, honey," I tell her. Her fear puts me on edge. "Talk so I can understand."

"It was on the news. They found her, Duke."

"That's great."

"*No.* You don't get it. They found her *dumped behind the garage* of the daycare. *He killed her.*" Voice breaking on *her*, she sobs uncontrollably.

"Almost home."

At the same time I disconnect, Boss gets an alert on his phone and turns to the group. "Fuckin' A."

20

CAITLIN

I wanted to stick. For him. For us. But Houdini killed Laynie Briggs. He killed her. Jade and I need to get out of here. He won't get my daughter. Her poor parents, sister and brothers. How can you ever be right again after something so heinous happens to your family?

With Hero out doing whatever he does when not guarding us, I jump on Duke's laptop and navigate to a travel-booking site. As I scroll, I see Nashville has a red eye to Ireland leaving tonight. I calculate it in my head. *Three hours for us to get to Nashville. The allotted three hours to get through security… if we packed now, Jade and I could be at my family home by lunch tomorrow.*

But only if we pack now.

My cell phone rings. Unknown number. Sydney, Australia. I cannot deal with him right now. For some reason I swipe to answer. "Aiden, I sold the locket. It's gone. So leave us alone." Then I hang up, not giving him the opportunity to turn his vitriol my way, and toss the stupid phone onto the coffee table.

I should have let it go to voicemail the first time. He calls and hangs up four more times. Four times.

Duke will be so angry with me. For talking to Aiden. For walking away. But he has to understand I'm not leaving him. I'm saving my daughter from ending up dead behind a garage. *No. No. Quit second guessing yourself, Caitlin.* I let out a breath and walk over to the island to grab my purse.

Credit card in hand, I click to purchase two tickets to Ireland. Though, once my confirmation pops up, it hits me that our passports are at the rental house with all our other stuff. And I know I'm not supposed to leave without a guard, but he can't know we're leaving anyway. Because I know for a fact Hero would try to stop us.

While Jade plays in her room, I walk into mine to grab our bags from the closet, pack quickly for myself, then head out to the laundry room to pack Jade's clean clothes that I hadn't put away yet. We won't be gone forever. If she needs more than this, I'll just have to buy it for her.

After loading the bags into Duke's truck, I go back in to get my daughter.

"Teeny, sweetheart. Jade and I have to leave. So you need to head home, okay?"

"Sure, Dr. Brennan." Teeny stands, but bends forward to give Jade a hug. "See you tomorrow, Jade." She won't. But she doesn't need to know that.

"By Teeny." Jade hugs her back. "Where we gowing, mama?"

"Out," I tell her. "Now get your shoes."

She does without asking.

At the last minute, I grab my cell up and shove it into the pocket of my jean shorts before heading outside. Then after getting my daughter buckled in to her booster, I back out of the spot and turn around. There are always bikes and trucks coming and going, so the prospect guarding the gate doesn't give Duke's truck a second look. Now it comes down to waiting. Because he's not going to let me out without a guard with me.

But then... but then a busty young woman in an electric blue tube top drives up in a little convertible. It's older, but cute. Red. Her over bleached hair looks windblown, but the way the prospect glares hungrily at her, he doesn't seem to mind. No, he seems more concerned with something else as he looks behind him nervously, and then opens the gate to let the convertible in. With his head, he motions for her to drive a little ways in. She climbs in the backseat. He climbs on top of her.

And that's it. The damn horny prospect forgot to close the gate.

I shift the truck into drive and slowly ease off of the Lord's compound. We're free. Pointing the nose toward town, Jade oblivious to everything watching her princesses on her tablet, we take road after road until pulling into the driveway in front of our rental. It's been forever since we've been here.

Climbing out, I reach in the backseat to extract Princess Jade and set her down on the pavement. When I open the front door to the house, I expect the place to smell of dumpster. But it smells clean and fresh, instead. Duke taking care of me. He had someone clean out the trash and food. Damn it, I'm going to miss him.

We climb the stairs and walk to my pre-Duke bedroom. That's where I have the passports. In a safe in the closet. Since I don't know how long we'll be gone, I collect our other important papers, shoving them in my purse. This whole time Jade keeps quiet, trusting me. Trusting that I know what I'm doing.

There's nothing to grab from her room. She and Duke had moved it all over to his house, so we move back downstairs, and I stumble back a step. Blocking Jade with my body.

"H-how did you find us?"

"I have my ways, *Caitlin*." He says my name with such distain it almost makes *me* start to hate me. "Now let's go. The truck. That fucking biker has eyes on the SUV. But we'll still have to ditch for another vehicle as soon as possible." He's very handsome with his in-need-of-a-cut, light brown hair dusting around his ears and that full, trimmed beard. Too bad his soul is pure evil.

"Mama," Jade whimpers from behind me. "Who's dat man?"

"What?" He sort of snarl-laughs. "You haven't talked about me?"

"No." I tell him defiantly. "I try to shield her from evil."

Before I can raise my hands to block the swing, his fist cracks against my jaw. His fist cracks against my jaw. I'm stunned. My mouth begins to pool with blood. I've never been hit in my life.

He leans around me. "All in good time, sweetheart. All in good time. Now walk."

Jade begins to cry but every time I open my mouth to comfort her, blood dribbles down my chin. Instead, I hold my hand out to her. She takes it, and we begin to walk. I need to keep him calm enough to give me time to formulate a plan. If it weren't for the gun he held in the hand opposite the one he punched me with, I'd grab Jade and make a run for it. But the manic look in his eyes screams that he'd have no problem killing me, my girl or any samaritan I get to help us.

I lift my girl to put her back in her booster when he rips her from my arms. She cries harder. I cry harder.

"You drive," he orders me. Reluctantly, I climb behind the steering wheel. He climbs in the passenger side with my girl in his lap. The gun he keeps pointed at her temple. "Try anything stupid, and she dies. Got me?"

Tremors shake my body from head to toe. My palms sweat profusely. I think I might vomit. Because of this, I don't answer him fast enough and he strikes out, backhanding me along the cheek. Pain burns from jaw hinge to behind my eye socket.

"I asked you a question, bitch. Got me?"

Slowly, I nod and swallow down my tears and blood. "Got you," comes out garbled, and I back out of the driveway.

We take the back roads out of town, his attempt to keep a low profile. But it makes me nervous. He doesn't want me taking the highway. No highway. Back roads. He's taking me somewhere no one will find our bodies. Or my body. Because I still don't know what he wants with my daughter. Why he'd come after her?

Winding up the mountain, eventually he has me turn onto a dirt drive pocked with deep potholes. We bounce around the cab, my head hits the window. Jade he keeps a firm hold on, even though he jostles on the seat. We pass black walnut trees and thick brush. Finally we reach a decrepit singlewide. It's been abandon for years. It has to have been, the place looks uninhabitable.

"Park," he orders. I pull up along the blunt end of the trailer and cut the engine. There's a small window, so probably a bathroom. Not a useful bathroom because I doubt the place was hooked up to a septic tank, but a bathroom nonetheless. "Out," he commands next. "Keys on the seat."

I do as directed. But while he is distracted by my daughter, I casually slip my hand into my front jeans pocket, remembering the phone. Fingerprint ID unlocks the screen and from memory, I hit the call app, hoping it's Duke my cell connects with, as his was the last call I made, but am willing to take whomever. And then I get out, leaving the keys on the seat.

Jade in his arms, he carries her with the gun still pointed to her temple, me out in front. There's a wretched smell coming from the trailer. And I know that smell. Death. In this Kentucky heat, a body would begin to draw insects rather quickly.

"Please, don't bring her in," I beg.

"I will put a bullet in her brain if you don't move."

There are two metal steps, no railing. The backdoor is open. A mouse or rat, or something scurries across the floor in front of me, scurrying across the toe of my sandal, and thus, my toe. I scream and jump. That's when I feel the blunt end of his gun push me forward.

It's filthy inside. I wade through the trash and debris of a kitchen into the living room. The flies have already found him. The man lying face down on the floor. There are syringes and used needles spread around the body. The dead guy has a band tied around his arm. His pallor is a gray/blue color. As I bend down to examine the man, I'd guess him to not have died more than an hour or two before.

Jade screams at the sight of the dead man and begins to outright sob.

"Please don't make her see this," I beg.

"Unfortunate turn of events," is his only answer.

21

DUKE

"Sneak, step it up," I growl to Sneak. I got a bad feeling. The closer we get to home, the worse it's getting. Too bad I can't put my finger on what's troubling me, just got that unwavering prickly feeling on the back of my neck.

I call Hero again. "You at the compound?"

"Almost there," he answers. "Something wrong?"

I laugh into the phone. "It's all wrong, brother. We're almost home, too. Brief you then." Then I hang up.

Sneak grunts his reply and then picks up speed. He turns twenty minutes into fifteen. Some of those corners coming down from the mountain are too sharp to go as fast as we want to take them. Though we finally reach the compound, my lieutenant stops short. The gate sits wide open. Wide open, with no guard that I can see.

"What the fuck?" Boss shouts. "Wasn't Jimmy on the gate?"

Slowly, Sneak turns in and drives through the gate, parking and shutting off the engine. We exit quietly, unsure of what we're walking into. Could be a fucking ambush for all we know. Guns drawn, we spread out.

I see a car I don't recognize. A little red convertible. As I make my way over, I see the back of a cut with a prospect patch and a bare ass rise up then thrust back down.

You gotta be shitting me. *"Jimmy."* I bellow. His head shoots up like a groundhog popping his head out of a hole in the ground. "You better not be fucking some bitch while you're supposed to be guarding the gate."

The brothers hear me and come running. "You left the gate open with Houdini still on the loose? *My wife and kid are here,*" Boss roars. He's got a rage film covering his eyes, the man's out for blood as he comes at Jimmy. It takes Blood and Sneak to hold him back.

My eyes inadvertently move past Boss, just a glance over his shoulder when I notice my truck missing from the carport next to my house.

"When did my truck leave, Jimmy?"

He hems and haws for a few seconds. Now I'm losing my patience fast.

"When Jimmy?" I repeat myself. And I fucking *hate* to repeat myself.

"I… I don't know," he finally responds, looking ten kinds of guilty.

Before I lose my shit all over him, I pull my phone from my pocket and hit Hero's number one more time. *"Prez,"* he answers. First ring.

"You in my truck?"

"No."

My hackles rise. "Doc with you?"

"No…" He draws out the o several beats. "She's at home."

My stomach drops. *"Shit."* Then I take off running toward my home. "Drop your cut and get the fuck out." I call over my shoulder toward Jimmy.

Boss rumbles, "Take your bitch and go. Somthin' happens

to one of our women or kids, you better fuckin' get out the country 'cuz I'll kill you myself."

And then I realize Hero is still shouting in from the phone. "Prez? Prez?"

"Truck's gone," I reply, sharply. I'm barely aware of the wheezy engine from that crappy convertible leaving my compound in the background when my brothers join me. Including Hero who had to have booked it from the road. His tires squeal as he takes the corner onto club grounds. That's dedication. That's a man who's earned his patch.

Inside, the brothers spread out, calling for Doc and Peaches, checking each room. I head to the coffee table where Doc left my laptop open. The screen is black, but I run my finger over the touchpad and it lights up.

To a confirmation page.

From a travel site.

I have to read the page twice before the words click. Ireland. Two tickets to Ireland.

My woman finally broke.

"Dammit." I shout and bring my fists down onto the coffee table's salvaged wood, swiping my arm across the top until the damn computer crashes to the floor. The brothers come running again. "She bought two tickets to Ireland. Departing from Nashville."

Hero puts his hand to my shoulder. "Sorry. I should have been here. She never leaves the house anymore."

"Not your fault." I grind out. "You were off duty today. I should never have left her without a guard in place."

"Need passports for that." *Blood.* "Would those have been here or her place?"

"Her place." That's what I call to my brothers as I tear out of my house.

Men right on my heels, we head for our bikes. Way my heart beats a million beats a second, if I don't get control of myself, I'm liable to lay my bike down. And that won't help either of my girls.

We strike a menacing picture, engines rumbling. Nothing sounds like a Harley roaring down the road. It's as unmistakable as it is beautiful. Five Harleys, all with men wearing Lords' cuts, we inspire both fear and awe. Cars part for us, taking the shoulders as we pass them. Even the cross traffic at the intersection we come to waits their green light for us to pass.

Before long we're turning down Doc's street. The truck ain't parked in the drive. Shit. Not what I wanted. We park there instead and head up to the front door. I knock. Door was shut but not latched and pushes open from the force of my knuckle.

"Doc?" I call out. "Caitlin? Honey, you here?" Nothing. Starting to panic again.

While the boys check the downstairs, I run up, taking the steps two at a time until I reach her bedroom. Her closet door's open and inside the closet, an empty safe. That's where she'd have kept her important papers like passports. I'm too fucking late.

Time to regroup. That's it, I need time. I close my eyes, drop my chin and bring my hand to the back of my neck, holding on. Seems not just to my neck. Feels like my sanity needs holding, too.

After a couple deep breaths, I pull myself together.

Even though I know it's pointless, I check out the other two bedrooms and the bathroom while up here just to make sure they ain't hiding or something. Then Boss calls me from the base of the stairs.

"Duke, brother. Get down here. Something you need to hear."

When I meet the brothers in the kitchen, Boss passes me a phone receiver. "She has a landline. Most have voicemail set up. So I checked it. Listen," he orders, grinding his teeth so hard they might crack on him.

I will never in my life forget that voice. My gut clenches. "Hello Caitlin... or should I call you Dr. Brennan?" He sounds like that crazy Lecter guy from *Silence of the Lambs*. Hannibal Lecter with a Kentucky accent. "You should have stuck to doctoring. Club presidents make poor bedfellows. We'll be in touch. Oh, and tell the *Hollister whore* I can't wait to meet my nephew."

Then the next voicemail starts up. "Caitlin, you can't keep ignoring me." Fucker has an Irish drawl. Didn't Caitlin say her ex was Irish? Fuck him, he thinks he's gonna come crawling back into my woman's life. Those are my girls.

I throw the phone down with such force the face and number pad pop off when it hits the floor. "One more thing we don't fucking need. Seems on top of the Houdini mess, Peaches' father might be looking for her." Palms to my eyes, I press down, trying to clear my head and think. Then I let out a resigned breath. "Don't know where to go from here. Blood, you and me, let's get on it. The rest 'a you, head back to the clubhouse. Keep ready to mobilize. Yeah?"

All the brothers save for Blood and me exit Doc's house. But dammit, this ain't her house anymore. Her house, her home is with me. When I get her back, a few things are gonna change. First being the address on her driver's license.

Blood gets on his phone putting word out we're looking for a woman with curly red hair and a small kid to match. He gives a description of my truck.

It hits me, I roll up on my bike she's gonna hear me. And I can't take the chance she won't run. "Heading back to get the van. Pipes're too loud."

"I'll call if I get something." He's still looking down at his phone.

"Lock up if you leave."

I grow angrier and angrier the closer to the compound I get. What was in that woman's head? Never mind. I know what was in her head. Hearing about that little girl has finally broken her. But she knows better than to leave. She knew I was on my way to her.

Not even realizing I'd ridden here, I roll to a stop in front of Peaches' school. There's police tape tapping off a large area and several cruisers block the parking lot. Their blue and red lights flash, but no sirens. In the distance, I see Tommy doing his thing.

When I get my hands on them, first thing I'm doing is kiss my Peaches, then kiss her mama. If Doc is lucky, if I've calmed down enough, I'll be fucking her when I spank that ass. If not, I'm gonna bend her over my knee and throttle her for putting me through this. As it stands, there's a whole lot of hurry up and wait going on. And if it's two things she should already damn-well know about me, two things I absolutely despise, it's to *worry* and *wait*.

Before long, I'm back at the compound to switch out my bike for the van. My old truck, although quieter than Harley pipes, still rumbles too loud to keep her from knowing I've shown.

My cell rings. I pull it thinking Blood has something for me, but the screen reads Doc calling.

Doc.

"Where are you?" I ask, no hello. No answer from her though. Well, not directly. I hear rustling, like something rustling over her receiver, but in the background I hear Caitlin. She's crying. My Peaches is sobbing.

"Please get her out of here," I hear Doc say to whoever has her.

"Shut up or I put a bullet in your brain right now. I need to think."

"Keep the gun on me if you have to, just let me hold her."

And I assume he puts my girl down when I hear Doc. "Careful of the needles, baby. Look at Mama. Not the man, okay. You look only at me, Princess Jade."

"Oh-k-kay," Peaches sniffles her response.

Needles? A man? Could she mean a dead man? Like a dead man we left face down in a trailer off Rabbit Hole Road?

Un-fucking-believable.

I manage to shave ten minutes off the half hour drive. Turning down the bumpy, pocked driveway, passing the black walnuts and the thicket of trees where not that long ago, me and my brothers plotted our invasion, my truck sits alongside the trailer. Before I get too close, I pull off into the tree line and walk, well, silently jog the rest of the way.

"*Shut up.*" I hear him roar at my girl, still crying. "Outside, let's go." Then the front door opens and he pushes Doc out first, Peaches in her arms. He's got a gun trained on my woman. I hide behind the corner of the trailer and watch.

Caitlin begins to beg. "Please, please let Jade go." I see the silent tears run down her face.

He abruptly stops. Peaches clings to her mama's legs. The fucker moves one hand to squeeze around my woman's throat, not to choke her, but hard enough to show her who's in charge. She wears her pain and fear all over her face.

Her glossy eyes catch my movement. Only those eyes turn to me. I bring my finger to my lips and mouth, "Shh…" but it's unnecessary. She's a smart woman.

Then he looks around, and I don't know if he's just paranoid or senses me, but he moves the gun to press against Doc's temple, saying something. She gives him no response. She gives me the response though, through her eyes.

"…so now you have to die, Cait. And I'll be taking my girl."

"Why Aiden?" she whimpers. And although I can tell

she's scared, that little act is for his benefit. To keep him thinking he's got the upper hand.

"Ah, Caitlin. Here's the thing, I fell into a bit of a financial situation. My research grant fell through. Research takes money and I'm so close to..." He clenches his jaw and shakes his head to clear whatever's swirling around in there. "I was so close to closing the deal with Cartland Pharmaceutical, but they won't back me without the research. So I borrowed some money to fund the research. Only, guess what? The facts no longer add up. But I've run out of money once again, and cannot pay my debts.

"Now I have men trying to kill me unless I pay them back. I'm not ready to die, you see. So here we are. You out of the way, Jade comes back with me. I've already taken a hefty policy out on her. Got Rachelle hidden, locked away. I'll get twice the payout when I lose my wife and daughter in the same unfortunate accident. Which means Caitlin, it's time to say goodbye to Jade."

It's there on his face, he's ready to pull the trigger, leaving me no choice. I step free from the side of the trailer and stand to my full hulking height, towering over the assclown. Now, gonna just have to wing it.

His head whips toward me, face snarled with madness, and he twists Doc around to use as a shield for his body. I keep my gun hidden for now so maybe he'll push her away to take aim at me. It ain't a great plan, but the way she's positioned, I risk hitting her if I fire.

"'Fraid not," I tell him calmly. "Those are *my* girls, and they ain't going nowhere."

The crazed bastard pulls the gun away from Doc to aim at me like I hoped, only he don't push her or Peaches away. *Shit.* I take a step closer, letting the little cunt-wad know he don't scare me. Slowly, calmly, I start moving forward again. Face set. He knows I mean business.

There's a loud bang, and I see smoke drift up from the gun as my body jerks and pain radiates from my left shoulder. But I keep moving. Fucker thought I'd fall.

"My woman and my girl are coming home with me."

Peaches turns her head. "Duke?" she begins to cry.

"I'm here, sweetheart." And I hold her eyes with mine.

"*Shut up.*" Aiden yells.

"I don't wanna go wiff him."

"Not going anywhere, Peaches."

"I said *shut up.*" Aiden calls again. There's another two pops from the gun and I feel my body jerk again. Left side, below my ribs and right thigh. Pure adrenaline keeps me up and walking.

"*Chief,*" Doc gasps.

At the same time Jade shrieks, "No!"

Aidan cuffs my girl along the jaw. "I'm your dad, Jade. You listen to me. Shut up, now."

"Duke," she calls to me. "He says he's my dad. I want you to be my daddy."

"I *am* your dad, sweetheart. Forever." Then I turn my gaze to Doc and nod once. She understands my wordless command and turns Jade's face to press into her legs again. Caitlin holds her hands over both 'a Jade's ears. It distracts that fool enough to take his eyes off me to look down at her.

I swallow hard, knowing I can't be off even a millimeter and clear my throat so she knows it's coming. Caitlin bends her neck. That's when I whip the Glock from the back waistband of my jeans, flip the safety as I aim and fire.

One shot.

He crumples to the ground.

Dead.

Bullet hole between his brows.

My family is safe.

But then I hear Peaches cry, *"Daddy."* What the fuck? Is she talking about that asshole I just killed?

She wrenches from her mama's arms and runs to me, crying. "Daddy. My Duke daddy."

Seeing her. Hearing those words. Words I'd prepared to go my whole life without hearing. My adrenaline must be crashing, and I drop to my knees as Peaches reaches out to me. Ass to heels, I start to sway. Don't want my blood on my little girl, so I position her hands on my cheeks. She leans her forehead against mine and sobs.

22

CAITLIN

"Love you," I hear him whisper as he slumps, then falls to the ground.

Jade begins to scream. "*My daddy.*"

I move her to drop down next to the unmoving form of the man I love more than *almost* anyone else in the world. The man who not only claimed me as his, but claimed my daughter, even when he didn't have to. Taking bullets to protect her when her biological disappointment could think of nothing but hurting her.

Tears sting my eyes, but I can't think of him like that right now. Years of training kick in as I gently but swiftly push Jade back completely out of the way and reach into my pocket for my cell. With no service up this part of the mountain, connecting with Duke drained my battery.

Crossing my fingers that he has it on him, I reach inside his cut for his cell phone. His battery is only at twenty-five percent, but it's enough. I call 911 as I begin to assess the situation better, tearing at his shirt to not only get a better look at his injuries, but I use it to help staunch the blood flow while speaking to dispatch.

The sirens and flashing lights couldn't have been more welcome. Once the paramedics were on site and I'd handed off custody, I was able to switch from physician to partner. And old lady to the Brimstone Lords' president. Never had I been so happy to see police cruisers and ambulances come barreling down the bumpy, dirt drive where they immediately moved to action.

Guns drawn, the lawmen move about looking for more danger. "It was just him," I tell them. Satisfied the situation is safe, I watch each man holster his gun then start taking in the scene. Tommy sends a man over to take my statement.

But before answering any questions from the officer, I dial Boss's cell.

"Prez?" He answers. "Got a lead?"

I sniffle into the line. "This is Caity. He's down, being transferred to Mercy as we speak. They'll need to stabilize him, then transfer him out. He'll need a level one trauma center. My guess Lexington or Nashville."

"Jade?" he asks, which is sweet because I can hear the emotion in his voice for his fallen friend.

My sniffle deteriorates to a cry, but I manage to pull it back. "He saved her, Boss. He saved my girl."

"Right. Sneak, Carver, Blood, get to Mercy. Duke's down."

I hear loud gasps and "*Fuck.*" Then the rumble of engines.

"Caity, me and Hero are comin' for ya. Tommy there?"

"Yes. He's... well he's dealing with Aiden."

"Aiden?" he asks.

"Mmm... my ex. Jade's biological father."

"So not Houdini?" He sounds disappointed. Not that I can blame him. If Houdini didn't come after me and Jade, that means he's still roaming free, which is a scary thought in and of itself.

"No. It was never Houdini."

"Duke get him?"

"Yes." I repeat my answer, as my voice cracks.

"Stay strong, Caity. I'm comin'."

Only after I hang up do I allow myself to cry. And then remember there is a very patient police officer waiting to take my statement. So I wipe at my eyes with the back of my hand and square my shoulders. "Okay," I say. "I'm ready."

Once I've given every last detail from the moment I made the stupid decision to leave the compound, to when Duke took Aiden out in self-defense, making sure to clarify any details the young cop needs me to go over for him, my eyes naturally veer to where Aiden had fallen. Tommy Doyle has dropped a gray tarp with neon yellow stripes up each side over Aiden. Then he walks to his cruiser to grab out a warm blanket, which he brings over to drape around me and Jade as I'm holding my girl on my lap.

"You okay, Caity?" He asks. "You're shaking. Might be going into shock. Let me get someone over here to check you out."

"No. They already did. I'm fine. Jade's fine. Just nerves. I'll be fine after I have time to ruminate on all that's happened. That's once I know Duke will be okay."

"Duke." My daughter whimpers. "He said he's my daddy."

I kiss her forehead and snuggle her tighter against my body.

"Alright." Tommy places a hand on my shoulder while the other officer types on the tablet where he'd recorded my statement. "You told Officer Woodward everything?"

I nod.

"Good girl," comes his patronizing response.

Before I get sucked into a depression, because forcing a person to relive such a hideous situation especially so soon after it occurred can cause a person to get sucked into a depression, bike engines and an extended cab pickup rumble onto the scene. The pickup about thirty seconds behind the bikes.

Hero and Crass hop off their bikes to head first to a very dead Aiden. Tommy leaves me to join them. Boss and Elise hop out of the truck to get to me. "Had to drop off the bike. Figured you'd like your friend."

Elise kneels down at my side to wrap her arms around me and Jade. The hug is so welcome and comforting, I almost break down again.

"Can she go?" Boss asks Officer Woodward.

"Sure, she's finished her statement. She's free to go."

Both he and Elise take an arm to help pull me—and thus my daughter, who has her legs wrapped around my waist, holding on for dear life—up onto my feet. They walk me over to Duke's truck, but before I get in, I yell over to Tommy to remember the dead druggie inside the trailer.

With Jade in her booster, Elise takes the keys from my hand. "I'm driving you to see Duke. Beau will meet us there."

And like a true friend, she doesn't ask me to go over anything that happened, choosing to turn on the radio instead. I need that reprieve. Then once we're down the mountain, back in town, she pulls into a drive-thru to get me a large hot coffee before continuing on to Mercy Medical Center. It takes us another twenty-five minutes to get there.

Duke is already in surgery when we arrive. They're trying to stabilize him enough to be moved. I won't cry. Not here. Not now. Though my resolve starts to slip when a sleepy Jade's eyes begin to water. "He's my daddy," She tells the receptionist.

We're dirty and look like we've been to hell and back, which we have. But I don't have two cares to give at the moment. I want my Duke. I want to hold him, cuddle up next to him while we watch movies. I want to make him stuffed peppers and Limoncello cake again. To kiss him, to love him.

To wake up every day for the rest of my life next to him. Is that so much to ask?

No. No it's not. We deserve our happily ever after.

Mercy transfers him over to Lexington where they keep him for a week. A very long week since when my biker old man begins to feel better, he begins shouting down the walls that his woman is a doctor so he can be discharged. Thankfully Lexington doesn't agree with him, although I assure them I *can* take care of him. I'd prefer not to.

I drive the new truck to pick him up, smoother ride and all. He bitches at me to hand over the keys, but for once he has to take *my* orders. His doctors haven't cleared him to drive. Funny thing is, I was gone for maybe three hours tops. But when we walk back inside the doublewide, literally all my furniture is there, and they've even situated everything exactly as I had it at the rental.

None of Duke's old furniture remains.

"What's all this?" I ask, practically stumbling over my words.

"Moved you in. No sense you paying rent on a place you're never gonna be at. This is our home Doc. You, me, and Peaches. Ain't letting you go."

There it is, his declaration.

The man is a horrible patient. I'll bet Lexington was glad to be rid of him. Never a man to stay idle for long, the continued bed rest and recovery time begins to weigh on the both of us.

Though even if we haven't said the words yet, this is us. For better or worse. I've had to remind myself of that a couple of times.

Two weeks after that night, after I made him stuffed peppers and Limoncello cake. After he helped me tuck Jade into bed despite the pain it caused him to bend over, and against my advice, I might add. After I'd undressed him and we're lying in bed, he begins to tease me, rubbing his finger over my most sensitive areas. It's torture. He grows hard right in front of my eyes.

"What are you doing?" I, well, pant would be the word for it.

"What's it look like. We're gonna fuck, but you're gonna have to do the work tonight, honey."

"We can't have sex. You were shot."

"Yeah, I was shot. Didn't break my dick. Now climb on."

"I'm not climbing on." I protest.

"That fine ass won't hit my thigh wound, so we ain't got nothing to worry about."

"You're still healing."

"Listen woman, you either climb on my dick right now, or I'm gonna pick you up and drop you on it."

And I can tell how serious he is, so gingerly, I climb on and ride, if only to set the pace. When he climaxes, his shouts are as much from pain as ecstasy.

"Maybe I shoulda thought that one out better," he admits.

"Really? You think?"

"Don't wanna hear it." That would be a grouse, if I ever heard one.

"Man you're a pain in my ass. You're lucky I love you, Duke Ellis."

"Now that's the damn truth. Lips," he then orders. And as I always do, I lean in to give him my lips.

23

DUKE

Eight months later…

"They came. *They came*." She runs into the bedroom waving a large yellow envelope around.

"Watch yourself honey, don't want you slipping." I got a tarp over the carpet and a tray filled with silver-gray paint she says the color matches my eyes.

Her eyes light up for a different reason. "Wow," she says. "It's really coming together."

I put the roller back down in the tray and walk over to her. "Lips," I whisper.

She leans in to give me her lips. While I wrap one arm around her shoulder, I rub her growing belly. It's the sexiest, most beautiful thing I've seen in my life. My wife carrying our child.

Once I got out of the hospital, to put an end to the Aiden ordeal, as she refers to it, I didn't waste any time in turning Dr. Caitlin Brennan to Dr. Caitlin Brennan-Ellis. She chose to keep her name for professional reasons. Which I completely understand. Hell, I was just honored she wanted to take my name however she decided to take it.

Neither of us wanted a big ceremony. Her folks came in from Arizona. It was the first I'd met the in-laws. They didn't even know she was seeing anyone, let alone the relationship being serious enough to get married.

And they weren't too thrilled to learn their only daughter and granddaughter were living in a biker compound. But they were even less thrilled to learn that bastard who'd abandoned my girls tried to kill them. When Doc told them how I'd claimed her and Peaches as my own and how I'd taken three bullets to protect them, they warmed up. Not saying we'll ever be best of friends, but they're already planning on a return trip once the baby's born.

The day I found out she was pregnant, I'd just gotten back from a long run. A distributor was dicking us around. Had to put a stop to that. And I had to check on Chaos. It's been rough on him since Liv left. Hopefully he can get that girl's head straight. But I know he's gotta do for his family. And Liv is his family.

I walk in and there's one 'a them baby onesies, the kind that snap at the crotch, laying on the island. It's black with a flaming devil's head patch sewn on. Above the devil's head, it says Brimstone Lords. Below it, *'in training'*.

At first, I think Trisha had the baby. And that my wife picked out a fucking awesome gift. Until Peaches comes racing out 'a her room. "Daddy. Yew're home. I missed yew." I hold my arms open, and she leaps into them. That's when I notice the T-shirt she has on. It's black like the onesie and has a devil's head sewn on too. But above the flames, hers says Big Sister. And below it, *'in training'*.

"In training?" I ask Peaches, who beams up at me. Then I bellow, "Woman, you better get your ass out here."

Doc strides out from the hallway positively glowing. "Hey daddy," she greets me.

"Are you serious? This is serious?" I know I sound like a lunatic, but shit. My heart feels so huge it might explode.

"Yes," she tells me. "I'm only about eight weeks along. But Dr. Mason over in Milford says everything looks fine."

Trisha had the baby not two days later. A baby girl she and Sneak name Briar Rose. Because even girls, if they're legacy, need kickass biker names.

This morning I woke up to my woman going down on me. Pregnancy hormones are a thing 'a beauty. Thought she liked sex before. Now she's insatiable. But before I came, I had her calves up against my shoulders. Then we got up, showered together, which led to another orgasm for her, this time using my fingers, and we got dressed. Because today she's twenty weeks exactly, and we had an ultrasound appointment.

I drove her and our girl the two towns over to her obstetrician's office. We got looks from the moment we stepped through the front door 'til they called us back. What, because I wear a cut and a patch that says president, I'm not supposed to support my old lady during her pregnancy?

My bike and tattoos just mean I'm cooler than other dads, not that I don't give a damn.

I help her up onto the table, this is after she's been checked by Dr. Mason. We heard the heartbeat, a sound I'll never grow tired of hearing. Then she used a tape measure to measure Doc's belly growth. That's when she told Doc and me to go across the hall where the ultrasound tech was waiting for us.

The tech lifts Caitlin's shirt again and pulls her pants down to just above the pubic bone. And after gooping Doc's stomach, uses a wand to check all the vitals. It's a 3D ultrasound, so we can see every detail. I see my baby's face. My chin and cheeks. My lips and forehead. Don't know about eyes, they're closed. But Caitlin's nose, for sure.

After she records all the necessary information the tech asks, "You want to find out what you're having?"

I look to Caitlin and we both crack a smile. "Yes." We say together.

While we wait for the tech to hone in on the hotdog or the bun, my wife squeezes my hand. "You nervous?" she asks.

"*Nah.* You?"

"Maybe excited is more the word. You want a boy or girl?"

"Don't matter, honey. Don't matter at all."

"Really? Not even a little girl of your own?"

"Peaches *is* my own. Don't ever forget that." But it don't matter because there's a baby dick filling the screen.

"Mom. Dad, meet your son," the tech says.

Right after the appointment we headed for the home store.

And that's how I end up in a room painting silver-gray walls. We're decorating in what my woman calls badass biker baby chic. Specialty Lords shit. Harley shit. For one wall, she has these decals of translucent silver Harleys. The accent color is black leather. The room'll be sweet when it's finished. And I can't wait to bring baby Diesel home to it. Fuck yeah, I'm naming my kid Diesel. As I said, badass biker babies get badass biker names.

"*Open it.*" Doc hands me off the envelope, excitedly. You'd think it was fucking Christmas for the way she's acting. Not like we didn't know it was coming. Caitlin and I put in the paperwork a few months ago. And with the bio-loser dead and gone, nothing else to stop us. I carefully tear open the lip of the envelope and pull out the most important paper. The one I've been waiting to see since the day Brutus put the idea in my head over beers.

Certificate of Adoption.

Jade Ellis.

Peaches is my girl. Caitlin is my wife. And baby Diesel's got about twenty more weeks to marinate. "Peaches," I call out to her. "Come'ere sweetheart. Got something to show you."

She comes racing into the room. "Careful," both Doc and I yell at the same time. Our hands shoot out in front of us to stop her from stepping in paint.

"Look sweetheart. You're my girl forever now."

"*Daddy!*" Peaches screeches. "I'm a Ewis now. Just wike you and Mama." Damn if hearing that don't bring tears to my eyes as I gather my girls in my arms. Because they're mine. Because I can.

Dawna was a good woman. Loved her with every breath I had in me. But she often lamented we couldn't have this. Hopefully she's smiling down on me. Happy knowing my club is clean. Happy knowing I finally got my family now.

At last.

Still Not the End

THANK YOU FOR READING! I hope you loved meeting Duke and Caitlin. The next book in the Brimstone Lords MC series is CHAOS CALMED. Find out who the sexy biker president can't stop thinking about and takes to his bed.

CLICK HERE TO READ CHAOS CALMED>>

Don't miss more badass MC brothers from The Bedlam Horde, starting with DEVIL'S ADVOCATE: VLAD

I appreciate your help in spreading the word, including

telling a friend about the Brimstone Lords. Reviews help readers find books! Please leave a review on your favorite book site. A review on Amazon helps the most.

SIGN UP FOR SARAH ZOLTON ARTHUR'S NEWS-LETTER: Sassy, classy and a little bad-assy newsletter

Now, how about reading the first chapter from CHAOS CALMED...

FIRST CHAPTER from CHAOS CALMED

God, he's so loud. Every breath, through his nose and mouth simultaneously. The room. I'm in the room, not the box. I'm in the room. Next to him. The black, just black.

The black, just black.

I grab my head, holding my face with my hands, squeezing, tears streaming down my face again. Heart palpitations. Pounding. Pounding.

And he sleeps.

I keep gripping my face to keep from gripping his neck to shut up that damn loud breathing or from grabbing those scissors just a pullout drawer away.

I could stop him.

But I couldn't stop him.

Because I can't move.

I can't breathe.

Houdini is still out there, plotting. Waiting. He got me before. He could do it again.

I feel the box filling up.

Sloshing.

Wet.

Wearing nothing but my man's T-shirt, forcing the panic down, I will my legs to move. Quietly, so quietly, keys in my hand and purse snatched from the dresser and slung around my shoulders, I creep out of our room. I leave my phone. Phones can be traced. Especially by people like my brother.

So late, it's early. A few hours before dawn. No one remains awake in the compound. Not with the way bikers like to party. Even with the VP's old lady, my friend Elise, and their new baby, Gunner, taking up residence until that piece of shit Houdini is captured. They got to go home. Shit happened. Doesn't shit always happen in the club? Now they're back—as a precaution. That's what they tell us. Not to worry. They'll handle it. Trust your man.

Trust your man.

But Elise is back, isn't she? Elise and Gun, they're back. Because shit never ends.

Gun, the sweetest baby in the world, keeps her up but keeps her sane. Despite the badass biker name, Gun got his name from our friend Crass. Biker name Crass. Given name Gunner.

He lives back in Chicago, part of the Illinois chapter, no matter how many times I've, well, *we've* begged him to transfer down to Kentucky.

Maybe Crass would take me in.

No.

Gage, Chaos to the club—he'd find me. Biker name Chaos. Given name Gage, also known as my man. That would be the first place he'd look.

Damn him for coming back into my life. I couldn't say for making me care again, because to say that would be to insinuate I ever stopped. Which he and I both know I didn't.

He totally screwed up my world coming back for me—turned the whole place upside down.

My older brother, Raif, hasn't talked to me since I got out of the hospital after Boss and Chaos rescued me from the box. The blackness. The wet. The place Houdini meant for me to die. I miss him. My brother, not Houdini.

Half the time he'd been a shit brother, all entitled from being not just a man in a motorcycle club, but the son of a founding chapter member and his old lady.

We may have grown up together, but our lives couldn't have been further apart since I'm the worthless *daughter* of a founding chapter member and his *club whore*.

That's how I grew up. The worthless daughter of a club whore. Women, old ladies included, are nothing more than second-class citizens with the Lords. The Brimstone Lords. My brother's club. Our father's club. Chaos's club.

He didn't grow up in the life, just hung at the fringes. Knew my brother from school. Best friends from, like, kindergarten on.

Once upon a time I thought he could give me a life away from all this. If it weren't for that stupid bro code, the one that says you don't fuck your best friend's younger sister, which kept us apart for so long.

Until he couldn't stay away any longer, which happened to be the night my father was murdered and my brother, the stupid idiot, avenged his death—along with his best friend, my love. The love he pulled from my bed and didn't even know it, not until a few months ago, which would be why he stopped talking to me. And Chaos.

Two guards, newly patched, guard the front gate. But that's okay because I have no intension of waltzing out the front gate.

It took some time, but eventually I started to venture outside again, after my kidnapping and subsequent rescue, after Elise's kidnapping and subsequent rescue the day of her wedding—well, the rescue happened a day later. But that doesn't matter. What matters is how Houdini accessed the Lord property from an old access road at the back of the property, a road where they keep an old pickup truck parked to block the unguarded back gate. A pickup for which I have a key, a gate for which I also have a key hanging on the keyring next to my car keys.

Keys that neither Chaos nor my brother, nor Boss or even Duke know I grifted.

So as Blaze and Blue stare out at the road in front of the compound, I run silently through the short, mowed grass running along the singlewide trailers off to the side of the main clubhouse and into the tall never-been mowed grass leading back to the access road and my freedom.

The truck is loud but far enough away from the compound that it shouldn't wake up a bunch of drunken bikers. And if it does, I'll already be far enough away before they mobilize and figure out it was me who'd run off.

I've tried to stay.

But I just can't do it. Can't be here anymore, slowly drowning on the phantom water filling up the blackness of the room where Chaos, Gage, sleeps.

The truck turns over after a strangled start but rumbles to life. End of the access road joins a back state highway.

By the time the distant rumble of bikes disturbs the night, I've already turned off the old highway to cross the bridge into Ohio. Bridges connect Ohio and Kentucky at various spots all the way up the Ohio River. We stay near one such bridge.

My stomach hurts being off the compound, making me vulnerable to Houdini once again. But he couldn't know my escape would come tonight.

By the time dawn breaks, I'm firmly inside the border of West Virginia. To fool them, to fool Gage, I crossed from Kentucky into Ohio. But they'd expect me to head north again, wouldn't they? Back to Chicago.

I'm smarter than that.

I drive east. A destination in mind.

Several hours into my getaway, my mouth parched,

eyelids drooping and gas tank sputtering, I coast into a truck stop.

Truckers openly gawk at my dress, or lack of dress. A Lords T-shirt, no pants, no shoes. But they could never understand I had to get out. Gage, he'd have known, heard me moving around the room. Can't live the life and sleep deep. Everything had to be the same. Same. He'd have seen through a change in routine, even down to what I wear to bed. Besides, I have money. I have money to fill the gas tank.

I have money for coffee. Coffee to fill the Livvy tank.

I even find a cheap pair of pink jersey shorts with a West Virginia logo in white on the right leg corner, and a pair of plastic flip-flops.

The shorts, a size too small, hardly cover my ass cheeks, but cover enough to not get me arrested for indecent exposure when I tie up the T-shirt, so reports of a crazy woman in nothing but a T-shirt don't find their way back to The Lords.

The very last thing I do is walk over to the meager electronics department where they sell replacement phone cords and car chargers, and thankfully exactly what I'm looking for. I pick up the package for one of those cheap, disposable flip phones, one of those *untraceable* flip phones, and a card with triple the minutes. This card has a thousand minutes, which means three-thousand when I load it onto my account.

Twenty minutes after sitting in the parking lot of the truck stop setting up my phone account with those minutes and new number, the open road calls to me again, eastward bound. Disturbingly toward the sea.

If I allow myself to think about it, finding myself anywhere near a large body of water in my state of mind is probably not the smartest choice.

But this is an escape from bikers and murderers, so I hardly allow myself to think about it.

SEVERAL HOURS of highway behind me, mountains turn coastal, heat turns light breeze and the briny scent of freedom wafts through the truck cab along with the call of the gulls flying overhead.

I'll be safe here.

I have to be.

THE LITTLE TOWN OF SMITHFIELD, Virginia, yes, the very same town known for ham, smells of bacon and sits near the Chesapeake Bay.

Small town Americana in every way a girl from the Windy City would think of Americana.

Sweet.

Charming.

Quaint.

Storefronts for artisan galleries, shoppes and cafés. A tourist's dream. From stories of my mother's childhood, I know this place swarms with them in the summer months.

I'll get to look around more after settling in. Right now, with no sleep, crashing is imminent.

Following the handwritten directions my mother had given me years ago. I'd handwritten them from memory. My mother, when halfway lucid, told me about her home. When the mood hit, she'd tell me bedtime stories as she tucked me in at night. Right before she'd go off to get high and let men she didn't care about use her body however they felt fit because it was the only way she could sometimes get the attention of the man, the only man, she ever loved. Leaving me alone in our crappy, cramped apartment for hours.

Once I figured out she'd left, I couldn't sleep until she

came home. Sometimes she got there on her own, but most times dumped in our living room by some man who'd gotten what he wanted and had no more use for her.

How a young, beautiful virgin from Smithfield, Virginia could end up a cracked-out biker whore in Chicago?

My dear old dad.

The man only meant to roll through town. He met her at her grandfather's gas station.

He stayed a few days more.

He took her virginity.

He convinced her to run away with him. To the big life in the big city.

What he'd neglected to tell my beautiful, innocent mother was that he had an old lady back home. Not just an old lady, a wife. A wife and a one-year-old son. My brother. Raif.

My brother doesn't know about this place. Gage doesn't know about this place. Anyone, aside from me, connecting the Lords to this place died years ago.

Freedom.

From Raif.

From Gage.

From Houdini.

Maybe here, the nightmares will stop and I can finally get some sleep.

Out the other side of town, closer to the Chesapeake, I turn the truck down a dirt lane off the main road. Barbed wire fencing lines the trees leading up to the dirt lane, all with NO TRESPASSING signs in bright orange lettering tacked to each tree.

I'm not trespassing. This land belongs to me. Inherited after my mother's grandfather passed away. I'd paid the hefty inheritance tax and keep up property taxes every year. The gas station had been sold to afford assisted living for the old man before he passed. Too bad. I could use a readymade place to work. Since the kidnapping, I haven't been able to get myself back into the phone sex, my main source of income while I worked on my finance degree from DePaul. It paid well, and I could set my own hours. A great job until the moment he took me. Now I'm a skittish woman always convinced the douche calling is Houdini threatening to finish what he started. I know I'll have to find a job. Just one more thing to check off my list.

The long lane ends at the mouth of an inlet off the bay. So maybe the house has seen better days—it's mine. Everything else can be fixed.

Without a second thought, I park the truck, jumping out to the brackish smell of ocean mixed with vegetation and walk to the overgrown flowerbed under the front window. Flowers have long since been choked out by grass and weeds. Mostly weeds. I head to the fake cement rock, which looks surprisingly like a real rock, the one my mother used to wax on nostalgically about before she'd get too high for coherent speech.

Not because of it being a fake cement rock, the nostalgic waxing, but because it sat directly under a tiny hula dancer in the window sill. Despite the overgrown vegetation, I know exactly where to find the rock.

The hula girl still sits in the window. One of those meant for a car dashboard. Mom's grandpops brought it back from Hawaii after WWII. He'd been a navy man. Saw combat. He'd been career. It was how he'd ended up in Virginia. The plastic, that old 1950s hard plastic, the kind that breaks just as easily as glass, has been sun bleached and hair-line cracked over the years from a lifetime stuck in her sentry spot.

Her deep Hawaiian skin now looks as pale as mine. What was once, I'm sure, a vibrant red on her lei and headdress now appears a shade lighter than pastel pink. Her green-grass skirt, a pastel green. Though, despite her age, she looks poised to hula with the best of them.

Mom.

She loved that hula girl.

Using the outside sill for balance, I squat down, ripping large handfuls of weeds from the flowerbed, tossing them to a pile I might actually get to clearing later, until my knuckles scrape the rough cement surface of the rock.

I toss over that last pile of flora, prying up the rock, and immediately drop it back to the ground. So many bugs, from long roly-polies to earwigs, wriggle their bodies over the edge, scurrying across the damp mud-bottomed stone to get back to the safety of the soil. The problem being, I have to touch that muddy bottom to unscrew it from the top of the rock to reach the treasure, also known as the spare house key, inside.

But I'm so tired. Not just from the drive but from days, weeks, months of not sleeping. I need to see if this will finally be the day. The day I can close my eyes and not fear the darkness.

I have to bash the fake rock against a real one to loosen the two sides enough to separate the top from bottom.

Upending the top, a brass-colored key spills into my hand.

Door successfully unlocked; I push it open. The space appears shadowed but not dark. All the curtains pulled closed years ago, but being so bright outside, the rays try desperately to infiltrate. Hence, shadowed.

All the furniture sits covered by white sheets, which is good, seeing as after almost twenty years of no occupancy, a blizzard of dust swirls up from just walking in.

Cleaning could wait.

Exploring could wait.

Well, except for finding a bedroom. I walk down the one

hallway in the house because it seems the most plausible spot to find a bed.

At the very end of the hall, I open the door to a kind of deconstructed bedroom. Deconstructed because only the skeletal bones of the bed, headboard and footboard and springs, were left for whatever reason.

So I go looking. Nothing bed-worthy in the bathroom or second bedroom.

The third bedroom, pay dirt.

All bedroom furniture, as in tables and dressers and thankfully, mattresses, fill the room. The mattresses up on their sides, leaning against the wall.

It isn't hard to find the one for the back bedroom. The only queen.

Why does sleep have to be so difficult?

Moving the other two twin mattresses to an adjacent wall, I then take up the arduous task of switching between pulling and pushing the queen out the narrow doorway, back down the hallway to finally flop the mattress down onto the springs of the big bed.

Now I'm not just tired, but too fatigued to go any longer without some shuteye. I give up and belly flop onto the naked mattress. Because although I have a naked mattress beneath me, I *have* a *naked mattress beneath me*. Sweet surrender.

The moment my face plants against the soft, fluffy surface, my eyes close and sleep finally, finally, *finally* finds me in a shadowed room outside Smithfield, Virginia.

Get it today! Chaos Calmed (Brimstone Lords MC 3)

MORE BY SARAH ZOLTON ARTHUR

Skydiving, Skinny-Dipping & Other Ways to Enjoy Your Fake Boyfriend

D.I.E.T. (Dating in Extreme Times)

WTF Are You Thinking? (Coming 2021)

Holiday Bites (A Lake Shores, MI World)

Baby, It's Cold Outside (Book One by Sarah Zolton Arthur)

Always Be My Baby (Book Three by Sarah Zolton Arthur)

Standalones

Summer of the Boy

The Significance of Moving On

Audio

Summer of the Boy

Skydiving, Skinny-Dipping & Other Ways to Enjoy Your Fake Boyfriend

Flight: The Roc Warriors

ACKNOWLEDGMENTS

Thank you to the best sons a mom could ask for. You two are truly my best friends and I couldn't do this life without you. Thank you for being my biggest cheerleaders. Guess what? I'm yours, too! Finally, thank you to my favorite baristas (Hello, *coffee*). I literally couldn't do my job if you weren't doing yours so perfectly.

But who I'd really like to send a shout out to is all of you who read *Bossman* and wanted more. I love that you love the characters, care about their lives enough to devote your precious time to catch up and that you're ready to root for new loves.

It takes a village to raise a novel, and you all are my villagers. The people who helped turn a project I was proud to have completed into a project I'm proud to present to the world.

ABOUT THE AUTHOR

Sarah Zolton Arthur is a USA TODAY Bestselling author of pretty much all things romance, but she loves to get down and dirty with her MC bad boys. She spends her days embracing the weirdly wonderful parts of life with her two kooky sons while pretending to be a responsible adult.

She resides in Michigan, where the winters bring cold, and the summers bring construction. The roads might have potholes, but the beaches are amazing.

Above all else, she lives by these rules. Call them Sarah's life edicts: In Sarah's world, all books have kissing and end in some form of HEA. Because even outlaw bikers need love.

Read More from Sarah Zolton Arthur
www.sarahzoltonarthur.com

Made in the USA
Las Vegas, NV
23 October 2021